Award-winning author Heather Peck has enjoyed a varied life. She has been both farmer and agricultural policy adviser, volunteer covid vaccinator and NHS Trust Chair. She bred sheep and alpacas, reared calves, broke ploughs, represented the UK in international negotiations, specialised in emergency response from Chernobyl to bird flu, managed controls over pesticides and GM crops, saw legislation through Parliament and got paid to eat Kit Kats while on secondment to Nestle Rowntree.

She lives in Norfolk with her partner Gary, two dogs, two cats, two hens and a female rabbit named Hero.

Also by Heather Peck

THE DCI GREG GELDARD SERIES
Secret Places
Glass Arrows*
Fires of Hate**
The Temenos Remains**
Death on the Rhine (novella)**

BOOKS FOR CHILDREN
Tails of Two Spaniels
coming soon:
The Animals of White Cows Farm
The Pixie and the Bear
More Spaniel's Tails

*shortlisted for the East Anglian Book Awards 2021
**Firebird Book Award Winners

DIG TWO GRAVES

DCI GREG GELDARD BOOK 5

Heather Peck

Ormesby Publishing

Published in 2023 by Ormesby Publishing

Ormesby St Margaret, Norfolk

www.ormesbypublishing.co.uk

British Library Cataloguing in Publication Data

A CIP catalogue record for this book is available from the British Library.

Page design and typesetting by Ormesby Publishing

With thanks to Gary

for everything

Acknowledgments

Many thanks again to my readers Geoff Dodgson, Alison Tayler and Gary Westlake for their constructive criticism and extremely helpful comments. This book is all the better for your help.

Thanks also to Sharon Gray at 'CluedUpEditing' for her meticulous and sensitive proof reading and to Helen Morrish for the cover design.

If seeking revenge, dig two graves - one for yourself

Chinese proverb

A mutilated body, a missing colleague and a bent copper...

Greg and his team have to move fast to rescue a friend and convict a vengeful crime-lord.

Contents

Key Characters XII

Glossary XIV

1. Crisis 1

2. Cock-up or conspiracy? 10

3. Briefings 18

4. Underground 22

5. Post-mortem 27

6. Moved on 34

7. Clean boats? 39

8. Drugs and more drugs 45

9. Some progress 50

10. Informers 58

11. Out of the mouths 70

12. Alarm and arms 78
13. Fun? 85
14. Aftermath 89
15. Coping 95
16. Breaking bad news 103
17. Explanations 112
18. 2nd post-mortem 126
19. Proper policing 132
20. Into hiding 142
21. A new search 149
22. Horses Mill House 156
23. One hour earlier 166
24. Family and friends 171
25. No comment 178
26. Inquest 1 186
27. Inquest 2 192
28. Consequences 197
29. At Acle 203
30. Cat antics 207

31. Cat-astrophe 213
32. Cornered 221
33. Siege 228
34. Negotiations 238
35. Survivors 244
36. None so deaf 249
37. Inquests part 2 255
38. Witness protection 262
39. Inquests part 3 271
40. Safe house 279
41. January 2020 289

Key Characters

Police

Chief Superintendent Margaret Tayler
DCI Greg Geldard
DI Sarah Laurence
DS Chris Mathews
PCs Bill Street, Jill Hayes, Jenny Warren, Steve Hall & Phil Knight
PC Jeff Fellowes transfer from the Metropolitan Police
Ned George crime scene manager
PD Turbo springer spaniel
Neil Simpson psychologist / negotiator
DCI Ram Trent previously of the Serious Fraud Office
DI Newton of the 'funny buggers'
CI Richard (Rick) Lake of Great Yarmouth
PCs Newton and Foxton ditto

Legal Services

Frank Parker Crown Prosecution Service
Sir Frederick Seymour QC Prosecution Counsel
Sir Bernard Rhys QC Defence Counsel

Judge Helena Westlake QC
Roger Goodwin Coroner
Yvette Pullen Assistant Coroner

Medical experts
Dr Paisley police pathologist
Professor Bailey Professor of Pathology

Baddies
Dragan Bakalov first met in Glass Arrows, now in prison
Constantin Gabrys Lithuanian Mr Big
Eva, Mica and Helen Gabrys his wife, son and daughter
Ralph Menton his butler
Peter Ashfield (aka Peter or Patrick Ashton/Shinfield,)

Other participants
Madame Trieste deceased proprietor, Nails Galore, aka Adelina Laurentiu
Mr & Mrs Geldard senior Greg's parents
Nathan Standish & Emily Atkinson, students at the East Norfolk Academy
Mary & Clive Westerby residents of Billockby

Glossary

ANPR	Automatic Number Plate Recognition
APB	All Points Bulletin
CCTV	Closed Circuit Television
GP	General Practitioner (local doctor)
IOPC	Independent Office for Police Conduct
PIRH	Pre Inquest Review Hearing
SCCT	Specialist Crime and Counter-Terrorism

1

Crisis

A row of emergency vehicles sat outside the beauty salon. DCI Greg Geldard was leaning on his car, shouting into his mobile phone. After a moment, he rang off, smacked both hands on the roof, then wrenched the passenger door open.

'Forensics are stuck on the A11,' he snapped. 'In heaven's name, how long is this going to take? Every moment that passes makes it harder to catch up with them before something happens to Sarah.' His short brown hair was on end, his face as red as Chris's was white. He took a hasty step toward the salon, stopped at the crime scene tape, then marched back to the car, every step clipped and unnaturally loud.

'Sit down a minute,' said Chris from the passenger seat. 'There's nothing you can do until forensics get here. You know that.'

'I need to get on! I need to do something!'

'I know. But, at the moment, you get on best by letting the specialists do their job. You don't need me to tell you that!'

Greg wavered, then stamped round the car and flung himself into the driver's seat and sat, drumming his fingers on the steering wheel. The fascia on the salon beside them read 'Nails Galore' but the old name 'Chips with Everything' was clearly visible underneath the newer lettering.

'Did you ever find out whether the old shop was fish and chips, or mobile phones?' asked Chris, just to break the silence. DCI Greg Geldard looked up.

'Phones I think,' he said. Then, 'At last! Here comes Ned.'

A small van was pulling up behind the two cars with blue flashing lights, the ambulance and a Mercedes with a 'Doctor on call' sign propped up on the dashboard. Greg shot out of his car as though fired from a cannon. Behind him, uniformed officers were erecting yet more crime scene tape to reinforce the message that this Norwich suburb was now out of bounds. A few rubberneckers were already collecting at the boundary now enforced by two polite but firm uniformed constables. By the time Chris caught up, Greg was already speaking to Ned, his Crime Scene Manager.

'As far as I know,' he said, 'Chris and I were the first to enter the salon after the perpetrators had left. Everywhere was locked up. I forced an entry and found the proprietor, Madame Trieste, dead and nailed to the kitchen cupboards. Chris and I made it as far as the kitchen door, then left the kitchen and reported in by radio, as it was obvious she was dead. I did notice that car keys looking like Sarah's were on the kitchen table. We both then conducted a swift search of the remainder of the property, just a quick look really, to see if Sarah was around and to check for any other casualties. There are two rooms upstairs, apparently used for storage, and a number of small treatment rooms downstairs as well as the main salon reception. No sign of anyone else anywhere.'

Ned paused in hitching his paper overalls over his long body. 'Any indications of how the perps got in or out?'

'Nothing obvious. I forced the back door with an old spade. It was locked or wedged before I got in. The front door is still locked, and all the windows shut. Either they had keys or took Madame Trieste's with them. Ned,' He waited while Ned pulled the hood over his shaved head and reached for his gloves. 'I imagine you got the message. That it looks as though they took DI Laurence with them. Her car is down the street and her keys are in the kitchen. There's no sign of her in the immediate vicinity and her phone is off.'

'Yes, I heard,' replied Ned. 'We'll have a very careful look round, believe me. If she was there, we'll find traces.'

'Yes, I know you will,' said Greg.

'One other thing,' said Ned. 'There're rumours back at the office about what triggered this. Some are saying that Sarah asked that mutt from the Met to do a discreet check round the home of our number-one suspect, and he went in with blue lights blazing.'

'Oh God. That might explain the cryptic message from Sarah on my phone.' Greg had no difficulty recognising the specific officer from Ned's description. DC Jeff Fellowes, formerly of the Metropolitan Police, had banged heads with quite a few of his new colleagues for a range of shortcomings, from a pronounced tendency to mansplain to rabidly macho behaviour. Subtlety was not his dominant characteristic and Greg was surprised Sarah had given him any task requiring discretion. It might also explain why Margaret was complaining about calls from the "funny buggers".

And I still haven't rung her back, he realised. 'Damn. Chris, you heard what Ned said. Can you check exactly what happened at the office? Who did Sarah send where and with what instructions? I'll ring the Chief Super before she has my guts for garters.'

Margaret was brief and to the point.

'Greg, I know you've got your hands full in Norwich and Sarah's safety is clearly the priority. I'll hold the funny buggers off for now. What you need to know, if you don't already, is that phone traffic to a number on GCHQ's watch list went through the roof yesterday. It seems Sarah has been chatting to our old friend Newton, I believe with your say-so, and he's now been on to me. He says he warned Sarah that the extra traffic might mean the Lithuanians were looking for the leak in their midst, and she should get her whistle-blowers to a safe space.'

'I'll check the prison visitor she was talking to is okay,' replied Greg. 'That might explain why she shot off to Madame Trieste without waiting to speak to me. I missed a call while I was with the CPS and picked up a voice message only this afternoon. It's looking black for Sarah then.'

'Keep me briefed,' replied Margaret. 'For now, let's keep the details between ourselves. We don't want any leaks.'

'Will do,' replied Greg, wondering if he was meant to read something between the lines. 'One thing I should mention, I gather the office rumour is that she sent DC Fellowes to take a quiet look round a particular location and he went in with his size elevens. I've got Chris checking precisely what did happen.'

'Good. Speak later.'

Following Ned across the road, Greg hung around at the entrance to the Nails Galore kitchen, waiting for the OK to enter.

'Stay by the door for the moment,' said Ned, looking up. 'It's getting a bit crowded in here and we don't want anyone stepping where they shouldn't.'

Dr Paisley looked up from where she was bending over Madame Trieste. 'The bad news is that it looks to me as though her eyes were removed while she was still alive. The good news is that the nailing was done after she was dead. I'll know more when I've had a proper look at her on my table. I take it you haven't found her eyes, Ned?'

'Not yet,' he said shortly.

'Well, I'll be surprised if you do. I rather think I'll find them later. She was probably made to eat them.'

Greg could feel himself turning green.

'Time of death?' he managed to ask.

'Not too long ago. I'd estimate between three and five pm. With the usual caveats.'

Greg took his phone out to check. 'If the earlier time is right, that's only half an hour after Sarah left me the last message saying she was coming here. That probably puts Sarah here at the time Madame Trieste was attacked. Or shortly after. That's not good. Anything from you yet, Ned?'

'Lots I need to double check,' he replied. 'But there's blood spatter here that might have come from someone other than the Madame. It doesn't look right for the picture emerging of what was done to her. This looks like a blow to the head or face of someone between the table and the door, and there's no such injury on the body here. But it could, of course, be someone else.'

'Enough for a DNA test? Sarah's profile will be on file of course.'

'Possibly.'

Chris interrupted from the yard. 'I've been speaking to Jill,' she said. 'She says that Jeff Fellowes was tasked to make some low-key enquiries around Greater Ormesby, but it seems he may have gone straight to the address under suspicion. I'll have a chat with him when I get back. More importantly, there're a couple of businesses in this street with CCTV and Constable Peake out here has used his initiative and found two houses with video doorbells. I'm just going with him to check them out. Then I'll go back to Wymondham, if I can find a lift.'

'I'll be heading over myself once I'm sure we've wrapped up here. Meet me after you've checked the CCTV and we might be able to go back together.'

Chris backed carefully into the yard and nodded to PC Peake: tall, young and keen. She sighed mentally for the days when she'd felt so excited by a new challenge. Today, she just felt tired, and more than a little depressed.

'Okay,' she said. 'Where're these two houses with the high-tech doorbells?'

'Over there,' he said, pointing to two doors overlooking the entrance to Nails Galore. 'I think they're the entrances to flats above the shops. I expect they got the doorbells with cameras to save them coming downstairs every time the bell rings. With these, you can monitor them from your phone. There may be more further down the street,' he added, 'but I thought these would be a priority.'

'You thought right,' said Chris. 'Come on then, let's see if there's anyone home.'

The first bell rang without response. The second was answered almost before Chris got her finger on it.

'I wondered if you'd be after our videos,' the disembodied voice said. 'Come on up.' With a buzz the door swung open.

The stairs were plain, with no carpet on the painted wood. A bike filled half the tiny hall and the pair edged past it with some difficulty. At the top of the stairs, they found another door; this one opening onto a bed-sitting room, rather elegantly dressed out in pale greys and white. The young man waiting for them, ready with his iPad, was a good match for the décor: taupe shirt, cream chinos and beige hair.

'The doorbell records anyone coming to the door, and also any motion it detects across the street. I usually ignore everything except the people coming to the door, but the other recordings are here for most of today. How far back do you want to go?'

'Say to around 14:30,' replied Chris.

'Take a seat.' He waved to the stripped pine chairs by his grey table and set up the iPad in front of them. 'Here you are.'

They watched in silence, except for the scratching of PC Peake's pen as he made notes, and one exclamation from Chris. At the end she looked up.

'That may be very important,' she said to the young technophile. 'Can I have your name, please?'

'Brian Caterham,' he said. 'I work at Aviva.'

'Okay, Brian. Thank you for showing those videos to me. I need copies. Is that straightforward?'

'No problem,' he said. 'I can email them to you right now.'

'Good. Please do that.' She handed him her card. 'My email address is on here. And I hope it goes without saying, I don't want to see copies turning up on the news or social media. These recordings are now evidence.'

'Got it,' said Brian, nodding vigorously.

'Before we go, did you yourself witness anything going on at the salon opposite? I mean directly witness anything, not through your doorbell,' asked Chris.

'I didn't get home until gone five,' he said. 'And I don't think I looked out of the window until all the blue flashing lights and sirens told me something was wrong. Sorry.'

'No problem. The video may be helpful. What about your neighbour? I see they have a similar set-up.'

'Yes, they got it on my recommendation,' he said. 'But they won't be home until later. She works nights mostly, and he's on shift work as well. I haven't seen them in the early evening all week.'

'Okay, we'll try them later. Thank you, Mr Caterham. We'll get back to you if we have any further questions.'

Once outside she said, 'Good call,' to the young policeman. 'Well done.' Then went back to where Greg was leaning on his car, apparently on the phone. When he turned to her, she said, 'I think you're going to want to see this. It's not great quality on a phone but the magicians can probably do something with it back at base.

'What it does show is a number of cars passing by, just before and in the hour after three pm. On most you can see the number plate. One is Sarah's, going past to where we've seen it parked up the street. This is the one that's really interesting. It parks outside Nails Galore by the ginnel to the back alley. As far as you can see there's a driver and a passenger, both sitting in the front seats. They get out and go down the ginnel. After about forty minutes the camera picks up some more motion. One of the passengers seems to push something into the back seat from the pavement side of the car and then get into the back seat after it. The driver comes round and gets in the front, then they drive off.'

'Can you see exactly where they come from?'

'No, but it looks as though it's the ginnel again.'

'And you're thinking?'

'I think that's Sarah being pushed into the car and driven away.'

2

Cock-up or conspiracy?

Looking over his shoulder, Greg reversed his red BMW out of the narrow space between emergency vehicles still parked askew the street. The ambulance had left. The mortuary van had collected the sad, despoiled remains of Madame Trieste. Only the forensic services' van and two police cars with blue lights remained. Soon the street would return to an apparent normal, except for the fluttering blue and white tape and the uniformed police ensuring the crime scene was secure.

Once they were back on the ring road, heading for Wymondham and Norfolk Police HQ, Chris put her notebook away and turned as far as her seatbelt permitted to study the grim face of the man she loved.

'I think it's time you explained what's been going on,' she said. Greg flashed her a glance, then returned his attention to the road.

'You're right,' he admitted. 'And now is as good a time as any. I need to go back a bit, to a few days ago. Soon after we charged Colin Brown with the murder of Marilena Dalci and the other women, Madame Trieste asked to see Sarah. It seems she was grateful that we had taken her seriously, and that we hadn't just written Marilena off because she was a sex worker. Anyway, she asked to see Sarah and gave her the name and phone number of a Lithuanian she claimed was behind a lot of crime in Norfolk including supplying the Semtex that was used in the recent terrorist attack on the government lab, and the modern slavery case involving Dragan Bakalov last year.'

'You always said Bakalov was an important link,' agreed Chris.

'The key point now, is that Madame Trieste was emphatic Sarah should say nothing about where the intelligence came from, because the subject had contacts in Norfolk Police. The Madame insisted that Sarah share the name with only one other person. Me. She was terrified she'd be at risk if the intelligence went any wider.'

'And she was right,' said Chris. There was a silence in the car. 'So that was why you wouldn't tell me what Sarah had been discussing with you?'

'That's right.' Greg was glad the traffic meant he could rightly keep his eyes on the road. 'I know you're discreet Chris, but in this situation, I had to play by the book. I couldn't apply one rule to Sarah and another to me.' He considered adding to his explanation, then decided to apply the maxim 'surplus words turn septic' and shut up.

'Okay, I get that,' said Chris. 'What about this afternoon?'

'Sarah left a voicemail this afternoon while I was talking to the CPS. She'd been trying to get hold of me. She said she'd been tipped off by the funny buggers, DI Newton to be precise, that traffic to and from a phone number they'd been monitoring had just gone mad, and they thought the reason was a hunt for a grass. She'd warned the prison visitor she'd been talking to about Bakalov to go to ground, and then she was coming over to warn Madame Trieste. It seems she arrived at exactly the wrong time.'

Chris was silent for so long, they were turning into the HQ entrance before she spoke again. 'You've spoken to Margaret about this?'

'Yes. And she said something interesting. She said to keep the details between her and me, because we "don't want any leaks".'

'Did she mean to the press? Or does *she* think we've a bad apple too?'

'I don't know. I'm seeing her now.' He pulled the car up with a jerk and turned the engine off. 'Chris, when you check out what Jeff Fellowes has been up to, be careful of the details. I need to know whether he was being a cack-handed idiot, or whether there was something more sinister going on.'

'Got it. I'll check back with you after you've spoken to Margaret.'

***

Clearly the phone had been humming. Greg could tell that, both from the Chief Superintendent's harassed expression and the dishevelled state of her hair. One of the first things he'd noticed about his boss was her tendency to run her hands through her hair when under stress. She wasn't alone. Already sitting at the table were DI Newton of Special Branch and a dark man he didn't recognise.

'DI Newton you know,' she said. 'This is DCI Trent, from Merseyside. He's been posted to us via Special Branch to assist with this case. It was good luck he was meeting with DI Newton in Cambridge.' Greg tried to hide his knee-jerk reaction.

'Does that mean you're taking me off the case?' he asked.

'No. I want you to work in tandem with DCI Trent. I will take the formal role of SIO. You'll both report to me. Until recently, DCI Trent was working in the Serious Fraud Office. He has useful contacts and experience. It's been agreed he will lead in tracing the movement of money, and especially the money laundering activities of our main suspect. I want you, Greg, to lead on finding Sarah and identifying the murderer – or murderers – of Madame Trieste. If, as we suspect, both investigations follow routes that end in one destination, all the better. Clearing up the little chaps is all very well, but it's not got us very far. Put a few away, and another twenty are recruited and set to work before we turn round. We need to take the head off this organisation, and that means cooperation from all involved.'

She paused and looked at the three men. 'It also means discretion. Special Branch are suspicious that someone within Norfolk Police is leaking to our Mr Big. Sufficient to tip him off when we're about to take action anyway. That's why this investigation is going to be very tightly controlled. You two,' she nodded to Greg and Trent, 'you report to me and me only. You'll get a small team to assist, and nothing goes outside that team.'

Greg cleared his throat. 'I've already asked Chris Mathews to investigate what Jeff Fellowes got up to in Ormesby,' he said.

'That's okay,' said Margaret. 'In fact, I'd say good choice. Who else would you recommend?'

Greg paused for thought. 'Jill for sure. She's good on detail. She might be able to help DCI Trent as well. Steve and Phil. If we can use civilian staff, then—'

'No civilians,' said Newton.

'I can borrow some resource from the SFO,' said Trent. 'Working remotely, I can make sure there's no crossover with Norfolk.'

'Okay,' said Margaret, standing up. 'Then I'll leave you to it. Keep me posted. DI Newton, can you stay a moment, please?'

Greg and DCI Trent took that as their release. Outside in the corridor, the two men each took the measure of the other. Greg saw a wiry, dark-skinned man with brown eyes alight with a sharp intelligence and a long nose above a wide mouth.

'Ram,' said the stranger, holding out his hand to Greg. 'I imagine you're feeling that you need me like a hole in the head.' Greg grinned, despite himself, and Ram saw the rather surly expression on the muscular man before him suddenly evaporate with the smile.

'Exactly what I was thinking,' Greg admitted, 'but I think we've got much bigger problems to worry about than a turf war between us.' Ram's smile vanished.

'Yes. Whatever I can do to speed up finding your colleague, I will, believe me. Now, first thing I need is somewhere to lay my laptop.'

'There's a spare desk in my office if you don't mind sharing,' replied Greg.

'Well, let's give it a try shall we,' said Ram. 'If we irritate the hell out of each other, we can always think again. It would have the benefit of keeping everything close.'

Ram Trent had barely plugged in and logged on, when Chris came bursting through the door in her usual precipitate fashion. If Ram was surprised by the dazzling effect of primrose and fuchsia worn on the same person at the same time, he didn't blink. Chris stopped short and looked to Greg for an explanation.

'DCI Trent, also working on this investigation, specialising on the money side,' said Greg. He added, 'This is Sergeant Chris Mathews, who has just, I hope, found out what happened to provoke the sudden crisis.' Chris took the seat by Greg's desk, and angled it so she could see both men.

'Pleased to meet you,' she said. Then to Greg, 'I've got a pretty good idea about that. After Sarah got the tip-off from DI Newton, she went looking for someone to make some discreet enquiries in the village of Great Ormesby. As far as I can see, it was just bad luck that the only officer available was that spare part the Met dumped on us.' Ram Trent raised an elegant eyebrow but said nothing.

'His orders were to scout out the ground and ask some quiet questions, if he could without making a stir,' went on Chris.

'How do you know that?' asked Ram.

'Sarah put it in the record. I've checked. She was always meticulous about making notes, but I think in this case she was probably also worried that she couldn't send someone more reliable, so she was covering her back.

'Anyway, it seems that Fellowes's interpretation of this order was to drive through the village and park right outside our

Mr Big's home, where he then got out and wandered up and down. He was definitely seen by one of the residents or their staff, because a man with a lawnmower came out of the drive and had a chat with him. Just in case the subject hadn't got the message, Fellowes then went back into the village and asked questions at the garage, the newsagent's and the village shop, to name but three. The timing coincides with the increase in phone traffic that triggered the second call from Newton and the alarm being raised thanks to Fellowes clomping about in his size elevens.'

'So, you're thinking cock-up rather than conspiracy?' asked Greg.

'Well, yes. But...' Chris hesitated, glancing sideways at Ram.

'It's okay, Chris, he knows the whole story,' said Greg, interpreting her caution correctly.

'Okay. I think that bit was cock-up. I think Fellowes is an unmitigated arse but I don't have any reason yet to suspect him of being actively on the take. But something else worries me.'

Greg nodded. 'The speed of the focus on Nails Galore.'

'That's right. Looking at how fast they got there, I mean, in order to be there at the same time as Sarah. Well, it makes it look as though they went straight there after Fellowes set the fireworks off.'

'So, were they already suspicious of Madame Trieste, or was there another trigger? Did they get a very precise tip-off? Chris, have you found anything that suggests anyone else knew where Sarah was going?'

'No. She didn't put that on her notes. Apart from the message she left you, obviously.'

***

After Chris left the room, Ram looked at Greg, his eyebrow raised quizzically again.

'Is that sort of description of a colleague common round here?' he asked.

'Sergeant Mathews has good reason for her, rather bluntly expressed, view,' said Greg. 'And you'll find blunt expressions are her usual mode of communication. Think yourself lucky. The first time she met me she called me a numpty.'

Ram laughed. 'And the unfortunate DC Fellowes?'

'An unreconstructed macho male who thinks with his...' Greg stopped himself. 'Let's just say, he doesn't use his brains much. He's no advert for the Met.'

'What do you think about this idea someone may have tipped them off from here?'

'At this point, I'm not sure what to think. I've been here a couple of years now, and I've had no reason until now to suspect anyone even of taking backhanders. But there are two obvious points for investigation. First, could Sarah's message to me have been intercepted? In other words, was her phone bugged? Second, could she have been overheard as she left the message, or could she have told anyone else where she was going?

'The first thing we need to do is corral our chosen few in a separate office and brief them on how these investigations are going to run. We can also check on whether we've got anything from forensics yet, and the CCTV footage. We're only just outside the golden hour. The faster we find something on Sarah's movements after the murder, the better.'

3

Briefings

Emerging from his office, Greg was surprised, but pleased, to find he'd walked into a whirlwind. Civilian assistants and researchers were bustling in one direction, burdened with the paperwork and laptops that had been in use on the serial killer investigation just concluded. Heading the opposite way were Jill, Steve, Phil and a couple of chaps in uniform, similarly burdened with laptops, screens, cables and filing trays.

'What's going on?' he asked Jill. She paused in her canter up the corridor.

'Chris told us to set up a mini ops room in the conference room down the corridor, and to get it up and running tonight. She said no one went home until we did! The chaos is because admin also told everyone to clear up the main ops room now the Colin Brown serial killer case is going to court.' Jill shrugged as well as she could while burdened with her high-end laptop and a large screen. 'I'm setting up as fast as I can so I can go back over the CCTV images we got from Norwich.'

'Good. Thanks, Jill. Tell everyone I'll be along in five minutes with a briefing. Seen Ned?'

'No. But Steve says he's back from Norwich too.'

By the time Greg and Ram reached the conference room, its main table was supporting a circle of laptops, looking very much like the wagons had been drawn up to fend off attack. At one end the white boards were in place, ready for updates on key issues. At the other were maps pinned to the walls; one a detailed Ordnance Survey map of the area around Great Ormesby. The other a street map of the part of Norwich that contained Nails Galore.

Ned followed Greg and Ram into the room. Ram closed the door and took up a stance near it. Greg headed for what small space there was by the whiteboards and wrote on one 'Find Sarah'. The other he headed 'Moneybags'. Then he turned to face the room. Jill and Steve were sitting in front of their laptops, either side of the conference table. Phil and Ned sat down just in front of Greg, leaving Ram still at the back by the door. At that moment Chris came in, almost knocking Ram over as the door flew open. She was followed by DI Jim Henning.

'Jim,' said Greg, startled. 'I thought you were still tied up with the county lines brief.'

'I was. I am,' he corrected himself. 'But Margaret told me to join you here. She said she thinks it'll be part of the same investigation anyway.'

'Great to have you on board. This is DCI Trent.' Greg performed swift introductions, then, with a glance round to check everyone was present, called for order.

'Okay, everyone. It's late and time is passing. I'm as keen as any of you that we find Sarah as rapidly as possible, but we need to be intelligent about this. When it's time to act fast, we will. When it's time to stop and think, we'll do that too. The clever bit is knowing which is which. So, as it's now…' He paused and checked his watch. 'Nearly midnight. The first thing we need to know is, do we have any red hot leads we should be chasing down now?

'Ned?'

Ned shook his head. 'Not much yet from me. I should know a little more tomorrow when results of analyses start coming in and you get the post-mortem report on Madame Trieste. At this point all I can tell you is what you know already. Sarah was there in that room this afternoon, and there's some evidence that she may have received an injury creating blood spatter. That's all so far.'

'Chris? Jill?' Greg changed the focus of his attention. Jill spoke up.

'That video footage Chris got from someone's front door shows what looks like Sarah being bundled into the back seat of a Range Rover. I've managed to get a partial on the number plate.'

Chris chipped in. 'I've put an APB out on the description and partial number. Nothing yet.'

'What about CCTV around the city?'

'Nothing yet,' replied Jill. 'But it takes time to trawl through that sort of footage.'

'Yes, I know.'

'What're we doing about that house in Great Ormesby?' asked Phil.

'Good question,' said Greg. 'And the answer as far as I know is nothing. DCI Trent?' Ram spoke up from where he was leaning by the door.

'I believe Special Branch and the Serious Fraud Office are monitoring communications. That's all so far. They'll tip us off if we need to know.'

'Jim,' said Greg. 'Can I leave that to you? Sort out some low-key surveillance. Use drones and the helicopter where you can without causing a stir. You know the area better than most. They'll be expecting something, so I'd suggest giving them something to look at, then sneak something more discreet in while they're distracted.'

Jim nodded. 'Any problem with me using Fellowes as the red herring?' he asked.

'Good idea. Provided you don't share any more with him than you need. Let them think we really are that stupid. Get him out there tonight, then again tomorrow morning. Anything he spots, he reports to you.'

'Okay.'

'Ram, anything you want to add?' asked Greg. Ram Trent came forward.

'No. I don't think so. DI Henning, can you keep in touch with me? I'll let you know if there's anything from the comms surveillance that needs tying in.'

Jim nodded. 'Will do.'

Greg looked round the room again. 'Then, reluctant as I am to say this, I don't think we can do any more tonight. I'll attend the post-mortem first thing tomorrow, then catch up with you all here. Sleep as well as you can, and be here early. Tomorrow needs to be the day we find Sarah.'

4

Underground

Coming round with a pounding headache, the first thing to hit Sarah's awareness was the sensation she was being suffocated. She gasped involuntarily and sucked some of the rough cloth covering her head into her mouth. Panicked, she gasped again and struggled as violently as she was capable. Someone growled at her in a language she didn't recognise and pushed her violently face down. Her air supply shrank still further and another voice, slightly further off, said something sharp. It sounded like an order.

The hands pushing her down relaxed, and the cloth was pulled tighter over her head, pulling it out of her mouth. She heaved a huge sobbing sigh, and then another. Oxygen reached her brain and while the pounding in her head continued, memory started to filter back.

A sudden picture filled her eyes, of Madame Trieste as she had last seen her, spread-eagled against the kitchen cupboards; of the burly man in polo shirt and jeans who'd turned round abruptly, a hammer in his hand, nails in his mouth; of the scream in her own throat echoing the one from Madame Trieste that ended in a sickening gurgle. Sarah vaguely remembered trying to turn back to the door, reaching for her phone and taser, but remembered nothing else.

She brought her mind back to the present. Her head ached with sickening thuds that felt as though blood was going to burst out of her temples. She could, indeed, taste blood in her mouth through the overpowering flavour of dirty cloth. She felt around her, trying to make out where she was, and something slammed into her right hand. She groaned, convinced that at least one of her fingers was broken, and lay still. Her ears though, she could use those.

From the sounds and the motion rocking her from side to side, every swing now transmitted excruciatingly through her damaged hand, she concluded she was in a vehicle. A car perhaps, from the feel of upholstery beneath her. She tried to listen to the sounds of the road and to note the sensations as the car took the bends. She concluded that working out your route and location by sound was an urban myth. She had no idea where she was, nor how long she'd been in the car.

She could hear voices, two she thought, and muffled conversation. None of it was in English as far as she could tell. Eastern European, she guessed, but couldn't narrow it down any further.

She stifled a groan as another bend in the road threw her against the back of the seat and jarred her hand. Certainly, the worst pain was in her hand and head. She remembered reading that you couldn't feel two different pain sources at the same time. Well that's a lot of cobblers for a start, she thought with a very wry smile. On the other hand, her ribs, back and legs seemed to be okay. Perhaps making a run for it might not be out of the question. If the opportunity presented itself.

The car seemed to slow down and bumped along a rough track before coming to a halt. Cold air blew in onto her legs, and big hands pulled at her, catching hold of her thigh, clothes and arms. She cried out through the muffling sacking over her head, as her broken hand jarred on the doorsill, then she was in the open air with a brisk wind blowing and the sounds of tree branches moving overhead. The commanding voice gave an order, and the other man pulled her arms behind her and grasped both wrists in one hand. She cried out again and the other man punched her in the stomach, doubling her up. For a moment she thought she was going to be horribly sick inside the sack over her head, but, swallowing hard, she managed to control it.

'Be quiet, or I hit you again,' said the deep voice from the man in front of her. 'And the next time, not so soft. I break your neck. Easy.'

She was pushed forward over rough ground. She stumbled often, each time jarring her hand, held firmly behind her, but now she bit the inside of her cheek until she bled, rather than make a noise. She had no doubt that the man would make good on his threat to kill her. If she'd had any doubt, she had only to look at the picture of Madame Trieste imprinted inside her eyelids.

They came to a sudden halt. There was the sound of something grating. Metal on concrete she guessed, then suddenly was seized by both arms and pushed forward. There was nothing under her feet and she couldn't help but cry out again as she hung, suspended by her arms, convinced they were pushing her to her death off a cliff.

'What did I say,' snarled the man in charge as she hung in their hands, her arms and shoulders screaming with the sudden pain. Then they let go and she choked back another scream as she dropped ... and landed on a pile of soil and rubble.

She crumpled to the ground, barking her shins on what felt like half bricks and shattered tiles. Her head hit the wall opposite her and, for a second, she thought her neck was indeed broken. Then she heard the voice again.

'Keep quiet, and we come back for you. Make a noise and you die here.'

Then there was the grating sound again, followed by silence.

Sarah listened. No sounds intruded, except for her own breathing, harsh through the muffling sacking, and the faint rasp of soil falling and settling. She waited for what seemed like an hour, but was probably only minutes. Her breathing gradually settled down from heaving sobs into something steadier. Her heart rate started to drop too, less thunder in her ears, more steady pumping. She tried moving her arms, and apart from the damaged hand and the strained shoulders, all seemed to be well. Her legs were painfully curled beneath her on the rough surface below. When she moved them, she lost her balance for a moment, instinctively put out a hand, and almost fainted with pain as it hit a wall less than a foot away. With her good hand she felt for the sacking over her head and pulled it off.

The relief of unimpeded breathing was huge; the disappointment she felt, almost as great. Even without the sacking, she could still see nothing. She felt around with her good left hand. There was a wall within reach on every side, surface crumbling, but firm. The floor beneath her was uneven with builder's debris, but solid. Above her, she could feel nothing but emptiness. As far as she could tell, she was entombed in a cell or shaft no more than four feet square. From the drop she assumed it was at least nine feet deep. She wriggled round, trying to find a less uncomfortable sitting position, her curled legs already beginning to cramp, her damaged hand cradled on her lap. With her good hand she pulled the sacking over her shoulders and prepared to wait. She wondered how long they planned to leave her there. No light, no food, no water. She refused to contemplate what would happen if they didn't return.

5

Post-mortem

Starting the day with a post-mortem would never be on anyone's wish list, reflected Greg, smearing the trusty Vicks on his upper lip. He smiled at Chris through the fumes as she did the same, then they both turned to Dr Paisley.

'Ready?' she asked, and led them over to the stainless-steel table, where rested what was left of Madame Trieste. 'You'll be pleased to know I've completed the autopsy,' she added. 'There's just a few things I think you'll need to see for yourselves.'

The standard Y-shaped incision had indeed already been stitched up and the scalp returned to its normal position.

'I'll take you through the stomach contents in a moment,' said the doctor, blithely oblivious to the unfortunate phrasing. 'These are the marks I wanted you to see. They've been photographed already.' She pointed to contusions on the neck and under the jaw. 'See here. These look to me like one hand. A large one. He's taken a grip on her neck and half choked her, then shifted his grip to just under her jaw here,' – she pointed with her pen – 'in order to force her mouth open.'

'You said "he", and "half choked",' said Greg.

'Yes. Hands this size are unlikely to belong to a woman. And half choked, because she didn't die of choking. She died of blood loss from this wound here.' She moved closer to the body and pointed to an incision just beneath the jaw. 'This one cut the carotid artery and she bled out in minutes. But only after she'd been tortured.'

Greg swallowed hard and from the corner of his eye he saw Chris's knuckles whiten where she gripped her clipboard.

'I'm sure you're going to tell me,' he said.

'Afraid so. This was a very vicious attack, designed as a clear warning to others. The evidence here suggests she was first half choked, as I said, by a very powerful man with large hands. Either he, with his other hand, or an accomplice – most likely an accomplice – then removed her eyes with a knife and forced them into her throat. The stab wound which caused her to bleed out was the last and fatal wound.'

'What sort of weapon are we looking for?'

'Two different blades in my opinion. The one used on her eyes was a short-bladed sharp knife, a bit like a scalpel, or perhaps even a scalpel. The one which killed her was a bigger knife. It had a blade at least ten centimetres long and sharp on both edges. What I think is called a spear point. I'm no expert on militaria and you might want to consult one, but I think this wound was made by something similar to a trench knife, only smaller. I'll give you the precise measurements in my report.'

Greg glanced at Chris, scribbling notes. 'Do we have an expert we've used before?' he asked.

'I'll check,' she said, still scribbling.

'Anything else we need to know?' asked Greg.

'Just that the final flourish, the nails, were inserted after her death and didn't contribute to it. Bog-standard galvanised nails, the sort you'd buy from any hardware shop, or find on any building site.'

Greg walked round the body on the table, studying the marks he'd been shown. 'Did you find the eyes?' he asked.

'I did. As I guessed, she'd been forced to swallow them.'

'Why do the thing with the eyes while she was still alive?' he asked abruptly. 'It'd have been much easier after she was dead and nailed to the cupboards, and the message to anyone finding her would've been the same. You're sure it happened before she died?'

'I'm sure,' replied Dr Paisley. 'And in answer to your first question – perhaps because he enjoyed it.'

Outside and breathing deeply of the fresh air, Greg glanced at Chris.

'Okay?' he asked.

'Okay. For now. Although I'll probably have nightmares,' she replied. 'We need to find Sarah fast, before he decides to have a bit more fun.'

'Perhaps knowing she's a police officer will affect how he treats her?'

'Perhaps so. But which way? And which of them is the sadist. The man in charge or the other one?'

'We don't know for sure there were two involved in the torture,' objected Greg.

'No. But thanks to the local IT expert's door camera, we do know there were two men putting her in the car.'

By the time they got back to HQ, there was already a buzz in their makeshift operations room. Jill met them with a wave and a big smile.

'We might have a lead,' she said.

'You've not spotted something already?'

'Not me, no. I'm still going through CCTV feeds. But I got the images from the door camera enlarged and cleaned up, then shared them with Highways England. They have people monitoring cameras on all the main arterial roads all the time, and I thought it was worth asking if they'd spotted anything like the car in the images we have. It was a long shot, but it's come up with a possible lead.'

'Which is?' Greg sat down in the chair next to Jill.

'Here.' She tapped swiftly on her keyboard and pulled up a hazy image of a car on the side of a dual carriageway. It was dark and the nearest street lighting was some distance away, casting shadows that obscured the scene rather than illuminating it. She used the cursor to focus on the back of the vehicle and the number plate.

'This matches the partial registration number we got from the door camera footage. Highways England spotted it last night and checked it over, but it was burned out and, they thought, empty. They logged it for retrieval later today, as it wasn't causing an obstruction.

'I've asked uniform to send someone out to tape it and ensure it's undisturbed until forensics have had a chance to check it over. I hope that's okay,' she added slightly anxiously.

'Well done, Jill. Absolutely the right thing to do,' replied Greg. 'Where is it exactly? We'll get over there.'

'I'm surprised you haven't recognised it. It's the A47 near Blofield, just before the single carriageway section with the speed limit.' Greg looked again, his nose practically touching the screen.

'So it is. That's the slip road. Okay. We'll get out there right away.' Chris interrupted. 'There's a message on your desk. Margaret wants to see you and Ram in her office.'

'Damn. Okay. Chris, you get over to the car with Ned. I'll catch up with you later.'

Ram was just taking a seat and Margaret looked up as Greg entered her office.

'I've had the short version emailed over from Pathology,' she said. 'Very nasty.'

'Yes.' Greg took a seat. We think we've found the car that took Sarah from Nails Galore. I was just going over there.'

'Leave that to the team,' said Margaret. 'I understand the wish to get stuck in, but you need to take a more holistic view, Greg. This is a big case with a lot of ramifications. So, what do we have so far from your side?'

'In summary, evidence of two men, probably neither of them our main player, one with big hands and another with a tendency to enjoy torture. They were armed with at least two blades, one of them an ex-military trench knife or something very similar. Then, what looks like Sarah being forced into the back seat of a car caught on camera footage, and the remains of the same car, burned out, on the road heading east from Norwich toward Great Yarmouth and the coastal villages. I haven't confirmed with Ned yet, but it's likely Sarah was injured in some way at Nails Galore before being forced into the car.

'Jim has sent Fellowes round Greater Ormesby to provide a distraction, and separately has some discreet drone and helicopter surveillance. Nothing new to report as yet.'

'Ram?' asked Margaret.

'Phone activity still high, and at the moment they don't seem to be aware we are monitoring. Translations are coming through now, as this operation has priority. I've got transcripts to share with you, but the main points of interest deal with money laundering operations in Great Yarmouth and Norwich. There's also what looks like a connection with drugs. Possibly grow-houses.'

'You need to share that with Jim,' said Greg. 'He's been leading on our county lines operation. He found one small grow-house producing cannabis on the edge of Great Yarmouth, but I know he's been following up some leads in Caister and the coastal villages.' Ram made a note.

Margaret looked up. 'Just make sure no one moves too soon,' she said. 'Number-one priority is Sarah. But number two is nailing the head man. We don't want to go too soon and end up with only small fry again.'

'Has Jim identified the recruiters?' Ram asked. 'The folk grooming the kids moving the drugs about?'

'He's put away a couple,' replied Greg, 'but that isn't getting us very far, as Margaret has just said.'

'Any pattern?'

'We need to talk to Jim. But as far as I remember, the recruiters are usually fairly well-known lowlifes making a career move. The recruits tend to be youngsters, either just out of school or even still at school.'

'And who's recruiting the recruiters?'

'That's not so easy, as you know.'

'I'd suggest looking at the money launderers again,' recommended Ram. 'I'll have a chat with Jim, see if there's any crossover.' Greg shifted uneasily on his seat.

'Yes,' he said. 'But let's not forget Sarah. Time's running out for her. I need to catch up with Ned and Chris to see if we have any more leads.'

6

Moved on

With no way of reading her watch, Sarah had no idea how much time had passed. It seemed to be endless. She started to construct a balance sheet in her head. On the positive side, she was still alive, and her headache was gradually subsiding. On the negative side, her legs were now so cramped she doubted they would move even if they had the opportunity. The cold had chilled her beyond shivering and she'd long since given up the unequal struggle with her bladder. At least that had produced a transitory sensation of warmth. Searching through her pockets with her good, left hand, produced a crumpled handkerchief and one remaining super-strong mint in a scrap of paper. She hesitated over saving the mint, wondered what for, and popped it in her mouth. She made it last as long as she could, but all too quickly it was gone. She licked the paper in case there were any crumbs of sweet left, then had another thought and licked it some more, before tucking it in the corner of the shaft by a broken brick.

After that, there was nothing else to do but strain her ears in the silence and her eyes in the dark. Sometime later, after how long she had no idea, she woke suddenly to some sound.

'Either woke, or came to,' she said to herself grimly.

The noise was more a vibration than a sound: a sort of pulsation reverberating through the ground.

'A vehicle moving above,' she said to herself, and then realised she'd said it aloud. She could shout. Perhaps rescue was only a few feet away. She opened her mouth to shout, had second thoughts and closed it again, then had third thoughts and shouted as loud as she could manage.

'Help. Help.' It was little more than a croak. Her mouth and throat were dry. She could hardly hear herself. No one else would. Especially not someone driving a heavy vehicle above ground. That was the point at which she gave up and resigned herself to dying in that rank, miserable hole. She cried a little, although she was too dehydrated to produce many tears. Then she either slept or lapsed back into unconsciousness.

When she woke again, the metal cover was off the shaft and she could see the grey light of dusk. Some drops of rain fell on her head, and she tried to lick them off her face and arms. There was an exclamation of disgust, then someone dropped down beside her, landing partly on her feet and ankles. She groaned, then passed out again.

The man beside her passed a rope swiftly round her body below her shoulders. It tightened, and with him boosting from below, she was lifted swiftly from the shaft and placed in the back of a white transit van.

***

When she regained awareness again, she realised she was on the move. The floor of the van was naked, ridged metal and agonisingly uncomfortable, but the realisation she wasn't lying dead at the bottom of the shaft buoyed her up. The van took a corner sharply, and the only reason she didn't roll around was the man sitting opposite, his back braced against the van side, his feet in her belly. This time there was no sacking over her head. She couldn't decide whether that was a good sign or a bad. Was she effectively dead already, so it didn't matter what she saw? Or was there some other reason for their carelessness? Perhaps they thought she was beyond taking anything in. Her eyes half closed and looking out through her lashes, she tried to note any special characteristics of her jailor. He was a big man with big hands and large features. His head was bald or shaved and there was a tattoo of some kind on his neck. At this distance she couldn't make out what it depicted. He was wearing what looked like black jeans and a black sweatshirt with some sort of logo on the front. Another swerve of the van gave her the excuse to let her head loll back so she was looking at the cab. The driver had short hair and a baseball cap. That was all she could see from her place on the floor. Another swerve, some more bouncing over a rough track, or possibly speed bumps, and the van came to a halt. The man wedging her against the side wall didn't move. The driver got out, and after a short while the rear doors were flung open. Sarah, making out she was only half conscious at best, was slumped on the floor and stayed that way, even to the extent of ignoring, as far as she was capable, a kick in her side. She suppressed the groan, but couldn't help but huddle up in a foetal position.

There was a swift exchange in the language she didn't recognise and, even semi-conscious, Sarah could detect the note of disgust in the driver's voice. He seemed to want to keep clear of her, and Sarah couldn't blame him. She stank.

The big man seized her by her left arm and dragged her toward the open van doors. She half dropped out onto a road or driveway, almost dislocating her shoulder in the process, and there was another sharp command from the smaller man. Now she saw them side by side she realised he was not just smaller but small, probably shorter than herself and slight in build. As she was trying to calculate his height, she was swung over the big man's shoulder and hung head down as he carried her through a door, along a corridor and into a filthy bathroom. He was grasping her arm in one hand and that too had a tattoo. She had time to see it was a dagger, before he dropped her down in the filthy bath and turned the shower on full. The water was cold. She gasped in the flow and tried to fight back as her clothes were ripped off, but a blow to the side of her head made it ring again and she flopped down under the gouts of icy water.

More shouts, and a woman came in carrying a small tray and with a bathrobe over her arm. Sarah tried to stand up, but her muscles weren't obeying their signals and she sagged down again, half in, half out of the bath. Her soaking hair straggled over her face, but she saw the woman, youngish but deathly pale and with terrible skin, hold out the tray toward the big man. He wrenched Sarah's arm toward him, braced it over his knee, and plunged a needle into the big vein in her elbow. He laughed as he depressed the syringe, and that was the last she knew.

7

Clean boats?

Mindful of Margaret's injunction that he be more 'helicopter' and less 'JCB', Greg restrained himself from dashing off to the A47 and picked up his phone.

'Ned, any news?' he asked. In the background he could hear voices and the sounds of traffic passing.

'Not much yet,' replied Ned. 'A couple of bits of evidence from Nails Galore I don't think I've passed on yet. One is that the blood spatter that overlays everything from Madame Trieste is definitely Sarah's. From the placement, height, angle, etc, I'd suggest a blow to the head. There are scuff marks in the yard and down the passageway to the road that support the images we got from the door camera, ie that Sarah was dragged from the back door all the way to the high street and then pushed into a car. Given they were perfectly happy to have the other body found on the premises, that implies to me that Sarah was alive at that point, and there's nothing in the forensics to suggest otherwise. And one other thing, we found marks on the kitchen floor, consistent with chunky-soled trainers. You know the sort I mean. The ones that look as though they've been bred by Goodyear out of Michelin. And there are two distinct sets of marks. One pair size sixteen or thereabouts and one size eight. So, we're looking for a big chap, probably more than six feet four, and a little one, around five feet five.'

'Could the smaller shoes belong to a woman?' asked Greg.

'Yes, I suppose they could, although size eight would be big for a woman.'

'What about the car you're looking at now?'

'Well, the good news is, it *is* definitely the car we have on CCTV outside Nails Galore. The bad news is that the interior was burned pretty thoroughly. There's nothing much left. Hang on, let me pass you on to Chris.'

There were muffled sounds of a handover and Chris picked up. 'Hi, Boss. I assume Ned's told you there's not much to see here. The number plates are no help. They were nicked more than two months ago off a Defender belonging to a farm just outside Boston in Lincolnshire. However, one of the chassis numbers is still visible. Obviously the one on the windscreen went when the glass shattered, but the one on the right doorsill is readable.'

'That's something,' said Greg. 'We can check it.'

'Already checked,' said Chris with a note of triumph in her voice. 'The car was originally registered to a business operating out of Great Yarmouth. I very nearly rang them straight away but had second thoughts and spoke to Jim first. Lucky I did. It's one of the cleaning businesses he's had on his radar for some time. They supposedly provide cleaning services for hire boats on the Broads. He thinks they've links with modern slavery and cannabis growing, but he hasn't been able to connect anything dodgy with the top of the organisation and Margaret stopped him from hauling in the small fry.' She paused for breath.

'Any idea who's the car was? I mean within the company?'

'Not without asking, but it is, or was, a high-end car. It's not going to be allocated to a secretary. But get this, the company chairman, at least according to Companies House, lives in Greater Ormesby.'

***

'Jim?' Greg was chasing round the building when he saw a familiar rear view disappearing into the canteen. 'Jim, grab your sarnies and back to my office, please. I think you, Ram and I need a chat.'

Diverting via the ops room, Greg managed to catch up with Jill, also engaged in her lunch. 'Jill, have you had an update from Chris on the burned-out car?'

'Yes,' said Jill rather warily.

'I've got a job for you and Steve, and anyone else you can coerce into helping. I want ANPR and CCTV scanned for any vehicles moving in the vicinity of the A47 where the car was found, between the hours of, say midnight and six this morning.'

'What're we looking for, Boss?'

'That's the problem. I don't really know. I'm hoping the numbers will be manageably small and I want the plate on any vehicle capable of transporting an unconscious woman discreetly, checked with DVLA. I want to know whether we can identify any that are registered to this company in

Yarmouth – Clean Boats Inc.' He handed over a Post-it with the name written on. 'I also want someone to check with Companies House and then anywhere else that occurs to you, to see if any locations between the A47 and Great Ormesby are linked to that company. Go to it.'

Jill looked at Steve and shrugged. 'Some of us have all the luck!' With wry looks and a heavy sigh, Steve got down to work.

Back in his office again, Greg was pleased to see Jim had arrived and was chatting to Ram around a doorstep bacon sarnie.

'Hi, Boss,' he greeted Greg. 'Any more news on Sarah?'

'Not yet. That's what I want to talk about.' He succinctly brought the two men up to date with recent developments then added, 'I thought it might help to see if cross-referencing our intelligence on Clean Boats Inc. threw up anything new.

'Jim. What've you got?'

Jim unfolded a much-fingered Ordnance Survey map. 'Mind if I pin this up on your board?' he asked. Greg nodded his assent and got up to help Jim fix the map to the corkboard alongside those of Ormesby and Norwich already decorating the wall. 'Just to orientate us a bit,' said Jim. 'Here,' and he pointed, 'is where we found the burned-out Range Rover on the side of the A47, just before it changes from dual carriageway to single. Here—' and he went to stick a pin in but Greg stopped him.

'Just point,' he said. Jim looked at him quizzically but nodded and used his finger again to point to a spot near the Ormesby Broad.

'This is the house that Jeff Fellowes was asked to investigate discreetly. "Horses Mill House." As you can see, it's some way off the main road, down a long private drive. The entrance Fellowes was checking out when he spoke to the chap on a mower, that's around two to three hundred metres from the house itself as you can see from the map. The estate seems to be surrounded by a wall except where it backs on to the open Broad. And this,' he pointed again, this time to a heavily built-up area in Great Yarmouth. 'This is the registered head office of Clean Boats Inc. On the face of it, it's just a small rented office acting as a post box and possibly a call centre. But I think it may be more. It's one of those buildings with mainly shops on the ground floor fronting the street, and quite sizeable flats above.'

'Cobholm Island,' read Ram, peering at the map. 'Why's it called an island? It doesn't look like one.'

'It was an island once,' replied Jim. 'Bounded by the river Yare to the east, and Breydon Water to the north. They're both still there, but the third expanse of water to the southwest, Lady Haven, has long since dried up and the land been built on. All that remains now is its name on the bridge: Haven Bridge.'

'Anything from your investigations on Clean Boats, Ram?' asked Greg, impatient to bring them back to the point.

'Nothing specific, but I'll change the focus of my research now, and see what I can find. You know already that one of the phones GCHQ has been monitoring has been linked to this general location, but this is a very built-up area. It's difficult to pin it down to one particular property.'

He was interrupted by Jill, entering the room with an unusual degree of precipitancy.

'Got something,' she said, and consulted her notes. 'The car in the CCTV we found burned out on the A47... It didn't go there directly from Nails Galore. According to ANPR it went via the new Northern Distributor Road, and it seems to have taken its time about it. Looking at the data, I'd say it stopped somewhere en route.' She spotted the map on the wall and went over to it. 'Between here and here,' she said, pinpointing two spots.

'What's there?' asked Greg, peering at the map.

'Not much. A couple of farms – but the buildings aren't close to the road, so it's mainly fields and waste ground. Plus, a couple of roundabouts with side roads leading nowhere. That's about it.'

Ram was looking puzzled. 'The Northern Distributor?' he asked.

'New ring road round the north of the city,' replied Greg. 'Opened last April. I'm not very familiar with it, but Jill's right. There are several roundabouts with exits that lead nowhere. Presumably ready for more developments later.

'Okay. Let's get a team out to check over the areas alongside the road between the two points you've indicated, Jill. Asap. And I hope to God we don't find a body. Jim, can you get on to that? Ram, let's pick up on the Cobholm angle when you've had chance to check out Clean Boats.'

8

Drugs and more drugs

Sarah was floating on a warm sea of euphoria. Anxieties gone, pain gone, no longer cold or fearful, it felt wonderful. She allowed the thin woman with bad skin to help her onto a bed. The thin woman covered her with a duvet, and left the room, closing the door behind her. With the last remnants of self-preservation, Sarah looked round to see if the men were still there. No. She was on her own. She sank back into the pink, warm mists and slept.

Later, much later, she woke to renewed pain and panic. She felt desperately sick and leaned over the edge of the bed, retching, but having eaten nothing, brought up only saliva. The door creaked open and the woman with the bad skin returned. She had a damp cloth in one hand and a mug of what turned out to be tepid water in the other.

'Drink,' she said, and held out the mug. Sarah took it in a shaking left hand and drank. Some of it came straight back up. Some of it stayed down.

'Where am I?' asked Sarah, looking down at her swollen right hand, now twice its normal size and turning black and green.

'No speak,' said the woman, picking up the mug and turning to leave.

'Please,' said Sarah. 'Please tell me what's happening. I feel so odd. I feel...'

'Not allowed,' said the woman, handing her the damp cloth and turning away.

'Please,' said Sarah again, reaching out with her left hand and catching the edge of the woman's wrap. 'Please help me.'

'No,' said the woman and left the room, the door clicking to behind her.

After some while, as the whirling of her head seemed to subside, Sarah slowly and cautiously swung her legs over the side of the bed and sat up. She discovered she was naked under the thin, stained duvet, and pulled it around her as best she could. The room was small: not much bigger than the single bed on which she sat. Such light as there was filtered through a threadbare, flowered curtain, stapled, rather than hung, over the window. Apart from the bed, which had no headboard, the room held only a bucket and a small coffee table. The sort you'd most often see in a sale of garden furniture.

Very carefully, hugging the stale-smelling duvet to her, Sarah leaned over to the window and tried to see out. The curtain was too thick to see through. She tried to prise out a staple or two with her fingernails, and was just getting somewhere when a creaking of floor boards warned her someone was approaching the door, and abruptly it flew open, banging on the wall behind at the end of its swing.

The big man with the tattoo she remembered from the night before was standing in the doorway, another syringe and needle in his hand. Sarah shrank back, still clutching the duvet, and looked round desperately for some sort of weapon.

'Two ways,' said the man. 'One, you sit down and I give you this.' He held up the syringe. 'Take away all pain. Two, you fight, and I hit you and still give you this. Which is it? One or two?'

Sarah didn't answer. Still looking round for a weapon, she saw past the big man into the hallway beyond. In the shadows were the thin woman and someone else. A small man in dark clothes, smiling.

'One or two?' repeated the big man.

'Help me,' cried Sarah to the shadows and the small man laughed, before saying something she didn't understand.

'So, two it is,' said the big man as he hit her hard across the head with his open palm. When she slumped down, dizzy, he pulled her arm toward him and injected her again.

As she sank back into the pink mists, Sarah noticed that her heart was beating slower, and slower. *Maybe this time, too much,* was her last conscious thought, then she lay back again.

'Clean her up,' said the man to the thin woman, and he left the room.

***

Out on the spanking new Northern Distributor Road, Jim and Steve had already quizzed two farmers and stopped to check in with two uniformed teams searching field margins and ditches near the road.

'Nothing,' Jim reported to Greg, adding, 'We're just coming up to the last couple of roundabouts before the A47. We'll have a look round, but the chances of us spotting anything without a thorough search with a big team…' and he shrugged.

'Understood,' said Greg. 'They might have just stopped for a pee. Or at a burger van.'

'Are there any along here?' asked Steve with renewed enthusiasm.

'Not so far as I know,' said Jim repressively. 'And you're not eating burgers in my car anyway.'

As he spoke, he pulled over to the left-hand lane at the next roundabout, and parked across the second exit, which led to open fields and a big sign reading 'Storage and Light Industrial, ring…' and then a phone number.

'Obviously earmarked for development,' remarked Jim. 'Let's take a look round.'

Apart from the road leading nowhere and a few surveyors' stakes, there was little to see but tall grass, brambles and, where the soil had been disturbed, the remains of last season's poppies. They both inspected the ground by the road edge, but if anything had driven off the asphalt it wasn't obvious. Near the big sign the ground was humped into spoil heaps and the poppies were very much in evidence, some crushed into the poor soil.

'Someone may have been here,' remarked Jim. Going over to the sign with some idea of seeing better from the top of one of the heaps, he stumbled over some lumps of old mortar, then stopped. 'Steve, over here,' he said.

By the edge of the rough ground, oriented on a straight line between the sign and the turning off the roundabout, was a square of concrete with a mortared edge, covered with a heavy iron lid.

'Let's take a look.'

Sliding and heaving the lid sideways, the two of them sweated and cursed, but eventually it was lying on the rough grass and they stared down into a narrow shaft, maybe six to eight feet deep. At the bottom, the surface was covered with rough piles of builders' rubble and cement. In one corner Jim could see a small scrap of white. No Sarah.

Disappointed, Steve turned away and started to move back to the car. Jim stayed a moment, staring down into the chamber below, then also turned to go.

'Hey,' he shouted to Steve. 'We ought to put the lid back, it's dangerous like this.' Then he paused, looking at the ground on the edge of the shaft. He bent again, reached out, then thought the better of it and put his hands behind his back. 'Steve,' he shouted again. 'Radio for forensics. Get them out here as soon as.'

'Spotted something?' asked Steve, turning back.

'I don't know. Possibly. Might be blood on the edge of the shaft here. But I think it needs a closer look. Get them here quick, before it rains.'

9

Some progress

Greg heard the report from Ned's team with mixed excitement and disappointment. The blood smears, taken together with the ANPR data, suggested strongly, to a willing mind, that Sarah had spent time in the sunken chamber. He recognised, reluctantly, it could be some other captive or even some bizarre accident. But his gut told him it was Sarah and he wanted, so much, to believe it.

'What exactly is it?' he demanded slightly irritably. 'Why are people scattering the countryside with underground hideaways apparently expressly designed to hide bodies in?'

'It's an access chamber for a sewer,' replied Ned. 'The sewer isn't in use yet. In fact, it's only partly built. But the plans for that area allow for mixed light industrial and domestic development, hence a sewer.'

'Who'd know it was there?' asked Greg, then answered his own question. 'Anyone involved in the planning or the construction on that site. A fairly wide church I imagine. How long before we have DNA typing on your samples?'

'Twenty-four hours,' said Ned.

Greg rang off and turned to Chris. She was already half out of his room.

'I'm on it,' she said over her shoulder.

'On what?'

'Well, I assume we're operating on the basis that Sarah was hidden there. So there's work to do on who knows what about that site and movements round it. I need to catch up with Jill too, on her CCTV researches. Speak later?'

'Yes. Thanks, Chris.'

He turned back to Ram glaring at his laptop screen the other side of the office. 'If we're right,' he said, 'we've got Sarah taken by a Range Rover belonging to Clean Boats Inc, then hidden temporarily in a sewer access chamber before being moved again, who knows where? Anything you can turn up about links between Clean Boats, the county lines operation in Norfolk and road construction around the NDR would be really useful. Especially if it leads back to our Mr Big in Great Ormesby.'

'There's a risk that if I go looking for links to him, that's what I'll find,' said Ram. 'Or seem to find. Better I look with an open mind.'

'Happy to leave it to you,' said Greg. 'You're the expert. But in the short term, anything that narrows down the search for Sarah is my priority. We can tackle the organised crime after.'

'I'm not sure how far Margaret agrees with you,' remarked Ram, still looking at his screen. Greg opened his mouth to reply, then thought the better of it and went looking for Jill.

'Having that new location to focus on is really useful,' was her opening comment to Greg. 'That's helped me narrow things down a bit. My working assumption is that they might have used the same vehicle to pick Sarah up from the sewer as they did to collect the drivers from the burned-out Range Rover. After all, someone must have picked them up. It's a long walk to anywhere from where that car was left.'

'True. So, what've you got?'

'So far, too much. From the NDR to the A47 is a common route after all. I'm narrowing it down by time of day and type of vehicle, and when I get some closer matches I'll try and see if any took a long time between cameras in the vicinity of the sewer chamber. I'll report to Chris as soon as I have anything.'

'Good. Okay.'

Greg went back to his desk, pushed some paper about irritably, then stood up again.

'I'm going to catch up with Jim,' he announced to the room and Ram. And left before his colleague could object.

'Bugger helicopters and, for that matter, bugger JCBs,' he said to himself, and almost trotted down the corridor to his car, with relief at escaping inactivity. 'Jim, where are you now?' he demanded of his phone.

***

Jim was in Greater Ormesby, catching up with his drone operator. Masquerading as UK Power Networks, complete with appropriate liveried van, the story deployed to anyone who asked was that they were checking for damaged lines.

'Where'd you get the van from?' asked Greg, impressed. 'It looks very realistic.'

'That's because it's genuine,' replied Jim with a grin. 'I borrowed it from someone who owes me. We've only got it for today, but provided I hand it back with a full tank of diesel, we've got it for free.'

'What've we found so far?'

'Well, nothing yet.' Jim waved an arm at the open fields to either side of the road from Ormesby to Martham. 'We've been operating out here to establish our cover story, so's to disarm suspicion. I don't expect to find anything here. After this, we'll move over toward the edge of the Broad, and then down toward our prime target.'

Greg watched as the drone was packed back into the van. 'Heard anything from your contacts in Great Yarmouth?' he asked.

'Nothing new. They'll ring if they have anything. If I don't hear by this afternoon, I'll suggest a meet tonight.'

'Okay. Jim, I'll leave my car here for the moment and come with you to the next drone flight if that's okay. We don't want too much of a convoy and there's just a chance my car might be recognised.'

'Sure. Come on then.'

The next flight was over field margins and a quiet road running past a large house on the edge of the Broad. Greg watched on the iPad screen as the operator directed the drone toward the house, following the route of the electricity cables running beside the road. As the road neared the house, the cables cut across fields and through a small wood.

'That's the house,' said Jim softly to Greg.

'That's the one?' asked Greg surprised. 'I thought we were coming to it on the next flight.'

'We will, but from the opposite direction. This is one of the two possible routes by road. This lane doesn't lead directly to the house, but it goes near and they seem to have installed a gate in the wall. Strictly speaking it's a farm road, mainly used by the local farmers when they're moving machinery.'

Greg was concentrating on the screen. He could see a large house, with what looked like two new wings built at right angles to the frontage, creating a courtyard. Behind the house there were gardens running down to the Broad and a boathouse on the edge of the water.

'Can we get a closer look at the boathouse?' he asked.

'We can, but it'll blow our cover,' replied Jim. 'We're hovering a bit too long here as it is. We're inspecting power cables remember!' As they watched, a man came out of the house and looked up at the drone, shading his eyes from the sun.

The operator dipped the drone toward the power cables, as though inspecting a junction box on a pole, then followed the cables closely, away from the house and back toward the van. The picture of the man was lost.

'That's enough for there I think,' said Jim. 'We'll move on to the last site then do one more flight over the other side of the village and call it a day.' He reached in his pocket for his phone. 'It's buzzing,' he said. 'I'd got it on silent.' As he spoke, Greg's phone buzzed as well. They both turned away to answer as the drone operator packed his kit away again.

'Hi, Chris,' said Greg, then fell silent to listen. 'Jim,' he said, 'can you get me back to my car? Jill's turned up something about a van.'

'Sure,' Jim replied. 'Then I'm going into Yarmouth. My snout wants a meet.'

'I might be going the same way. The van in question belongs to Clean Boats.'

***

This time the struggle through the pink mists took longer, and was accompanied by the vague remembrance of dark shapes with evil voices. When Sarah eventually awoke it was to a vision of empty eyes staring ... staring. She woke on a scream, then struggled as someone put their hand over her mouth.

'Shhh,' said a voice. 'Shhh, or they'll come and hurt you.'

Sarah lay still – panting, covered in sweat, and suddenly aware she'd soiled herself. She looked away, embarrassed and disgusted in equal measure. Then, to complete her total humiliation, was violently sick.

There was an exclamation of disgust from the doorway, and a voice said, 'Clean her up! Again!' Then the door slammed.

The thin woman looked at Sarah and sighed. 'It happens,' she said. 'Come.' And she helped Sarah over to the tiny bathroom. The water was still cold, but better than staying in her disgusting, messy state. The woman left her there, and after a while, Sarah turned the water off with a trembling hand and sat down on the edge of the toilet. She looked down at her, now clean but bruised, body and wrapped her arms round herself.

Things surely can't get much worse, she thought. Then refused to think about the many, much worse, possibilities that instantly flooded her head.

The woman came back with a brightly coloured wrap in a shiny, synthetic material and handed it to Sarah.

'Thank you,' she said as she put it on. 'What's your name? I'm Sarah.'

The woman regarded her in silence for a little then said, 'They call me Cara. When they call me anything.' Sarah looked at her in silence.

'Cara is not your real name?' she asked.

'Best you call me Cara,' replied the woman. 'Or we both in trouble.'

The bedroom had been cleaned roughly while Sarah was in the shower. The bed was stripped of the duvet and the floor was smeared but at least not awash with body fluids. Sarah sat down on the bed, shivering and pulling the wrap around her. It wasn't clean. It smelled of cheap perfume and something else.

'I can't stop shivering,' she said.

'It the heroin,' said Cara matter-of-factly. 'You need another shot. They probably come soon.'

'Is that what they've been giving me?' asked Sarah.

'That, or coke. I think heroin from how you sleep. They give you more, then when you need it, they make you work for it.'

'Is that what happened to you?' asked Sarah. Cara nodded.

'I need to go, or they be angry,' she said. 'Listen, Sarah. Don't make them angry. Especially the little one. He mad.'

'Wait!' Sarah caught at the edge of Cara's clothes. 'Do you go out? Can you take a message for me?' Cara pulled away sharply.

'Not unless you want me dead,' she said.

Sarah, remembering how she came to be there, fell silent. *No more Madame Trieste's,* she thought.

Then the door banged open and the big man was there again, with his needle. On the spur of the moment she tried to push past him, but it was a feeble, wobbly-kneed effort and he pushed her back easily, laughing. The laughter was the last thing she heard as her heart slowed again, almost to a stop.

10

Informers

Jim found his contact in his favourite corner of The Feathers, an elderly Jack Russell on his lap. He looked up under his greasy tweed cap as Jim placed a brimming pint glass in front of him. A little spilled on the battered table and the dog stretched forward to mop up the liquid with a bright pink tongue.

Jim sat opposite, at an angle that gave him a view of the room behind him, reflected in the mirror opposite. He took a slurp of his beer and put his glass down, noting as he did so that there was no one nearer than two tables away.

'So, what've you got for me?' he asked. 'Might as well get the business out of the way quickly, while the place is quiet.'

His man opposite looked round nervously over the top of his pint glass. His eyes were pale blue and cloudy in a thin, red face, marked by a faint scar running from his left eye to the corner of his nose. He pulled his cap off, scratched his thinning scalp with the brim, then put it back.

'In an 'urry?' he asked. Then answered himself. 'Course you are. Got one of your detectives missing a'nt you?'

Jim said nothing, just looked across the table and placed a closed hand on the wet surface. The blue eyes sharpened with avarice, and the man reached across, but Jim moved his hand as he did.

'News first,' he said.

'I'm taking a big risk,' replied the man, 'so t' price is 'igher.'

'As I imagined,' replied Jim, put his hand back on the table and turned it so that a red bank note was visible between his fingers.

'Not enough,' said the man, and Jim returned his hand to his pocket.

'Too bad then.' Jim stood up to go.

'Hang on,' said his snout, 'don't need to be in such an 'urry. Get me another drink and we'll agree on that.' He nodded at the now hidden hand.

'Okay.' Jim went to the bar, still quiet this early in the evening, and fetched another pint of Landlord. 'Now, what d'you have for me? It'd better be good at this price.'

Both man and dog had another slurp of beer, the man from the glass, the dog from the table top again.

'Heard a white van's bin deliverin' again to a certain cleaning company. Women. The last one was delivered unconscious only last night. Might be yours.'

'Is that all?' asked Jim, disappointed.

'Int it enough?' asked the man in mock outrage, then after another swig of beer shared with his dog he added, 'She was delivered by two men. One of them was the little shit that belongs to the big boss. His son. He's the sort probably pulled wings off flies in his cradle, and graduated to crucifying cats in his nursery. Word is something bad 'appened in Norwich. If it was more than just revenge, it was probably 'im.'

'Got a registration number for the van?'

'Don't be daft.' The man snorted. 'What makes ye think I can see them sorta numbers at that distance? It had the same logo as the offices tho',' he added as an afterthought.

'There was signage on the van?' asked Jim. 'What did it say, apart from the logo?'

'Not a clue,' replied the man cheerfully. 'Can't read, remember? But I did see the logo. Sort of boat with a mop across it.'

Jim handed over the £50 note, under the table. The waiting hand took it and pocketed it.

'Don't get used to that much,' warned Jim. 'And take care.' As he got up to go, he said casually, 'I take it you mean the Clean Boats Inc. offices?'

The man took another look round the half-empty pub and nodded, then left in a hurry, the dog scurrying alongside.

Back in his car in the corner of the marketplace, Jim phoned Greg. 'Where are you now?' he asked.

'At the station. Got anything?'

'White van spotted delivering an unconscious woman – or at least an unconscious person assumed to be a woman – to Clean Boats Inc. last night.'

'Any ID on the van?'

'No number. My informant is very short-sighted, and he can't read. But he did describe what sounds like the Clean Boats Inc. logo, and it was their offices it delivered to. He also says one of the men involved was the son of 'the big man' and that he has some nasty habits.'

'If he can't see very well, how reliable is his story?' asked Greg.

Jim hesitated. 'The honest answer is, good enough for us to investigate, probably wouldn't stand up in court if we were depending on it for a conviction.' There was a pause while Greg thought.

'I doubt we've enough for a raid then, unless we can find some supporting evidence. Leave it with me for a few minutes and I'll get back to you.'

Greg's first phone call was to Jill.

'Jill, focus your search on vehicles linked to Clean Boats Inc. I need to know asap if any were moving around the NDR and the A47 that night.'

'Okay. I'll search my database and get back to you.'

His second was to Ram. He was blunt. 'Anything on Clean Boats Inc. that would help justify a raid. Anything at all? We have a witness who may have seen her being taken into their premises.'

'I'll get back to you', Ram replied. 'I may have something, but I need to check with the GCHQ data.'

'Make it as fast as you can,' recommended Greg. 'I want to go tonight. Otherwise, we risk losing her again. I'm tired of playing catch-up.'

Waiting impatiently for answers to his questions, Greg fetched himself a moderately horrible coffee from the machine down the corridor and went back to the interview room he was using as a temporary office. Then he had second thoughts and went along to the office of the Great Yarmouth Chief Inspector.

Receiving a quiet ‘Come’ in response to his knock, he went in. The man behind the desk looked young for his responsibilities. His hair was cropped short, and he was clean-shaven. His uniform was immaculate.

‘I need to introduce myself,’ said Greg, holding out his hand, ‘and to thank you for your station’s hospitality today.’ The man stood up to shake his hand.

‘I take it you’re the Greg Geldard who dived into the Bure at Acle,’ he said with a smile. ‘Your fame goes before you. Richard Lake. Usually known as Rick when people are being polite.’

‘Oh God,’ responded Greg. ‘I could wish I was famous for something else.’ He sat down when waved to the visitor’s chair. ‘Pleased to meet you, Rick. Sorry we haven’t met before,’ he said. ‘I think you’ve taken over since I was here last.’

‘That’s right,’ said Rick. ‘What can we do for you today?’

‘That’s the problem. I’m not absolutely sure yet. I have good reason to believe our colleague DI Sarah Laurence is being held at a location in the town, but I don’t yet have enough proof to launch a big operation.’

‘This is the DI who was abducted?’

‘Yes. I’m hoping we’ll be able to launch a raid this evening, so this is partly notice that a request is likely to be coming your way. But we have a problem. We’re told to keep it quiet until the last minute, and I’m also worried that between now and then, they might move Sarah again. You know the town better than me. How can we keep a close enough eye on movements to ensure Sarah isn’t moved through our net, without giving too much away?’

‘Where exactly are we looking?’ asked Rick, moving toward his wall map.

'Here.' Greg pointed.

'Okay.' Rick stood staring at the map for a while. 'It's near the river. That gives me some ideas. When you say keep it quiet, do you mean from the team too?'

'For the moment, yes,' said Greg. 'I'm already stepping over a line telling you.'

'Okay. Second question. How far off are you from getting the go-ahead to launch a raid?'

'Close,' said Greg, mentally crossing his fingers behind his back. 'I'm going to speak to the Chief Super shortly.'

'Okay. Do that. I can't redeploy teams without that authority. There're too many priorities as it is. But as soon as I get the go-ahead, I'll sort a team to create a ring round this location.' He pointed to the map. 'The cover story will be a hunt for illegal immigrants. As soon as the ring is solid, we can send a team in to raid the premises. That way, if any of our rats run, we can pick them up in the immediate vicinity.'

Greg opened his mouth and closed it again, recognising that was as good as it was going to get. 'Thank you,' he said. 'I'll get back to you.'

Back in his interview room, he picked up the phone to Jill. 'Anything for me?' he asked with a touch of desperation.

'Something,' she said. 'Chris spotted it. We've got a white van on the CCTV. The image is blurred but it looks like the boat cleaning logo. It was on the A47 at around the right time. We've also got a registration number on the ANPR that's registered to the company, but according to the DVLA, it belongs to a black transit not a white van. So, two possibilities, but no hard evidence either vehicle was doing anything other than going about its normal business.' About to ring off, Greg was startled when Jill suddenly added, 'Hang on! Chris thinks she has something. I'll hand you over.'

'Chris?' asked Greg after a few moments of silence and then a muffled scuffling.

'Here,' she said. 'Sorry, nearly dropped the phone. I've got something I think you should check with Jim. The last number, the one registered to Clean Boats and a black van? It came up in some of Jim's records connected with the county lines investigation. Mainly linked to one particular suspected groomer and showing up on CCTV as lurking round schools.'

'Was he ever arrested? The groomer I mean.'

'No. Not enough evidence. Certainly no one willing to dob him in! At the time, that is. Might be worth a chat with Jim.'

'Yes.' Greg was thoughtful, then suddenly realised the line to Chris was still open. 'Sorry, Chris. I'm still here. It seems ages since we had chance to talk. Are you okay? It sounds as though you've taken over the data collation. You hate doing that!'

'Needs must,' she replied. 'We don't have Sarah to do it, do we. Jill and I are doing our best to cover. And as for hating it, yes I'd rather be out and about. You know me too well. But I feel I owe her this.'

'Sarah you mean?' The silence was eloquent. 'Chris, are you coming over tonight? Please come over tonight. I think it'll be a long day for both of us, but even if all we do is sleep, let's do it together. Life's too short.'

'Yes. I'll see you later. When we know what's happening with the investigation. Love you.' And Chris rang off before Greg could reply.

'Okay. Now Jim,' said Greg to himself and redialled. 'Jim, where are you now?'

'Here,' said Jim, pushing the office door open. 'Anything new?'

'A link to the county lines operation,' said Greg and brought him up to speed. Jim was quiet for a moment.

'Chris was right. We couldn't get anyone to give evidence against the groomers at the time, but I've a damn good idea who was involved. It might be worth going back to them now, with the story about Sarah, and seeing if we can get one of them to talk. Would that be enough for a warrant and a full-scale raid?'

'Possibly. Let's try it. What's your idea?'

'Go to the school. Come on. The Head was sympathetic. They're as keen as us to put a stop to their children being exploited. I think they'll help.'

***

The East Norfolk Academy wasn't far away. Greg followed Jim in a mini convoy. He could see the two heads in the car in front of him – the second belonging to a female officer from the local team.

'The child I have in mind is male,' Jim had said, 'but you never know. And if it's a girl who comes forward, we need to be able to talk to them appropriately.'

The Head, a small woman with a neat grey bob, dressed in slacks and a dark jacket, was welcoming. It certainly seemed Jim had her confidence, as Greg noted.

'What are you asking me exactly?' she asked, once Greg had been introduced and Jim had explained the background.

'With your permission, and ideally in your presence, we'd like to explain to one or two specific classes what has happened to our colleague, DI Sarah Laurence, and seek their help. DI

Henning here, as he's said, has a pretty good idea that one or more of your students have had contact with the gang we're after.

'They're not in trouble,' Greg added hurriedly. 'If we're right, then they're victims too. When DI Henning spoke to them last, they were reluctant to speak up. We're hoping that the story of what's happened to Sarah might encourage them to come forward with what they know.'

'It might terrify them into silence again,' observed the Head.

'Yes. It might. If it does, we're no worse off. But in general, I find youngsters are pretty idealistic. What they wouldn't do for themselves, they might do for someone else. It's their idealism I aim to appeal to.'

The Head looked at Greg sharply. 'That's very perceptive of you,' she said. 'The general impression is that the police tend to see youngsters at best as a nuisance or at worst as troublemakers. If that *is* genuinely your view, then you might have some success. I'll send my secretary to warn the two top classes we're on our way.'

'Can we go straight there?' asked Jim. 'It would be a pity if someone we need to speak to disappeared before we have a chance.'

'Okay. Follow me.'

A short walk at a brisk pace down silent corridors that smelled faintly of polish and teenage BO, then the Head stopped at a classroom door.

'This is one of our two top classes. The oldest children,' she said. And pushed the door open.

It seemed a drama or English lesson was underway. Most of the teenagers present were arrayed as an audience, some on chairs and others perched on tables in order to see better. Five others were in mid scene at the front of the class.

'So,' said the teacher at the side, 'we've seen Bianca won over. How realistic do we think that is?'

There were rude sounds indicative of disbelief and a big girl at the front of the class remarked grimly, 'It's hard to take any of this seriously int it, Miss, given that blah about soft women!'

A diminutive boy at the back laughed raucously and said, 'Makes sense to me!'

Speaking at the same time another boy, with glasses and a mullet, said, 'I like the bit about rotten apples. That's good.'

Stepping forward the Head said, 'I'm sorry to interrupt this energetic debate, but these officers have something important to ask you.'

A silence fell abruptly, broken only by a surprised cough from the teacher at the front, and in the stillness Greg and Jim walked to the front. The female officer in uniform stayed by the door with the Head. Greg thought it looked uncomfortably like she was poised to intercept fleeing students but couldn't think of a way of adjusting the situation when, to his relief, the Head perched on a side table and indicated the officer should do the same. At the front, Greg cleared his throat, overcome with an unexpected attack of nerves, and sat down on the edge of the teacher's table.

'I think some of you have met Jim Henning before,' he started. 'I'm Greg Geldard and I'm here to ask for your help.' Heads turned to look at each other as he paused. 'I'm sure you're all well aware that one of our colleagues has been abducted this week by a gang who committed a particularly brutal murder. You're wondering what this has to do with you. I'll tell you.

'Jim here spoke to you some months ago about county lines and the fact that some of you have been, or are being, groomed to assist criminal gangs in the transport and sale of drugs.'

Jim stirred uneasily and there was a loud mutter of, 'You can't say that to us,' from the back of the room.

'I can and I have,' said Greg to the face at the back. 'I know, and you know, that we can't prove it yet. That doesn't make it untrue. As I said, I'm here to ask for your help. Being coerced into helping these drug gangs is no joke. Young people like you have died because of it. Some, not far from here. When Jim spoke to you, he appealed for your help so we could help you. No one would give it then. Perhaps the risks didn't seem real enough. Or the dangers of speaking out were too real.

'But today things are different. Today I'm asking you to help us rescue a young woman who may be being tortured even as I stand here in front of you. I'm asking you to help us get her back before it's too late. I'm asking you to take a risk to help rescue a young woman. It's not an easy thing to do. And yes, you will need to be brave. But I have no doubt at all that you have both strength and courage. I'm asking that you use both to help someone else.

'The officer at the back is passing round copies of my card. You can ring me anytime.' As Greg finished and stood to leave, a raucous bell cut through the silence. There was a clatter of chairs as every member of the class shuffled books and papers into bags and stood behind their desks.

'You may leave,' said the teacher from her position at the side, and the class filed out in silence. Except for two. A slim girl with long fair hair caught back in an Alice band remained behind her desk near the front, and the boy with the mullet remained sitting at the back.

'I'll talk,' said the boy and the girl turned round, taken by surprise.

'And me,' she said.

In the deafening silence, the Head stepped forward.

'You'd both better come to my office,' she said. And sailed off down the corridor with both pupils and three police in tow, like an ocean liner and accompanying tugs.

11

Out of the mouths

Jim caught hold of Greg's sleeve as they approached the Head's office.

'This is going to get us into all sorts of trouble,' he said. 'We can't talk to children without their parents or guardian present. And we absolutely can't put them at risk. I'm getting seriously cold feet about this. Even Sarah wouldn't want this.' Greg stopped.

'I know,' he said. 'To be honest, I wasn't expecting an immediate response. At best I thought we might get a phone call or two in response to handing out my cards. But we're in a bind now. We can't ignore these two kids, or they'll never trust us again.'

'So what do we do? If we go ahead and interview them, Margaret's going to hang us out to dry!'

'Best I can come up with is, we have a chat with each of them in turn, in the presence of the Head, if she's willing. The objective for that chat is to establish what sort of information they have, and whether it's likely to be of interest. If it is, we schedule a formal interview with parents present.'

They were interrupted by the Head reappearing from her office and closing the door behind her.

'I'm not willing for you to talk to either child unless I'm present,' she said firmly, and Greg heaved a sigh of relief.

'That's just what we had in mind,' he said. 'And only a general chat at this point then a follow-up, if need be, with parents involved. First, what can you tell me about these two?'

The Head glanced down the corridor to make sure it remained empty.

'Well, to start with, I'm very surprised that Emily has stepped forward. Not because she isn't an ethically minded girl. She is. She's a Queen's Guide and volunteers in a local old people's home. And that's what's sticking in my mind. Why would a girl like that, from a good and affluent home, be involved with county lines? And while I wouldn't have put Nathan in quite the same bracket, he's another with generous parents and no apparent shortage of money. It doesn't fit the expected pattern.' Jim shifted on his feet and Greg nodded for him to comment.

'It fits the latest intelligence,' Jim said. 'Most recently, right across the country, we've seen a shift in the nature of the children targeted. It used to be the poorest. The ones with neglectful or distracted parents. The children who were easily tempted by treats and easily seduced by adult attention. But those are the children that are easily spotted by us. And, therefore, the most likely to be intercepted as they are delivering. The gangs are not as stupid as we'd like. Some have worked this out and are targeting middle-class children instead. They're much less likely to be stopped by a police patrol and can move freely in places other children might stand out. Looks like this shift in behaviour has caught us up in Norfolk.'

'What's the lever?' asked the Head. 'What gets them involved?'

'How about we go and ask,' suggested Greg.

They followed the Head into her outer office. The school administrator was working at her laptop, Nathan slouching in the seat opposite.

'Emily is waiting in your office as you suggested,' she said to the Head.

'Thank you, Sue,' she replied, then to Greg, 'Who do you want to speak to first?'

'How about we go and have a chat with Emily first, if Nathan's willing to wait a few minutes?' The boy shrugged, which Greg took for assent. Greg and the woman police constable followed the Head into her office. Emily was sitting on the leather sofa in the corner. The Head took a seat beside her desk and waved the two police officers to the easy chairs by the sofa.

As they sat down, Greg said, 'I gather your name is Emily. You know I'm Greg Geldard and this is...'

'Sally Newman,' said the PC. 'Pleased to meet you, Emily.'

Emily had a tissue in her hands. Outwardly composed, her fingers were nonetheless quietly shredding the tissue, then balling up the remains in the palm of her hand.

'What's your surname, Emily?' asked Greg.

'Atkinson,' she replied quietly.

'Thank you for coming forward, Emily. Sally here is going to make a note of what you say and your headteacher is going to stay with you, as your parents aren't here. But I think we'll just have a preliminary chat to establish what you want to tell us, if that's okay with you.'

There was a silence. Greg glanced at the Head, who nodded, and then looked back at Emily.

'It was brave of you to stay behind, Emily,' said Greg. 'What was it you wanted to tell me?' There was another pause, then Emily looked up with the air of one who had made a decision and dropped the shredded tissue decisively into a nearby waste basket.

'I was trapped by one of a gang,' she said, hurriedly as though she wanted to get the words out before she changed her mind. 'At least, it turned out he was one of a gang. I met him at the pleasure beach. He seemed nice at first. We started meeting up and he took me for drinks and meals. It was nice being treated like a grown up. He told me he loved me.'

She started to turn pink, hesitated, then said almost inaudibly, 'He took some photos of us. Then he threatened to show them to my parents and to put them online if I didn't do what he wanted.'

'Which was?'

'To carry drugs for him to clubs and bars.'

Greg looked at the horrified expression on the Head's face and her effort to wipe it clear. 'When was this?' he asked.

'About two months ago, when he made the threats.'

Greg hesitated over what to say next, looked at the Head again, then said, 'Emily, I'm really sorry that happened to you. Sorrier than I can say. That shouldn't happen to anyone. But if you were willing to identify that man for us, it might help stop it happening to other girls.' Emily opened her mouth to reply, but Greg held up his hand to stop her. 'No, hang on a moment before you say anything else,' he said. 'I think this is a conversation that should continue with your parents present. Are you okay with that?'

'That's what I was trying to say,' said Emily. 'They already know. When he threatened me I got in a panic. I didn't know what to do. I knew what he was asking would get me into big trouble, but the photos he had were *really* embarrassing. I couldn't sleep. I couldn't eat. I couldn't stop worrying about what to do. Then my mum cornered me and asked what was wrong. I really, really didn't want to tell her, especially about the photos, about how stupid I'd been, but she worked it out of me, and once I started talking, it was a relief. She told my dad for me, and he said leave it to him, he'd sort it. And he did. He emailed Pete and told him to back off. That I'd told him everything so there was no mileage in threatening me, and that if any pictures of me surfaced on the web, he'd live to regret it. I haven't seen or heard anything from him since.'

Greg heaved a big sigh. 'You've been unlucky in your boyfriend,' he said, 'but it sounds like you got really lucky with your mum and dad.

'In that case, are you willing to come to the station with one or more of your parents and make a statement? We'll probably have some photos for you to look at too, to see if you can identify anyone.'

Emily sat up straighter. 'I'll do it', she said. 'It'll be a relief. What about Nathan?'

'I'll have a chat to Nathan in a minute. Just let me brief Jim Henning and he'll sort out the interview with you and your parents while I talk to Nathan.'

A short conversation and some phone calls later, and Emily was on her way to Yarmouth station with her mother and DI Henning. Greg returned to the Head.

'Not what you expected I think,' he said.

'Not at all. But poor Emily. So embarrassing for her. I hope this doesn't damage her A-level results. She has a bright future ahead of her.'

'She was lucky in one way,' said Greg. 'It could all have been a lot worse. Okay, let's have our chat with Nathan now, before he gets tired of waiting.'

Nathan was leaning back, his chair precariously balanced on two legs, his head wedged against the wall and his eyes closed. Judging by the waving feet and the EarPods, he was living with the beat of a different drum to the rest of the room.

'Nathan,' said the Head, and then said it again in rather more stentorian tones. The front legs of the chair hit the floor with a crash and Nathan jerked forward, opening his eyes in surprise.

'Yes, miss,' he said, and climbed to his feet.

'Thank you for waiting,' said Greg, and waved him into the Head's office before him. Nathan chose to sit in the upright chair by the desk, leaving Greg and Sally Newman to take the rather lower armchairs by the sofa. Introductions and preliminaries complete, Greg paused and looked hard at the boy before him, currently polishing his glasses assiduously on his shirt tail. Nathan looked up in the sudden silence.

'I suppose you want to know what I know,' he said.

'That would be helpful,' agreed Greg.

'Well it's simple enough. My father does the accounts for Clean Boats Inc. and he's involved in the money laundering.'

The silence in the room was so absolute Greg could hear the administrator's fingers tapping on her laptop through the office door. He cleared his throat.

'Do you know what a serious allegation that is?' he asked Nathan. The Head had her mouth open, and closed it in a hurry.

'Oh yes, I know,' replied Nathan. He put his glasses back on and jiggled them on his nose until they were comfortable.

'What makes you think that?' asked Greg.

'He said so, to my mother just before she left. He said, and I quote here, "Don't think you're going to get your hands on a deal of money if you go. Most of what passes through my accounts belongs to the boss, and it'll disappear like Scotch mist if anyone comes looking".'

'That could have meant a lot of things,' said Greg but Nathan interrupted him.

'So I had a look to see for myself. Dad's pretty naive when it comes to passwords. I've been into his laptop loads of times. Last time I looked, there was a stream of cash sums coming into the business, all of which were matched by similar sums leaving it to purchase investments. Sometimes gold. Sometimes bitcoin. And other stuff. None of this showed up in his accounts. They just passed through without touching the sides.'

'How can you be sure—' began Greg and this time the Head interrupted.

'Nathan is a very good mathematician and statistician,' she said.

Greg paused for thought. 'You do realise the implications for your father?' he asked.

'Yes. And the sooner you put him away, the sooner I can live with my mother again,' said Nathan calmly.

'Where's your mother now?' asked Greg.

'She left when she found out about the money laundering. I'm in touch by phone and WhatsApp. She couldn't take me with her until she'd found somewhere to live, so the sooner he's put away the better. Then she can come home.'

'Nathan, do you mind waiting out there for a few minutes.' Greg nodded to the outer office. 'I'll be with you in a moment.'

Once the door closed behind the lad with the mullet, Greg turned to the Head. 'This complicates things,' he said. 'Can Nathan stay here while I contact his mother? He may need an appropriate adult so I need to get that organised, before we proceed with any further interview.'

'Of course,' said the Head. 'Until the end of the school day anyway. I think you should contact social services too.'

'My thoughts precisely. I'll be as quick as I can.'

12

Alarm and arms

This time when Sarah came round, the small man was there in the room. She realised he was younger than she'd thought. Early twenties, she guessed. He was sitting in a chair by the bed, playing with his mobile phone. As consciousness fought its way through the mists, she became aware of two things. First, that she was lying naked on the bed, and second, that he was taking photos with his phone. She cried out, the sounds blurred both by a numb mouth and the buzzing in her ears, and she lunged for the phone. She took him by surprise and for a few seconds the phone was in her clumsy grasp, then he smashed it out of her hand and pushed her back down on the bed. She squirmed away from his small but powerful fist, but he reached out again and banged her head on the wall at the side.

'I'll be back,' he hissed. 'And we'll have some fun. I'll bring my knives, and I'll have lots of fun.' And he left the room.

Sarah was left curled on the bed, pulling the cover around her as much as possible and shaking with shock. When the door opened again she was off the bed and staggering to the window before she realised that this time it was the woman who called herself Cara, not the small man.

'I got you some food,' said Cara, and put down on the bed a packaged sandwich and a bag of crisps. She took a can of Pepsi from her pocket and put that on the bed too. 'Eat,' she urged. Sarah had never felt less hungry, but mindful of the need to stay alert, forced herself to open the packet of sandwiches. Cheese. Could have been worse. She took a mouthful, heaved slightly, but breathed hard and managed to keep it down. Another mouthful followed the first.

'Who is that man?' she asked.

'He the boss's son. Mica. He bad news. Keep him happy, whatever it takes,' advised Cara. 'He too fond of playing with knives. My friend...' She stopped and started again. 'Another girl, someone I know, she scarred now, thanks to him.'

'What happened?' asked Sarah.

'He took her ear off. He gave her a choice. Ear or slit in nose. And after, he said it would be an eye next. He meant it, I think. Don't cross him.'

Sarah followed Cara in silence from the grubby, stuffy bedroom to a small, equally grubby kitchen. There Cara sat her down at a tiny table and put a mug of instant coffee in front of her.

'No milk, sorry,' she said. 'Sugar?' She proffered a paper packet with a couple of stained spoons sticking out of the top. The sugar inside was also stained with drips of tea or coffee and sticking together in lumps. Sarah helped herself to three lumps, on the basis that energy from any source would be useful. She looked round the kitchen. Apart from the table and a couple of chairs, there was a small sink with a gas boiler providing hot water, and a stained draining board. She noted that the cupboard underneath might contain something useful in the way of corrosive cleaning materials, then corrected her assumption with the thought that, so far, she'd seen little that suggested any cleaning took place. The drawers now, they might be worth checking for knives. She wondered how she could get Cara to leave her alone for a few minutes, but the thought died as quickly as it was born.

'We need go back,' said Cara, looking at a cheap watch on her wrist. 'You need shower and I find you more clothes.'

'Why? What's the hurry?' asked Sarah.

'Don't ask. Just do what told,' said Cara. 'And do it quick, or trouble.'

She hustled Sarah back to the bathroom she'd seen earlier and left her inside with a threadbare towel and a wrap dress in brightly flowered polyester.

'Should fit,' she said.

'What about underclothes?' asked Sarah.

'You not need,' said Cara, and if possible, Sarah's blood chilled still further.

Another cold shower later, her hair washed and hanging damp down the back of the flowered dress, and Sarah contemplated her image in the mottled mirror. The dress was large for her, but at least that gave her scope for wrapping tightly and ensuring maximum coverage. Up top at least. It was too short to cover her knees, and the continuing lack of undies nagged at her. She looked around for any sort of substitute, although what might qualify as such defeated her imagination and she resigned herself to sitting very carefully, knees firmly together. When she pushed on the bathroom door, without much hope, she was surprised to find it gave before her.

Moving quietly, she listened at the top of the stairs and heard voices below. She retreated to the kitchen door, listened again and, hearing no sound, went in. Nothing seemed to have changed since she and Cara were there. To give herself a credible explanation for her presence, she put the kettle on. Then, still listening, pulled out a drawer. Nothing except old takeaway menus, elastic bands and bits of string. She looked in the next drawer. Battered cutlery stared back at her, mostly spoons and forks. Nothing of use. The third and last drawer contained kitchen utensils. A slotted spoon, a fish slice, some other odds and ends and a knife. She stared at it covetously, then spotted something else. A carving fork. It was the work of seconds to snatch the fork, then one of the elastic bands from the other drawer. She'd just finished fixing the fork to her upper arm with the elastic when she heard steps coming quickly toward the kitchen.

She shook the sleeve of her dress down. 'Coffee?' she asked, pouring hot water into the two mugs in front of her. Cara was close to panic.

'Where you been?' she demanded.

'Nowhere. Here,' said Sarah. 'Coffee?' she said again.

'Never mind coffee. You come back to your room.'

Nonetheless, Sarah took the mug of hot instant coffee with her, and the small successes buoyed her up through the long hours that followed after Cara locked the door again. After some thought, she hid the carving fork under the mattress at the head of the bed but left the elastic band on her arm in case she should need it again.

***

On the phone to Margaret, Greg was keen to stress the positives.

'Yes, I know I went further than perhaps I should have,' he said, 'but events moved faster than I expected. And I'll be honest, I never expected to turn up the pure gold we did. We need to follow up with properly chaperoned interviews, but it looks very likely we'll have enough to pursue Clean Boats and their boss all the way to court this time. And I think we have enough now to justify a raid on Clean Boats.' Margaret hesitated, and over the phone line could be heard tapping a pencil on her desk.

'You're jumping the gun, Greg. You don't have enough yet to satisfy the CPS. And if those children back off, or have vivid imaginations, you still won't have enough.'

'Agreed,' said Greg with some impatience. 'But that's not what I'm saying. I agree we need to follow up thoroughly with Emily and Nathan, dotting all the i's and crossing all the t's. What I am saying is, we have enough to raid Clean Boats and we need to do it quickly if we're to have any chance of finding Sarah before they move her on again. So, do I have your go-ahead to get Rick Lake and his chaps on the move?'

Another hesitation. 'Yes. I'll sort the paperwork at this end. Go ahead, Greg.'

The drive through Yarmouth had never seemed so irritating. Every set of lights was red. Every zebra crossing seemed to be occupied by three chatting mothers with pushchairs. And every car in front seemed to be driven by a person of a certain age with a fixed conviction that exceeding 15 mph on a corner would cause it to fall over. Greg was in a fever of impatience by the time he got to the station. To his relief Rick was in his office and, better still, wasted no time getting his teams organised. Some swift phone calls later, and Greg found himself in a planning meeting with Rick's top team, a detailed map of Cobham on the wall in front of them.

'I've got a team keeping an eye on the access roads, and a drone over this area here,' – Rick pointed at the map – 'so we'll know if any of the targets make a move. We'll go at 19:45. The streets should be quiet then. The armed-response team will wait here.' He pointed. 'Team A will go in at the front. Team B at the back. Team C will wait here,' – he pointed again – 'to mop up any runners. You've got the stingers I presume?' he said over his shoulder to a grizzled sergeant in the corner. 'The most likely scenario is that one or more of the company vans hit the road and you'll need to be ready to stop them.'

'Yes,' said the sergeant economically.

'DCI Geldard, I'd like you to stay back with armed response. We'll give you the signal when we've got the place locked down.' Greg nodded, unsurprised. In Rick's shoes he wouldn't want a stranger getting in the way of a well-oiled team either.

'I'd like DI Henning with me,' he said.

'No problem.' Rick nodded too. 'Any questions anyone?'

'Any intelligence on arms held?' asked the armed-response tactician. Rick looked at Greg.

'Very little,' he said. 'We have clear evidence of use of knives in a variety of situations, and the data from GCHQ and their pals suggests they have access to firearms. But no detailed intel either on type, or on this location. However, they have demonstrably had access to old IRA explosives in the recent past, specifically Semtex, and it's probably best to assume the same applies to firearms. In which case the most likely worst case is AK-47s.'

'Caution then,' said the armed-response expert, and made a note.

Rick looked at his watch. 'No one leaves the station now,' he said, 'until we deploy. See you at 19:15 for an update briefing and then we go.'

13

Fun?

By early evening, Sarah had the shakes again, due, she assumed, to the drugs fading from her system. She found she was listening for the heavy footfalls of the big man coming down the passage to top up her dosage. As the shaking intensified, she was torn between fearing a further chemical onslaught and wanting it. When the door did open she was taken by surprise, with no footsteps to warn her.

It was the small man. He swaggered in and closed the door behind him, then leaned on it.

'So,' he said slowly. 'Now we have some fun.' Sarah backed up as far as she could against the wall by the bed. She gripped her upper arms, aware of the elastic band on her left bicep and wishing she'd left the carving fork there as well. She wondered how many seconds it would take to snatch the fork from its hiding place under the mattress, and how many seconds she would have.

Remembering the courses on hostages and hostage situations, Sarah took a deep breath, moistened her lips and tried a smile. It wavered but it was the best she could do, and she put a hand to her hair as she said, 'I look a mess I know. But at least I managed a shower. I guess you know I'm Sarah. What's your name?' She tried to study the man before her as she waited for an answer. Tried to judge his likely reaction. She realised that he was probably younger even than she'd guessed. Not much more than twenty, if that.

The man laughed. 'I've read the books as well,' he mocked. 'Make friends with your captor. Make him see you as a real person. Develop empathy.' Despite a pronounced accent, his English was good. 'Problem is,' he went on, 'that is problem for you; you're not a person. You're just a victim. Not real at all. Not to me. And I don't have any empathy. I'm a psychopath, didn't you know?

'So your problem is, how do you deal with a psychopath? And the answer, I have to tell you, is you don't.'

Suddenly he lunged forward and scored a line down her right arm where it was clenched across her chest. Sarah stared as a thin red line rapidly became a thick ooze of blood, running down to her elbow and then dripping steadily to the floor. The pain followed a few seconds later. She gasped and clutched the wound.

'That's just the opening move,' he said. 'What you might call pawn to king four.' Sarah sat down on the bed, near the wall. Near where she'd hidden the carving fork. Nearer her hidden weapon.

He lunged again, this time scoring a line over the back of her fingers. Again, the knife was too fast to avoid.

'This is fun,' he remarked. 'Just so you know, this is how our game will go. I'll keep cutting you, and you'll keep losing blood, until eventually you pass out or even just get a bit dizzy.

Then I'll cut some tendons, so you can't walk or move your arms. After that, well, after that will depend on my inspiration at the time. I could skin you or blind you first. But on balance I think I'll let you see what's happening while I flay you. I could start on your legs, for example.'

Sarah looked in his eyes, and believed every horrific word. The pale eyes were filled with large pupils, dilated with either a drug or just the drug of cruelty. There was no humanity there. Nothing she could appeal to. She felt a warm rush on her legs as her control went in the extremity of her fear. Panic filled her eyes and her ears. She could see nothing except the blank, blue eyes in front of her and the blood-streaked, sharp-bladed knife waving before her. Dimly she was aware of a bang, then another, then voices shouting.

The young man in front of her turned sharply and started to move toward the door. As he did, Sarah reached swiftly under the mattress left-handed, and pulled out the carving fork. The blood from her fingers made her grip slippery, but she clenched her fist hard and put her hand behind her back just as the man turned toward her.

'Don't try anything,' he warned. 'It seems you may have to wait a bit, but I'll soon be back.'

As he turned back toward the door, there was the sound of heavy boots moving swiftly down the linoleum floored passageway and cries of 'Clear! Clear!' came closer and closer. Through the haze of panic, Sarah recognised the sounds of a police operation and hope was reborn. Perhaps she wasn't going to die yet. As the panic began to recede, it left room for other feelings. Rage, hate, and a deep shame born of disgust with both her physical state and her feelings of helplessness.

The door flew open and hit the knifeman on his shoulder, hard. It partially spun him round and he wasted a few seconds turning back to the open door and the burly, uniformed policeman behind it. The officer took a stab to his chest on his body armour and brought his ASP baton down hard on the man's wrist. The knife fell to the floor and another officer, partly concealed behind the first, reached round to fire his taser. The young man followed his knife down to the floor, and as his taser-induced twitching began to stop, Sarah stepped forward and quite deliberately plunged the carving fork into his chest.

14

Aftermath

Greg was impressed by the speed and efficiency of Rick's deployment. Judging by the crashes, doors front and back gave way simultaneously and the designated teams entered swiftly. Then, from the perspective of those waiting in reserve, there was a period of quiet. Armed response had moved to their forward position but held there until needed. So far, at least, there was no sign they would be. A garage door between the property being raided and the shop next door crashed open. The grizzled sergeant with the stingers took the risk it wasn't a late dash for a Norwich train and brought the vehicle to an abrupt halt. He was right. It was a Clean Boats van and the three occupants were easily apprehended as they attempted to leg it down toward the river. The radio crackled and Greg headed into the property, confident that the situation was under control, his main concern that Sarah had been found, safe and well.

Just inside the front door was the reception with a desk separated from a waiting area by a frosted glass screen. Two uniformed police officers were standing guard over three recumbent and handcuffed forms, face down on the tatty carpet. Rick was behind the desk, using his radio. As Greg approached, he put the radio back in the shoulder pouch and came forward.

'Building secure,' he began, and Greg interrupted.

'Sarah?'

'Yes. We've found her. She's alive, but she has some injuries. I was just calling the standby ambulance in.'

'Where is she?' Greg was already turning to go, but Rick caught him by the arm.

'Just a moment. There's a problem.'

'What?'

'She stabbed a prisoner who was already disabled by taser. He's dead, Greg.'

***

Greg took the narrow stairs two at a time. A quick glance sideways, as he ran past a small kitchen, showed him a couple of girls cowering in a corner.. Along the narrow corridor, almost sliding on the slimy carpet runner, he pulled up sharply beside a half-open door. Two uniformed police were standing guard while a couple of paramedics kneeled by the body of a young man. Over their bent backs Greg saw Sarah sitting on a dirty bed. She was bowed forward, her face hidden in damp, grubby hair. He took in the skimpy, bedraggled dress, saw the urine stains on the front and smelled the results of her panic. Her bare arms were marked with bruises and scored with needle tracks. One was already bandaged. He was filled with immense compassion alongside what he was ashamed to recognise as strong revulsion – whether at what had been done to her, or at what she had become, he couldn't decide. He stepped up to the two police guards as he exclaimed, 'Sarah!' and she looked up.

She took in his face, his expression and with one move she was on her feet and waving him away with a fierce gesture.

'No,' she shouted. 'Keep him away. No.' The paramedics looked up and one got to his feet.

'Better you leave her with us for now,' he said in an undertone. 'We've finished here and she'll need to go to hospital first.'

Greg hesitated for a moment, then turned away. Back in the grubby corridor he bumped into Jim, hard on his heels.

'Sarah? Jim asked.

'Alive but wounded and in a bit of a state. Paramedics say leave her to them. They're taking her to the James Paget for a check-up and any necessary treatment. Someone needs to go with her, Jim, and I think it'd better be a woman. Can you find someone suitable?'

'Of course.' Jim hesitated. 'Do we arrest her?' he asked.

'Not at this point. But there'll need to be an independent investigation. I'll speak to Margaret.'

Outside in the street, Greg shivered in the sharp wind from the river. His phone to his ear, his attention was divided between Jim speaking to one of the uniform sergeants in the glow from the Clean Boats open garage door, and the ambulance, blue lights still flashing as it awaited its cargo for the James Paget Hospital. Just as he heard Margaret's voice on the phone, he saw Sarah, cocooned in blankets, being wheeled in a chair to the back of the ambulance. As he watched she was joined by a uniformed woman officer he didn't know and reflected that a stranger was probably the best option for Sarah in the circumstances. He couldn't shake off the picture of the shame on her face, when he'd tried to go toward her. The increasing volume of the voice in his ear brought him back to the matter in hand.

'Greg, can you hear me?' Margaret sounded more than a little impatient. 'What's been going on? Rick's reported a death in custody, but no details. He said you'd brief me.'

Greg took a deep breath and turned away from the street, the yellow-tinged bricks in front of him shutting out the image of Sarah being put into the ambulance. He leaned one arm on the wall above his head as he talked on the phone.

'First the good news,' he said. 'Sarah is safe. She has been harmed, but her injuries aren't life-threatening and she's on her way to the James Paget Hospital as we speak. She has some cuts and bruises and it seems likely they've been drugging her, but no worse than that. The bad news,' he went on, pre-empting Margaret's next words. 'As Rick has told you, there has been a death in custody. A young man, aged early twenties at a guess, and so far, not definitively identified, was stabbed by Sarah in front of witnesses. He was under restraint at the time.'

He paused, but Margaret was temporarily bereft of words. Into the echoing silence he added, 'Clearly, we don't know yet what preceded this attack, nor what provoked it. I've sent a female officer to the hospital with Sarah, both to keep an eye on her and as some protection in case there's a risk of a revenge attack once word of the death gets out.'

Margaret had found her voice. 'What a mess,' she said succinctly. 'How on earth did Sarah get hold of a weapon, let alone be free to use it?'

'The weapon was a carving fork. I've no other details as yet.'

Greg was interrupted by Rick approaching. 'One of our other arrestees has suggested an identity for the casualty,' he said. 'He claims it's the boss's son. They know him as Mack. It's a nickname I gather. Mack the Knife. Because of his propensity for using one.'

Greg turned back to the phone. 'Did you hear that, Boss?' he asked.

'I heard. Once word gets out, there's going to be trouble. Greg, this is one for the Special Crime and Counter Terrorism Division in London. They'll need to decide on the legal issues. And the IOPC will need to investigate.'

'What do we do in the meantime?' asked Greg. 'Do we begin the investigation here in Yarmouth, or what?' He held the phone out so Rick could hear the answer.

'Seal the building and make sure no one, and I mean no one, has access before Ned and his team arrive. I'll take advice and get back to you. It may be the IOPC will want you to investigate under their management, or they may want to investigate themselves. Given the seriousness of the allegation and the potential for a conflict of interest, it's likely to be the latter.'

'Got it,' said Greg. 'And Rick heard too.'

Rick nodded and said, 'I'll seal the building and place officers accordingly.'

'Thank you,' said Margaret. 'I'll keep you both posted. Greg, I would expect you can and should continue with your investigation of the deaths in Norwich and the original abduction of Sarah. Just keep out of the investigation of what happened in Cobham tonight. And keep me briefed.'

'Will do.' Putting the phone back in his pocket he looked at Rick. 'Just for my ears,' he said, 'what exactly did happen up there?'

'My officers had just put their man down – the one now being identified as Mack. They say that when they entered the room, he already had his knife in his hand, and they had to taser him to put him down. It was while he was on the floor, recovering from the taser, that Sarah stepped forward with the carving fork and plunged it into his chest. No doubt the post-mortem will let us know precisely what she hit, but my chaps say death was very quick. He lost consciousness within seconds and appeared dead within a few minutes. They tried CPR but got nowhere. The paramedics pronounced him dead at the scene.'

'That move must have taken some strength,' said Greg, thinking aloud.

'I think it'd have gone in easily,' replied Rick. 'Like most carving forks, it was sharp and stiff. It made a good weapon. Better than a knife in some ways.'

Both men fell silent for a spell. 'It's not looking good for Sarah,' said Greg at last. 'Unless she was under the influence of drugs, or something.'

'Best we don't speculate any further,' said Rick. Greg quietly nodded his agreement.

15

Coping

Greg drove home with the black dog on his shoulders. The midnight hour had come and gone, so the Acle straight was blessedly quiet. Even that small positive had no effect on his mood. The flat pastures between the road and the river were draped in a low-lying mist. Horned heads appeared here and there where the mist hung lowest. Closer to Acle, the grazing cattle gave way to horses just before the billowing mist enveloped the road. Greg cursed and slowed to a crawl, turning his fogs on and dipping the main headlights. Yellow light bounced back at him from the thickening vapours and two amber spots appeared in front of him. Another late traveller going the other way. A few yards further on he found his turning and bounced down the rough track to his riverside cottage.

To his surprise there was a glow of lights where all should have been darkness. He pulled up on the sweep of gravel near the back door and rested his head on the steering wheel for a moment. It had to be Chris. And he wasn't sure he was pleased about that. Right now, all he wanted was peace, solitude, and time to think. Sighing, he reached for his bag, got out of the car and slammed the door, the noise lost immediately in the deadening effect of the surrounding fog.

Just as he reached the door, it opened, and Chris was in the doorway. She stepped forward and put her arms round him in a warm hug, then stepped back.

'I heard,' she said briefly. 'There's soup on the stove, fresh bread and cheese, and I've run you a bath. Go and have your bath while it's still hot.' She kissed him lightly on the cheek and went back into the kitchen. Through the open door he saw her give the pot of soup a stir, Bobby twining round her ankles. He went upstairs with a slightly lighter heart.

The bath was so full of hot water he had to step in carefully to avoid it overflowing. He lay back with a sigh and closed his eyes. Imprinted on the lids he could still see Sarah in the skimpy flowered dress; a stranger to anyone who'd known the immaculate, smart, controlled DI before her abduction. He made no effort to reach for soap or sponge but just lay in the hot water, letting it wash away the aches from his muscles and the stress from his mind. Then as it cooled he sighed again, got up and reached for the towel warming on the radiator. By the time he came slowly downstairs in his towelling robe, with feet bare, he was calmer and the weight on his shoulders had materially lightened.

'How did you know when to run the bath?' he asked Chris. Not at all what he'd intended to say, but just what popped into his mind.

'Jim let me know when you were both leaving Yarmouth,' she replied. 'Go and put your feet up on the sofa. I'll bring the soup through.'

It was homemade pea and ham: thick enough to stand a spoon up in, and the bread was fresh and crusty. Not at all hungry, Greg plunged a spoon into the soup out of politeness, and was surprised to find, moments later, that the bowl was empty. He wiped up the dregs with the last of the bread, ate the last chunk of salty cheddar with his fingers and leaned back. Chris sat down at the opposite end of the sofa and pulled his feet into her lap.

'You'll catch your death wandering around with no slippers,' she said. 'Where're the ones I got you?'

'Upstairs somewhere.'

The silence fell again. Chris rubbed his cold feet and Bobby jumped onto his lap, turned round a few times purring and kneading, then settled down. He rested a hand on the cat and looked at Chris's downturned face.

'How did you hear?' he asked.

'It's all round the team. I think it came from Margaret's office, but only via rumour, until Jim rang me. Was it awful?'

'Yes.'

'Do you want to talk about it?'

'Yes. No. I don't know. I just feel so guilty. So sad. It's such a waste. If we'd got there quicker it wouldn't have happened. Now, her career's gone. Her life ruined. God knows what she went through to drive her to do that.'

There was another pause. Then Chris said, 'The rumour is she stabbed a prisoner. Is it true? Is there no doubt at all?'

'She stabbed a man, who'd just been tasered, in front of two constables. So no doubt at all, no. What had happened previously to drive her to that, well that we've still to find out.

But it's unlikely we'll be doing the investigating. It'll probably be the IOPC.'

'Jim said something about drugs. Is there any chance she was under the influence?'

'Possibly, but we just don't know. She wasn't out of it when I saw her, but I've no doubt the medics will be checking her blood for traces. No point speculating.'

Silence fell again, but Greg felt it was a good silence. He could feel the tension seeping out of his ears. The comforting food and foot massage were taking effect. He yawned. It was the signal Chris had been waiting for.

'Bed,' she said firmly. 'It's tomorrow already and it'll be another long day.' Greg swung his feet to the floor and as Chris stood up, pulled her to him for another hug.

'Thanks,' he said into her hair. 'I can face it now.' And they went up to bed.

***

The alarm went off at 07:00. Greg woke with a start and turned over to find the bed beside him empty. Chris came in as he got out of bed, rubbing her hair dry on an old towel.

'We've got better towels than that,' said Greg, distracted. 'That's a cat towel.'

'Not clean we haven't,' replied Chris. 'We've both been too busy to do anything practical. I put a wash on last night but everything's wet.'

'I hope I've got a shirt,' said Greg, heading for the wardrobe.

'A couple, then that's the lot,' said Chris. 'You need to get your house fairy in.' Greg grinned at the reference to his cleaning lady and nodded.

'Quick shower and shave then I'll be ready to go,' he said.

It was eight o'clock by the time they got to Wymondham and Margaret was already closeted with the IOPC. In his office Greg found Ram busy at his desk, trawling through multiple files on his two screens.

'Morning,' he said, looking up. 'I gather yesterday was a modified success.'

'That's one way of putting it,' agreed Greg. 'We got Sarah back alive, but until we hear from the hospital, we won't know how badly she's hurt. And you'll have heard what happened next.'

'Certainly have.'

'Has the casualty been identified yet?' asked Greg.

'Certainly has. Your 'Mack the Knife' turns out to be Mica Gabrys: only son, at least as far as we know, of Constantin Gabrys of Horses Mill House, Greater Ormesby, Chairman of the Clean Boats holding company, and strongly suspected of being our Mr Big!'

'Oh my God.' Greg sat down with a bump. 'Has the family been informed yet?'

'Not as far as I know. Margaret is discussing just that with SCCT as we speak. I understand the IOPC have also been informed and are on their way from London. The body was identified early this morning, by one of the men taken into custody last night. He's being held in the cells on other charges, and I think Margaret's hoping the news of the death doesn't leak before we speak to the family. I bet that's her now,' he added as the phone on Greg's desk rang.

It was.

'I need you and Ram in here now,' she said. Ram was already putting his jacket on as Greg looked up from the phone.

'We're wanted,' said Greg unnecessarily and both men walked briskly through the building to Margaret's office. Greg knocked on the door, then opened it on an empty office.

'Oh,' he said, turning to Ram, just as Margaret appeared in the corridor behind them.

'Go on in, gentlemen,' she said. 'I was just seeing the experts from SCCT off the premises. Take a seat.'

She settled herself behind her desk. Greg took the seat opposite with its back to the window, and Ram the other.

'This is what's going to happen,' she said, all her business-like qualities to the fore.

'First, SCCT advise that we need to create a Chinese wall around the investigation of the stabbing of Mica Gabrys while in custody. IOPC are going to lead, but they've already signalled they'd like to use personnel from here that can be regarded as not conflicted. That's you, Ram. From now on, until that investigation is complete, you will lead on it under the supervision of IOPC. You'll move out of Greg's office, and we can discuss shortly what team you have under you.

'Greg, you'll continue to lead the investigation into the murder of Madame Trieste and the abduction of Sarah, together with all its ramifications, the evidence of the children you spoke to yesterday and the issues surrounding Clean Boats Inc.'

Both men opened their mouths, but Margaret held up her hand.

'Before you start,' she said, 'I realise that we can't completely isolate Ram's investigation from yours, Greg. Clearly what you turn up about Sarah's abduction is likely to be relevant evidence on what led up to the attack with a carving fork. But that's the problem when an IOPC complaint becomes part of an ongoing investigation! So, think of it as a Chinese wall with a valve, and I'm the valve.

'You, Greg, will keep me abreast of what you find out and I'll share evidence with Ram that I judge to be relevant to the consideration of Sarah's actions. And you, Ram, will do the same and I will pass on to Greg anything I judge important to his lines of enquiry.'

A silence fell, and Margaret leaned back in her chair, the ever-present pencil in her fingers. Greg looked at her. Her fluffy hair was as dishevelled as ever, her uniform a little tight. The only difference, he thought, was that new lines of strain were showing on her plump face.

'Okay,' said Ram. 'Not ideal, but I can see the point.' Margaret turned her face to Greg.

'I agree,' said Greg. 'But one question. Who's going to break the news of his son's death to Constantin Gabrys?'

There was a silence, in which the cawing from the rookery beyond the window could be clearly heard.

'Make your pitch, Greg,' said Margaret. 'It would seem obvious it should be Ram, but the fact you asked the question suggests you think otherwise.'

Greg paused to clarify his thoughts. 'Two things,' he said at last. 'First, it's the best chance I've had, both to meet Gabrys and to get into his house. It's too good to miss. Second, setting aside for the moment who stabbed Mica, if the death had occurred during the raid in other circumstances, it would automatically have been my duty to deal with talking to the family. Up to this point, I think we should stick with normal procedure, but I should make it clear that Sarah's actions will be the subject of an independent investigation.'

There was another silence while Margaret turned the pencil over in her fingers, then smacked it down on her desk decisively.

'Okay. We'll go with that. Ram, you stay in the background until Greg's broken the news, then you make an appointment to see Gabrys and brief him on the investigation.'

'Okay. But I doubt he'll wait for that,' said Ram. 'From all accounts, his next step will be an appeal to the Police Commissioner, the Chief Constable, his MP, or all three.'

'It might be interesting to see who he thinks will listen, who's in his pocket so to speak,' said Greg, then took a look at Margaret's face and shut up quickly. 'I'll get myself off to Greater Ormesby,' he said. 'Unless, of course, we've intelligence that suggests he's in Lithuania or other foreign parts.'

'Not as far as I know,' said Ram, and they got up to leave.

Out in the corridor, they looked at each other in silence for a moment. 'I'll clear my things out of your room before you get back,' said Ram. 'Sorry it's turned out like this.'

'So'm I,' said Greg. 'But at least the investigation will be in good hands, and I don't envy you dealing with the IOPC.' They shook hands, then Greg turned to the car park, reaching for his phone.

'Chris,' he said. 'Join me at the car, please. We're going to Greater Ormesby. And we need a family liaison officer. Bring me one with a good head on their shoulders.'

16

Breaking bad news

Greg glanced up from starting his car and was delighted, if surprised, to see Chris coming toward him with Jill in tow.

'Hi, Jill,' he said. 'Delighted to have you along, but I didn't realise you did family liaison along with everything else.'

'You said a good one, and I got one,' said Chris smugly. Jill slid into the back seat, pushing a black satchel in front of her.

'I did the training a couple of years ago, but I haven't done a live case for a while. Chris thought my knowledge of the background would be useful, and from my perspective it's good for my CV if I'm going for the sergeant exams this time around. But I understand if you want someone who's done it more recently.'

'No, not at all,' replied Greg, looking over his shoulder as he pulled out onto the slip road to the A11. 'I think you'll do a very good job. And knowing who we're dealing with will be as useful for you as for me. What do you know about the family so far?'

'Just what's in the briefing from Ram,' she replied. 'Constantin Gabrys, head of the family, chairman of a holding company with interests in several Norfolk businesses and assumed to have other interests back in Lithuania. The local businesses that are public knowledge are the boat cleaning company and the chain of nail bars and hairdressing salons. The former cleans boats for holiday companies, and also does some work with the big chalet and mobile home sites on the east coast. The latter is run by his wife, Eva Gabrys, or at least she fronts it.

'In addition, he's been linked to cannabis factories, illegal immigration supplying workers for the cannabis factories, and drug distribution. But so far, we've no proof that would stand up in court.'

'How many children?' asked Greg. 'Was Mica the only one?'

'The only son, according to what we know. There's a daughter too. A couple of years younger than Mica and currently at university reading Law.'

They all fell silent as the car negotiated the A11 and the Thickthorn roundabout. Chris was consulting the emails on her phone. Jill was checking through the file in her bag again.

In the slow section before Acle, Greg said over his shoulder, 'Let's plan our approach. We'll be there in fifteen minutes or so. Judging from Jeff's experience, the first challenge will be getting in. I really don't want to give this news on the doorstep, nor to anyone other than the father or mother. On the other hand, they'll presumably be questioning why their son hasn't come home, and they must have heard about the raid last night. I'm guessing they'll be expecting an approach and news that we've arrested Mica.'

'Or, they'll have heard all the news already, in which case Wymondham is leaking worse than we thought,' remarked Chris. Greg glanced across.

'True. Now that would be very interesting indeed. In fact, whether they know or not will give us some useful clues.'

'As in, if they don't know, then the people who are in on it are presumably okay. While if they do know, we've got a bad apple in that group?' asked Jill.

'Yes to the last, but not quite to the first,' said Greg as he negotiated the very familiar bridge over the Bure. 'If they haven't heard yet, it could simply be that the news hasn't reached them. But how they react is going to be very important. Keep your eyes peeled.'

The seven-feet-high wooden gates were firmly closed when they arrived at the entrance to Horses Mill House. Greg pulled up just off the road and got out of the car. A security camera stared back at him as he walked over to the right-hand gate post. He pressed what appeared to be a bell and held his ID up to the blank electronic eye.

'DCI Geldard to see Mr and Mrs Gabrys,' he announced.

'Do you have an appointment?' asked the gate post.

'No,' replied Greg.

'Please contact Mr Gabrys's office for an appointment,' said the gatepost as Greg interrupted.

'I am a police officer on official business, and I need to see Mr and Mrs Gabrys now.'

There was silence for a few moments, then a different voice asked, 'Why do you wish to see both Mr and Mrs Gabrys?' Greg hesitated, then said, 'I need to speak to them about their son, Mica.'

Another pause, then with a low sigh the heavy double gates swung open.

'Please take the drive to the house. You will be met at the door,' the voice said. Greg got back in the car and started down the drive. As he drove slowly between the gates Chris looked back and said, 'The gates are reinforced.'

He nodded, and replied, 'Keep your eyes peeled both of you.'

The drive was bordered by lawns, looking a little tired after the long dry autumn. A few shrubs were dotted here and there, but sight lines along the tall walls had been kept clear. The house was visible at the end of the drive, an old three-storey farmhouse tarted up, as Greg mentally described it, into something akin to a manor house. The original farmhouse was apparent in the centre and the front door stood open. Wings had been added to either side. The left-hand extension, in external appearance very like an orangery, seemed to house a swimming pool. A fancy built-in barbecue adjoined. The function of the right-hand extension was less obvious. Greg pulled up by the open door and they all got out. A man in some sort of livery was waiting and curtly said, 'This way, please.'

The three of them followed him into the hall. Chris paused to take a good look round and noted that some of the original farmhouse rooms had been sacrificed to create an imposing hall, with a central stairway leading up to a landing. They were led across the hall to the right and it immediately became apparent that this extension now provided the main reception rooms.

'DCI Geldard and his colleagues,' said their guide, and a couple rose from a pair of sofas aligned at right angles to the fireplace at the far end. The man, a sturdy figure rather less than six feet tall and wearing mustard corduroys topped by a tweed jacket, stepped forward. His wife, or what Greg assumed to be his wife, hung back a little. She was an elegant, but too thin, 6 ft plus in her high court shoes. With her hair piled in a high chignon, she seemed quite a bit taller than her husband, but also rather frail, as though a stiff breeze might bend her to breaking point.

'Good day, Mr Gabrys, Mrs Gabrys,' said Greg. 'May I introduce my colleagues, Detective Sergeant Chris Mathews, and Detective Constable Jill Hayes. I am very sorry to say we have some bad news for you. Perhaps you would like to take a seat?'

Mrs Gabrys immediately sank into the sofa behind her. Her hands were shaking as she put them first to her mouth, then clutched the pearl necklace round her thin neck. Mr Gabrys took a step forward.

'I would prefer you tell me what you have come to say,' he said in slightly accented English. Greg glanced sideways at Chris and Jill, then he took a step toward Mr Gabrys. Keeping his eye on Mrs Gabrys as he spoke, he said, 'I am very sorry to have to tell you that your son, Mica, is dead.'

The words fell into the silent room like a brick. There was a pause, then a low moan from Mrs Gabrys. Her hands tugged at the necklace, the string snapped and a few pearls fell from it to the carpet between the sofas. She sat still, looking down at the broken string in her hands, tears pouring silently down her thin face. Jill stepped forward, bent to pick up the fallen pearls, then sat down beside Mrs Gabrys on the plumply stuffed sofa and put her hand over the shaking, heavily beringed fingers in the woman'slap. Mr Gabrys ignored his wife. His face may have paled a little, although with distress or rage, Greg found it hard to tell.

'How?' he asked at last.

'Mica was being arrested at a crime scene in Great Yarmouth, to be precise at the offices of Clean Boats Inc. He was the subject of an attack, a stabbing, while being restrained, and although emergency services were on the scene very quickly, I'm afraid they were unable to save him. I am very sorry,' repeated Greg.

'Where is he now?' asked Mr Gabrys.

'At the mortuary in Norwich,' replied Greg. 'There will, of course, be a post-mortem.'

'I wish to see him,' interrupted the father.

'Of course, and we will make the necessary arrangements as soon as the post-mortem is complete. I also need to tell you,' went on Greg, 'that because your son was under arrest at the time of the incident, there will be an independent inquiry into all the circumstances. This will be carried out by the Independent Office for Police Conduct.'

'Who killed him?' asked Gabrys.

'He was stabbed by a person whom we believe to have been illegally imprisoned at the site. I am not at liberty to give more details at this time. You will, of course, be kept fully informed of the investigation.'

Those words also dropped like a brick, but the reaction this time was different. This time Gabrys definitely changed colour. His face became so dark a red that Greg feared an imminent vascular event and stepped forward. Gabrys spluttered a word that Greg didn't understand and also stepped forward.

'Out. Out,' he shouted. 'Out of my house. I will be consulting my lawyers. I will have justice. I will have my revenge.' He switched to Lithuanian again and his wife visibly jerked.

Greg stood his ground. 'As I said, I am very sorry to bring you this news,' he said. 'My colleague, Jill Hayes, will stay with your wife if that would be helpful and will liaise between you and—'

'No. Out. Out, all of you. Out.'

'If that's your wish, then of course we will leave. Mrs Gabrys, please accept my most sincere condolences.' He turned back to Mr Gabrys. 'As I said, the investigation of this incident will be undertaken by a team independent of Norfolk Police. They will be in touch with you and I will have no further involvement in the matter of your son's death. There may, however, be other matters related to the issues around Clean Boats which took us there in the first place, and I may need to talk to you further, as a company director that is. But that's not a matter for now.'

Gabrys was still breathing hard and his face was still dark. 'Out now. I wish to talk to my lawyers. Out.' He moved toward Greg aggressively, who thought it better, in the circumstances, to step aside and take his dismissal.

The three officers walked back through the hall to the front door, walking as slowly as they dared and alert to their surroundings. Behind them they heard Gabrys snap at his wife in Lithuanian, and what sounded like high heels running over a wooden floor and then up some stairs. Gabrys's voice, apparently shouting into a mobile phone, diminished slightly as he moved away in the opposite direction toward the far corner of the drawing room. Then a door slammed and they heard him no more.

'This way, sir. Goodbye, sir,' said the man in livery. Greg paused on the doorstep and looked at him.

'If Mrs Gabrys should need help, you can call us,' he said and offered his card. The man didn't take it.

'More than anything is worth for me to take that,' he muttered. But I caught your name, Inspector Geldard.' Greg nodded and didn't bother to correct him.

'That's okay then,' he said, and followed Chris and Jill to the car.

They were silent as he drove slowly back down the drive. The big gates swung open as they reached them, and he turned the car toward Acle and the A47.

'Comments?' he asked.

Chris looked at Jill. 'You first,' she said.

'Initial reactions,' said Jill, 'Mrs Gabrys is scared of her husband and is probably anorexic or bulimic. When she ran away as we left, she went up some stairs that seemed to lead off from that sitting room. So her accommodation, at least, may be in that wing rather than in the main block. I'm sure they didn't know Mica was dead, but they may have known about the raid in Clean Boats. Oh, and the pearls she was wearing. They weren't real. At least, not the ones I handled.'

Chris added, 'I agree as regards the wife. It also seemed to me that Gabrys's office was at the far end of that sitting room. I think that's where he went as he made that phone call. Incidentally, I think it was on his mobile, so it'll be interesting to see if GCHQ can pick it up. Only other thing I'd add, it wouldn't be easy to raid that place, not even for an army. The walls and gates are solid and there's no cover between the house and the wall.'

17

Explanations

Over at the James Paget Hospital, Ram was still waiting in the corridor to see Sarah. He'd got to his feet several times as nurses had come and gone from the private room, but each time the figure in blue scrubs had shaken its head and he'd sat down again. As he checked his watch yet again, and sighed yet again, PC Jenny Warren smiled at him sympathetically. He took no notice, and shot to his feet as the door opened and the doctor emerged.

'You can go in now,' said the doctor, in Ram's eyes about twelve years old and enjoying his temporary power just a little too much. 'But don't overdo it,' he added. Ram nodded grimly and went in, followed by Jenny clutching her shoulder bag and notebook.

Sarah was in the bed, propped up and drinking a cup of coffee. Her bedside table had already acquired get-well cards and some grapes from a less-than-imaginative colleague. From the speed at which they'd arrived, Ram concluded that the source must have been the officers who'd accompanied her to the hospital the night before, presumably plundering the hospital shop for anything remotely suitable. At a quick glance, some of the cards seemed slightly out of place. Decorated as they were by flowers and cherubs, they looked more suitable for the successful conclusion of a confinement, rather than the precursor to one at Her Majesty's Pleasure.

'DCI Ram Trent,' said Ram. 'We haven't met, as I was posted to Norfolk only after your kidnap. Constable Warren you know.'

Jenny nodded, and Sarah managed a weak smile. 'How's Turbo?' she asked.

'Temporarily on sick leave,' replied Jenny. 'He cut a paw on a shout last week and it's taking some time to heal.' Seeing some bewilderment on Ram's face she added. 'Turbo's my usual partner – a springer spaniel.'

Ram nodded but went straight on, unwilling to be side-tracked. 'I've been asked to take charge of the investigation into what happened at Clean Boats Inc. last night,' he said. 'I'm sure you'll have realised that there would need to be an independent inquiry. The fact we'd never met before was quite convenient from that point of view. So, before we start, I need to ask, do you want a solicitor present? Or a representative from the Police Federation?'

'Do I need one?' Sarah asked.

'I've been advised that this should be an interview under caution, so yes, you have that choice, like anyone else.'

'No, I don't need a solicitor, or a rep, thank you,' she said, and leaned her head back on the mounded pillows. 'Go ahead. I've nothing to hide.'

'Okay then. Jenny here will take notes, and we'll record the interview too.' He placed his recorder on the table over the bed. 'For the tape, present in the room at the James Paget Hospital are DCI Ram Trent, PC Jenny Warren, and DI Sarah Laurence. Sarah Laurence, you do not have to say anything but it may harm your defence if you do not mention when questioned something that you later rely on in court. Anything you do say may be given in evidence.

'Also, just to confirm, you have been offered a solicitor or Federation rep and you have declined. Is that correct?'

'Yes.'

He pulled a visitors' chair over with his foot, and sat down between the bed and the window, so that the grey winter light fell full on Sarah's face. He studied her in silence for a moment, while Jenny settled herself opposite and got her pen out.

The face he saw was drawn and pale, with a livid mark on one cheek. There were bandages on one arm and one hand. 'How are you feeling,' he asked. 'I gather from the medics that you've been dosed with heroin or similar while captive, and I can see you have some injuries.' He nodded to her bandages.

'These?' She held her arms up. 'These are relatively superficial, although the one on my hand will probably leave some interesting scars across my knuckles and I've a broken finger. The drugs, that's the worst bit. Even in that short space of time, I think I was starting to get addicted. It's hard to come down from the sort of doses it seems they were giving me. Actually, correction! The worst bit is the nightmares.'

'Drug induced?' asked Ram.

'Partly. Mainly the memory of what that nutter threatened to do to me.'

'Which was what? I'm sorry,' added Ram. 'I realise that these are not things you want to remember or to talk about, but there has been a death in custody and you know what that means.'

'Yes.' She shifted restlessly in the bed and put the mug down on the side table. 'Not that I ever expected to be on the receiving end of this sort of interview.'

'No. I imagine not.' Ram paused, not quite knowing how to move on. 'I have to ask,' he said. 'What were the threats?'

'Various,' said Sarah, her voice tired. 'To blind me. That was one option he was considering. On balance, he thought he'd go for flaying me, starting with my legs.' Ram glanced involuntarily at the legs under the hospital blanket.

'Luckily, he didn't get a chance to start,' said Sarah. 'That was when the cavalry arrived.'

'Describe to me what happened,' prompted Ram.

'He'd just slashed my hand, then stepped back and started discussing what he was going to do next. How much fun he'd have. That's when he decided to flay me. I'd stepped back as far as I could go. Then the door flew open and two uniformed officers came in. I think one of them took a stab to his chest. Is he alright?' she asked.

'Yes. The stab vest protected him. What happened next?'

'Well, that's when it gets to be a bit of a blur. The nutter stabbed one of the officers, as I said. I think one of them may have struck out at him with his baton, then I snatched the carving fork from under the pillow and went to help. That's about it.'

'You were going to the assistance of a fellow officer?'

'That's right. What else?'

Ram paused to marshal his thoughts. 'Where did the fork come from?'

'I found it in the kitchen. They left me unattended for a while. At least, when I came round from the last shot of heroin I was alone, and when I tried the door, it was unlocked. I couldn't get to the stairs; I could hear voices. So, I went the other way. I knew where the kitchen was, and I went looking for a weapon.'

'Were there no knives?'

'I think there were a couple. It's hard to remember now. But I thought the fork would be easier to hide up my sleeve. And I remembered a pathologist telling me once that a carving fork made a good weapon because it's both sharp and stiff. Where a knife blade would bend when it hit ribs, a carving fork would go straight in.'

'How did you hide it up your sleeve?' asked Jenny.

'I fixed it to my arm with an elastic band. Once I got back to my room, I hid it under the pillow.'

There was another pause while Ram looked again at his notes and Jenny added to hers. 'The officers who came into the room,' he began.

'The ones he attacked?' said Sarah. 'Yes?'

'They say that they'd already subdued their attacker with baton and taser before you intervened.'

'Do they? I don't know anything about that. I've told you what I saw. The nutter turned and stabbed one officer, I saw a baton come down, then I stabbed him as I've already told you. Before he stabbed anyone else.'

Ram glanced at Jenny, then back at Sarah. Her head was lolling on the pillows and she looked, if possible, even paler. 'One more question, and then we'll leave you in peace. Did you know the man you refer to as 'the nutter'? I mean, did you know his name and had you come across him before in your professional capacity?'

'No,' said Sarah. 'No one mentioned his name and I'd never met him before. But in view of what he threatened, I'd make an educated guess he was the one who tortured and killed Madame Trieste. If I was in charge, I'd be checking Nails Galore and Madame for his DNA.'

***

Back in his car, Ram rang the boss. 'Tayler,' said the brisk voice. Ram recounted the results of the interview, to a silence that went on for what felt like minutes.

'So, her defence is going to be that she was defending a fellow officer,' said Margaret. 'Smart. But no one ever said Sarah was stupid.'

'You don't believe her?'

'What I think or believe is irrelevant. The question is what will a jury believe? Or IOPC. Make your report and we'll see what they say. I'll pass on the gist to Greg. The suggestion about the Trieste death is well made.'

***

When Margaret spoke to Greg, she found he was already on the case. 'Thank you, it's helpful to know how he threatened Sarah, but I'd already asked Ned to cross-check between samples. We're just waiting for the DNA team to profile Mica, then we can compare with the evidence from Nails Galore.'

As he spoke, a commotion arose down the corridor from his office. 'I'll keep you posted Margaret,' he said. And rang off hurriedly. The voice he could hear in full cry, like an entire pack of baying hounds, was Chris's.

He entered the team office, identifying the location of the noise with little difficulty. From the terms used he guessed Jeff Fellowes was the recipient of her ire.

'You complete and utter, plonking, toerag of a dingbat waste of space! I *had* thought some behaviour was below even you, but no, you have to go and prove me wrong. I even thought that, with training, you might be capable of rising just a fraction above the slime you naturally inhabit, but no. Caveman is too good for you! Moronic gorilla is too good for you! In fact I'm struggling to think of any animal, vegetable or mineral that wouldn't be insulted at being compared with you. Even slurry would take exception to a comparison. Words fail me,' she concluded and paused for a much-needed breath. Greg reflected that there was scant evidence of words failing her, and hastened to intervene before she reoxygenated and returned to the charge.

He put a hand on her arm and said, 'Chris. Report.'

She let the deep breath she'd taken whistle away unused, then took another and gestured at the big man cowering in the chair before her. 'This,' – she gestured in his direction – 'this inadequate in something roughly approximating human form has shared photos of Sarah on a WhatsApp group. I haven't yet found out how he got hold of the pictures, but *I will*,' she said with emphasis. 'Moreover, the photos are bad enough but the captions are worse. Look.'

She handed a phone to Greg. He flicked through a half-dozen photos, obviously taken at the scene of the raid the preceding evening, and read the captions. He swallowed hard and glanced round the rest of the room.

'Who else's seen these?' he asked. No one spoke. 'Steve? Phil?' They both shook their heads.

'I think you'll find that the WhatsApp group is mainly Met officers,' said Chris grimly. 'I had a tip-off and requested access to Fellowes's phone.'

Fellowes muttered something. 'What's that?' demanded Greg.

Fellowes looked up, red-faced and still not meeting Greg's eyes and said, 'It wasn't a request.'

'Okay, it was an order,' said Chris. 'Got a problem with that? Oh yes, perhaps you do have a problem with that. I was forgetting. You don't like taking orders from a "short-arsed slut in rainbow clothes" do you?'

'Chris, enough,' said Greg quietly. 'We'll take this into my office. Fellowes. Get.'

The door closed behind them; Greg sat down behind his desk. 'Chris, take a seat,' he said, nodding to the chair under the window. Then as Fellowes went to sit in the remaining chair snapped, 'At attention, Fellowes.'

He took a few moments to review the sloppy figure standing rigidly before him: ill-fitting leather jacket, creased and concertinaing trousers, battered suede shoes.

'Before I get on to anything else, Fellowes,' he said with some distaste, there's plain clothes and there's just plain sloppy. Unless you're undercover as a tramp, please see to it you present yourself better in future. If you have a future, that is,' he added, pre-empting a mutter from Chris. 'Now, Chris, let's hear your side of this.' Chris stood up herself.

'I had a tip-off almost precisely,' – she glanced at her watch – 'yes, one hour ago, that distasteful photos of DI Sarah Laurence were being shared on a WhatsApp group. My informant told me that the photos had been uploaded by Constable Fellowes. I went looking for him, but it took me a little while to run him to earth. Eventually he returned to the general office and I ordered him to unlock his phone and hand it to me. He refused at first, but when I pointed out that it was an official item of kit and that I had a right to review its use, he handed it over. I checked the WhatsApp site first, and when I found the photos, I also had a quick look at his browsing history, which is similarly seedy. That's when you came in.'

Greg turned his attention again to the phone in his hand. He glanced again through the WhatsApp images, then turned to the search engine. A quick look was sufficient.

'Fellowes, where did you get the photos? The ones of Sarah Laurence I mean.'

Fellowes stared over his head and said nothing.

'It has to have been from someone on the raid. That's a small list of possibilities and not difficult for me to find out who. You might as well say.' Still silence.

'Chris, go and speak to Chief Inspector Lake, with my compliments, and explain our problem. Brief Jim Henning as well. Come back here when you have a name.'

Chris left the room in silence, with no more than a disparaging glance at the scruffy figure in the centre. The door closed behind her, and silence reigned. Greg turned to the paperwork on his desk, pretending to ignore the continuing presence of Constable Fellowes.

After some minutes, the silence broken only by the squeaking of his biro on paper and the turning of pages, Fellowes cleared his throat and shifted his weight from one foot to another.

'Anything to say?' asked Greg without looking up. Still silence, except for more fidgeting.

Then Fellowes said, 'Foxton.'

'I beg your pardon?'

'Constable Foxton. He passed me the photos. I think he took them. I assumed he did.'

'And why did he pass them to you?'

'We met on a course. Last year.'

'Was he the official photographer?'

'No. I don't think so. I think he took them with his phone when he was left guarding DI Laurence.'

'And the captions?'

'They were just a joke. That's all. A joke. No one has a sense of humour any more.'

'Really? You find a photo of an abused fellow officer over headings that include the words 'Slut' and worse, amusing?'

Fellowes reddened some more and didn't answer.

'What'll happen now?' he said eventually.

'First, I phone Chief Inspector Lake and request he takes action against this Foxton. Second, I ring Chief Superintendent Tayler and inform her of developments. Third, I suspend you with immediate effect. Without pay,' he added. 'Then, we wait and see. Hand over your warrant card, security pass and any official car keys you have. I'm keeping this,' he added, gesturing with the phone. 'Then get out.'

Fellowes opened his mouth to object, took another look at Greg, and shambled away, shoulders down, head down. Chris passed him in the corridor on her way back to Greg's office. She said nothing and her vitriolic glare was wasted as he took care not to catch her eye.

'Foxton,' she said as she re-entered the office.

'I know,' replied Greg. 'Fellowes just told me.' He paused, his hand on the office phone. 'What do you know of Foxton?'

'Nothing really. Only what you can read in the unit directory. I haven't met him as far as I know. He's relatively new I think.'

'What happens next is up to Margaret. She can decide whether to leave him to Lake or take further action.

'Morning, Boss,' he said into the phone. 'I'm afraid we have another problem.' In a few words he explained the issue, then held the phone away from his ear to avoid permanent auditory damage. When the decibel level dropped, he spoke again. 'I've suspended him, and I told him it was without pay. I hope HR will stand by that. In the meantime, I've got other priorities.' Another silence while he listened again, then he put the phone down, sighed and leaned back in his chair.

'Margaret's going to speak with HR. For now, it's back to work for us. Let's catch up with Ned and plan the rest of our day.'

'What about Sarah? What's happening to her?'

'That's with Ram,' replied Greg. 'Margaret will let him know what's happened here today, but I don't think it'll affect his investigation. Come on, Chris. Let's do some proper policing. That's left a very nasty taste in my mouth. I'm going to have a chat with those two kids from Yarmouth – Emily and Nathan. You go and re-interview those lowlifes we picked up on the raid. I know Rick's team had a go immediately after the raid, but we know more now. And you might find it a refreshing change from talking to Fellowes.'

As they emerged from the office, Chris took a quick look up and down the corridor, then seeing it was clear, stuck her tongue out.

'That's for taking the micky,' she said.

'And that's dumb impertinence,' he replied with a grin. 'See you later.'

Chris ran her quarries to earth in the cells of the police investigation centre.

'They've been in front of the magistrates,' said the custody sergeant. 'If there hadn't been a hold-up with transport, they'd be on their way to prison. You're lucky you caught them here.'

'Can I have half an hour or so with each?' she asked. 'Probably won't need more than that. And what about the woman? Cara wasn't it, according to my notes anyway.'

'She's been released without charge and gone to a refuge. We'll need her as a witness, but there's no suggestion she's committed a crime.'

'Can you let me know where she is? I may need a chat with her too.'

'Okay. But it's confidential. The Chief said to be careful because of risks of witness interference.'

'Okay. I'll call back before I leave. That way you'll have time to check with your boss that he's okay me knowing.'

Her first two interviews were predictable. Sullen 'no comments' supplemented by demands for special treatment on grounds of anything from ADHD to arthritis, and complaints about poor food, cold cells and useless defence solicitors. Providing the standard responses, she noticed, all the same, that both men had something in common. Other than being well muscled and stupid, that is. They were afraid. It didn't take her long to conclude that they probably knew little and weren't going to share even that anytime soon.

The third was different. Unlike the hired muscle, this one was younger and slim. Quite good-looking in a flashy sort of way, with a beard which, she reflected, might have started off as long stubble before he was taken into custody. He also had a full head of dark hair, in contrast to the shaved or bald heads on the musclemen. He was still in the open-necked shirt and trousers he'd worn for his brief court appearance; again unlike the other, sportswear-clad, pair. She leaned back in her chair and pushed her notes away from her for a moment.

'You don't fit the mould,' she observed. 'What're you doing mixed up with those two gorillas?'

There was another silence, but she felt there was a calculation going on in the head opposite. Something was moving in the synapses, other than ritual moaning and fear.

'Come on, help me out here,' she said. 'Give me something, anything, and I'll see what I can do to help. At the least, I could see about separation from the hired muscle in prison. Maybe even a different prison.' Another pause and she looked down at the papers in front of her. A brainwave hit, and she texted Greg.

any details on the man who groomed Emily?

'Are we done here?' asked the young man into the silence.

'Not yet,' she replied, still looking at her phone. There was a *ting* as the reply came up on-screen.

man with beard going by name of pete ashfield, peter shinfield and patrick ashton

'Bingo,' she whispered under her breath looking at the name on the charge sheet in front of her. Patrick Shinfield. Close enough. 'So, Patrick, Peter or Pete, whichever you prefer, I gather you're good at grooming young girls. Anything you'd like to say now?'

As she left the station, reporting to Greg by phone, she explained, 'He did say something unexpected. He asked if Emily was okay. I think, down there in the dregs of his personality, he had a sneaking liking or respect for her. No, I'm not going soft!' she exclaimed. 'That's just the impression I got. That Emily, out of all the girls he's chased after, she got through to him. Not that I'd say that to her!'

'In that case,' said Greg, 'get back in quick and ask about Mica. Emily says he protected her from Mica.'

'I already did,' came the smug reply. 'He said Mica was a nutter and well known to be both a misogynist and a sadist. Not that he used those words, but that was what he meant. Then he said he couldn't say more unless we could protect him. I've left it there for the moment.'

18

2nd post-mortem

Ram was busy. A phone call from Margaret had set the hares running.

'Our Mr Gabrys has been making some phone calls,' she announced. 'I've already had calls from the MP for Great Yarmouth and from the Chief Constable. It's probably only a matter of time before I hear from the bishop as well! The gist of his demands is that he wants to see his son, and he wants to know exactly what's happened.'

'I'm on my way to the mortuary now to get the details of the post-mortem. Then I'll talk to Gabrys,' responded Ram.

Dr Paisley was washing her hands as he entered the cold space, masked and gowned.

'Good, glad you're here,' she said. Then, indicating the body, 'I'm all set to report. Cause of death was a penetrating wound to the chest. The weapon I'm told was responsible was this carving fork,' – she held up an evidence bag – 'and my findings are consistent with that. The fork went in here, between these ribs, and one prong penetrated the thoracic aorta. It looks to me as though either an attempt was made to remove the fork, or the victim moved. Either way, there was a movement of the fork from the aorta, making the wound worse. Blood loss would have been immediate and massive, causing death within minutes. I estimate not much more than four minutes from penetration to death.

'There are small wounds here,' – she pointed at the torso – 'consistent with the account of him being subjected to a taser, and one other finding I find interesting.' She turned to a microscope on the side table. I took a section from a growth on his prefrontal cortex, while carrying out a routine check of his brain. There's a small tumour here.' She pointed to the front of his head, close to the pituitary. 'I think it was probably malignant. We can send it away for tests.'

'What's the significance?' asked Ram.

'Many brain tumours cause behavioural changes, and some have suggested that tumours in this area might be a factor in the subject developing psychopathy. I'll do some looking up, although I suppose it's academic really. It's not going to affect any outcome for this chap. And it wouldn't have been implicated in how he died.'

'Interesting though,' said Ram. 'I'm seeing his parents shortly. I know they've been demanding to see their son's body. Is that okay now?'

'Yes, I'll warn the mortuary attendants to expect them, and to make the necessary arrangements.'

When Ram emerged into the waiting area, he found he had been pre-empted. A commanding figure in tweeds and corduroy was banging a fist on the reception desk. A dark-suited solicitor type stood at his right elbow, while a thin and elegant lady in a black coat lurked behind them, looking as though a breath of wind would blow her away. The middle-aged mortuary attendant who'd had the misfortune to be passing through reception when the Gabryses had arrived, was endeavouring to cool the emotional temperature. Obviously well-trained in managing stressed families, he replied in a carefully modulated voice, both pitch and volume low.

'I will just see what the situation is, and get back to you immediately,' he said. 'But I must ask you to stop shouting, and any further threats will mean I have to involve security.'

Constantin Gabrys took another breath, shaking his solicitor's hand off his arm, and Ram stepped forward.

'It's okay, I can deal with this,' he said, showing his warrant card impartially to both the Gabrys team and the mortuary attendant. 'I am DCI Ram Trent. Mr Gabrys, Mrs Gabrys, I was on my way to see you. I'm investigating the circumstances of your son's death. If you could come with me, I will explain what's happening, what's about to happen, and then take you to see your son. It would be most helpful if, at that point, one of you could formally identify him. This way, please.'

Constantin Gabrys followed him without waiting for his wife. The solicitor stood back in the doorway to allow Mrs Gabrys to go through, and then settled her in one of the low sofas pushed back against the office wall. Mr Gabrys had stopped dead just inside the doorway, and started to turn back to the corridor.

'I want to see my son,' he repeated.

Ram put a hand out, but stopped short of touching him, and gestured toward the sofa.

'Please take a seat, Mr Gabrys. This won't take a moment, and the staff need a minute or two to get everything ready for you.' The dark-suited solicitor added his encouragement to Ram's, and reluctantly Gabrys came back into the room. He took a seat – not next to his wife, as Ram noted. The solicitor also sat down, and took out an iPad.

'I'm Mark Johnson, of Norwich Law,' he said. 'I represent Mr Gabrys. You will understand, I'm sure, that the family are very distressed by what has happened and want some explanations. Also, a full investigation into the circumstances of their son's death. And an independent post-mortem.'

Ram took a seat also, and paused as he considered how best to approach the conversation. It was clear that Mr Gabrys was angry, possibly more angry than distressed. Mrs Gabrys, by contrast, was in pieces and was getting little support from her husband. He decided to address his remarks to her, and deal with the husband later.

'You know already, from my colleague DCI Geldard, that your son died during a police raid on your business premises at Clean Boats Inc. in Great Yarmouth. I am so very sorry for your loss, Mrs Gabrys, Mr Gabrys. In a few moments, when everything is ready, I will take you through to see your son so that you can give us a formal identification.'

'Then, it may not be Mica?' exclaimed Mrs Gabrys, clutching at straws.

'I'm sorry,' replied Ram, shaking his head. 'Your son has already been identified to us by someone who claims to have been a friend and colleague. There can be little doubt that this is indeed your son. But for reasons of process, it is very helpful to have the formal identification carried out by a close member of the family.' She subsided into her sofa again, sniffing. Ram offered her the box of tissues and she took a handful.

'So, what happened?' demanded Mr Gabrys.

'As I think DCI Geldard already told you, the Clean Boat premises were raided on the suspicion that a number of crimes were being committed at that location, including modern slavery, kidnap and possibly false imprisonment. During the raid your son was found in suspicious circumstances, including possession of a knife, and he attempted to stab an officer. He was restrained using a baton and taser and was in the process of being arrested when he was unfortunately stabbed himself by a person who had been illegally imprisoned at that site. As he was in police custody at the time, and as it is alleged that the attack was made by a police officer who had been illegally held prisoner, a formal investigation by the Independent Office for Police Conduct has been launched.'

A silence fell. Then Mr Gabrys said, 'The police murdered my son.'

'As I said,' repeated Ram, 'the circumstances of your son's death are being investigated.'

The solicitor opened his mouth to comment but was pre-empted by Gabrys.

'If the knife was held by a police officer, how can it be anything other than murder. I'll sue.'

The solicitor interrupted in his turn. 'I repeat, we will, of course, want an independent post-mortem,' he said.

'As is your right,' agreed Ram. 'But let's take things one step at a time. First, I'll take you through to see your son. Then you and I, Mr Johnson, can make any arrangements necessary for a further post-mortem. I will then be in touch further about the investigation. Just one question, however. Did you know your son was going to be at the Clean Boats premises yesterday?'

Mr Gabrys put a hand on his wife's arm – not, it seemed, to help her to her feet but to shut her up.

'We have nothing to say,' he said. And they left the room, the solicitor in tow.

After the viewing and formal identification, Ram picked up the phone to Jim Henning.

'He went no comment,' he said. 'Not in so many words, but that was the effect. But I don't think his son's whereabouts were a surprise, not to him anyway. Mrs Gabrys, she may have been in the dark, but my general impression was that she was terrified. Definitely of her husband, quite possibly of her son as well.'

19

Proper policing

Greg looked across as Jim put his phone down. 'Anything I need to know?'

'Gabrys has formally identified his son. Ram is certain he knew what was going on at Clean Boats and that his son was involved, but has no evidence to back that up. Gabrys is saying nothing and his wife is too scared to. At least, that's Ram's view.'

'Interesting. We may need to bear that in mind.'

'One other thing,' added Jim. 'The doc has found Mica had a brain tumour. Thinks that might, repeat might, have had something to do with his behaviour.' Greg filed that in his head in the category of interesting but not relevant and looked down at his notes again.

'Where were we?' he asked of the room at large. Chris, Jim and Jill all looked at each other. Jim took up the baton.

'You'd just told us that Ned hadn't got the DNA results through yet, and we were discussing where we go next,' he replied. 'In view of what we've just heard, I suggest we focus on finding that evidence of Gabrys's involvement. Starting with our young witnesses from the school.'

'When are they coming in?' asked Greg.

'In,' – Jim consulted his watch – 'about half an hour. Nathan first, then Emily. Nathan's coming with his mother and a social worker.'

'That was quick work. I thought we might be needing to line up an appropriate adult. Much better it's his mother,' said Greg with approval.

'The Head got involved. She had contact details for his mother, so I spoke to her before I left the school. She came and collected him before the end of lessons. She wasn't keen on social services being involved, understandably, but the Head made that referral herself, on safeguarding grounds. There might be a bit of tension there,' Jim warned.

'Okay. Chris, you go in with Jim for the interview. I'll watch on camera. That way we have Jim for continuity and fresh eyes as well. You know what we need. Enough to put the father away, and some good links to Gabrys.'

'Got it,' said Chris, gathering her things together. 'I've only got a few minutes to prep, so I'll get on to it.'

'Jill, I'd like you to go with Jim for the Emily interview. That okay?'

'Yes. Thanks, Boss,' said Jill, surprised but pleased.

***

Outwardly, Nathan was as composed in the 'soft' interview suite as he had been in the Head's office. He lounged on the sofa next to his mother, a short, dark woman who looked markedly less relaxed. She was fiddling with a pen and notebook when Jim entered with Chris, while occasionally darting irritated looks at the bead-strung social worker clutching her notebook in the corner.

'Hi, Nathan,' said Jim. 'Good to see you again. Mrs Standish, I'm very glad you could be here for this interview.'

'So'm I,' she replied. 'But it's Ms Raymond. I've gone back to my maiden name.'

'Sorry, Ms Raymond,' said Jim, making a note. 'I'm Detective Inspector Henning and this is Detective Sergeant Chris Mathews. Could you all state your names for the recording, please?'

Nathan removed his headphones and said, 'Nathan Standish.'

'Rebecca Raymond,' said his mother, and then glared at the lady in the corner, who seemed entirely undisturbed. 'I am Jean Price, social worker,' the latter replied in her turn.

'Thank you—' said Jim but was interrupted by Ms Raymond.

'I wish to make it plain that I object to social services being present. I am Nathan's mother, and I am fully capable of protecting his best interests.'

Jim intervened. 'I understand your concerns,' he said. 'No slur on your parenting is intended, I assure you. Ms Price is here purely to ensure that Nathan is treated fairly and his welfare is a prime concern. When social services were contacted you must understand that we didn't know whether it would be possible for you to be present, nor whether you were in a position to provide Nathan with a home. It was plainly not acceptable to involve his father in the circumstances.'

'Hmmph,' said Ms Raymond, and Jim decided to take that as an opportunity to move on.

'Nathan,' he began. 'When we spoke at the school, you made certain allegations about your father. Would you like to repeat them now?'

Nathan leaned forward, as if to ensure that the microphone on the central coffee table caught his words precisely. A lock of hair fell across his brow, and he brushed it back as he said, 'I told you that I had seen evidence in my father's online accounts that he was money laundering for one of his clients.'

'How did you get access to your father's accounts?' asked Chris.

'I told them earlier.' He nodded toward Jim. 'I'm good with IT and he's rubbish.' He said it with a sneer, leaving them in no doubt as to how he felt about his father.

'And your father is?' asked Chris.

'George Standish, of Standish and Partners. Although there are no partners. It's just him.'

'How exactly did you hack into his accounts?'

'I used his laptop. He's always leaving it lying around and it's not exactly difficult.'

'Isn't it password protected?' asked Chris.

'Yes, of course,' said the boy, the word 'stupid' as clear as if it had been spoken. 'That's what I mean about rubbish. His password is Standish1970, the year he was born. He always uses that, or else the name of the cat.'

'Which is?'

'Thumbelina. With a numeral '1' instead of the 'i'. Stupid name for a cat,' he added. 'Especially a big fat cat like ours. Anyway, neither of them is difficult to guess. I've been checking his mails and his porn habit for at least a couple of years.'

There was a choking sound from Ms Raymond, and Nathan glanced across at his mother.

'Sorry, Mum,' he added. 'That's why I knew you were well out of it. Don't worry. We'll be okay now.' Ms Raymond sniffed and wiped her eyes, as Nathan patted her knee. It was clear that if anyone was caring for the other, it was the son looking after his mother.

Chris glanced at Jim, then asked, 'What exactly did you find?'

It took a good hour to fillet the information offered by Nathan, but at the end of it, both Jim and Chris were confident they had good evidence of money laundering and possibly tax evasion as well. The links to Gabrys were less clear, as Jim said to Greg when he popped out for a quick word.

'So, what do we do now?' he asked. 'Pull Standish senior in and impound all his IT and associated data, risking that it tips Gabrys off and he deletes anything important? Or wait until we have enough to raid Horses Mill House?'

Greg tapped his teeth with his pencil, then came to a quick decision.

'May never happen,' he said. 'And Gabrys already knows we're looking at him. He's known that since we raided Clean Boats, if not before. Arrest Standish now and lay your hands on anything you can. If we're quick, we can probably even use the passwords the lad has given us. Incidentally, what happens to Nathan now?'

'I think his mother and social services are discussing that even as we speak. I left Chris in there as referee.'

When Jim returned, he found Ms Price already on her feet and packing her things away. He looked at Chris, who smiled and said 'All good here I think.'

'All good,' confirmed Ms Price. 'Ms Raymond, I'll be in touch by email and I'd appreciate you giving me your address when you're settled. For now, goodbye, Nathan, and I'll see you in a week or so.'

She left the room and Jim looked at Ms Raymond as he sat down. She looked a lot more relaxed and blew out a big sigh as she leaned back.

'I told you it'd be fine, Mum,' said Nathan, replacing his headphones.

'I gather everything's settled to your satisfaction,' Jim said.

'Yes, thank God,' said Ms Raymond. 'Sorry if I was a bit tense. I'd awful visions of them taking Nathan away.'

'I'm not a toddler, Mum,' he said indignantly. 'Like that was going to happen!' and turned up the volume on his phone, judging by the tinny sounds now escaping from the headphones.

'Yes, well, you hear all sorts, don't you,' she said. 'It's been preying on my mind ever since I got out and started looking for somewhere Nathan and I could live together. I'm staying with my sister at present, and although she's offered, there's really not much room.'

'I told Ms Raymond,' interrupted Chris, 'that we could help place her in a secure hotel for a few days while she sorted herself out. I'll get on to that now,' she said. 'Back in a minute.'

Outside the room, Jim looked at her with raised eyebrows. 'Budget?' he questioned.

'Realistically, it's only going to be for a day or two, then she can go home, can't she. Assuming, that is, we're arresting her ex.'

'True. You'd have been a bit stuffed if Greg had said no arrest, tho.'

'Not likely. Worth a punt I thought. Should I go and sort that while you get in with Emily? She's due any minute.'

'God, yes. Thanks. I was losing track of time.' And Jim ran down the corridor to collect Jill and the folder of images he needed Emily to review.

***

As Emily turned the pages of the folder, taking her time as he had advised, he introduced himself to her parents. Mr Atkinson, a business analyst by profession as he had explained to Jim, was watching his daughter with an air of mixed worry and pride. Mrs Atkinson, soft, light brown hair falling round her face, was sitting very close to Emily and holding her tongue with what seemed like some difficulty. She opened her mouth several times as the pages were turned, but thankfully thought the better of making an intervention.

Jim looked back at Mr 'call-me-Bill' Atkinson, his short, dark hair tousled above his smart, white, open-necked shirt and cord jacket.

'I wanted to congratulate you on how you handled Emily's situation,' he said, as diplomatically as he knew how.

'Thank God, she brought it to me,' Bill replied. 'It doesn't bear thinking about. Neither what she went through, nor what might've happened. She was very silly,' he added, 'don't think I haven't told her so. But it could've been an even harder lesson than it was.'

'It could certainly have been worse,' agreed Jim. 'We see it all the time. You did the right thing, calling his bluff. The only thing I'd say is,' – and he hesitated – 'if any of your friends find themselves in that situation, tell them to contact us. Don't recommend taking things into their own hands. For example, if you'd had to make good your threat, what would you have done?'

Bill looked embarrassed and admitted, 'God knows. Luckily, he didn't push his luck. I must've looked more threatening than I thought – or felt.'

Jim looked at him, and thought that, with the right scowl on his face, the well-built man who admitted to having boxed in his youth could probably look quite scary.

'You got away with it, but remember, spread the word that we'd be happy to intervene, and we can be discreet.'

Emily got to the end of the folder and looked up. 'I found the man who groomed me,' she said. She reopened the folder and pointed at an image of a dark-haired man with a closely trimmed black beard and one gold earring. 'That's him. Definitely.'

'You're quite sure?' asked Jim.

'Absolutely certain.'

'Let the record show,' said Jim for the recording, 'that Emily Atkinson has identified Pete Ashfield, aka Peter Shinfield and Patrick Ashton as the man who groomed her.'

'He called himself Pete Shinfield to me,' interrupted Emily.

'Noted,' said Jim. 'He has a number of aliases and a criminal record for minor drugs offences.'

'You mean he's done this before?' Emily's face was a study of horror and distaste.

'We've suspected it, but never managed to make it stick. Now, with your help, we can. We'll just complete the formal interview, then—'

Emily interrupted, 'There was one other face I recognised too.'

'Oh? Which?' asked Jim.

'This one.' She reopened the folder and pointed. Jim found himself staring at a photo of Mica Gabrys. 'He was always with Pete. He tried to muscle in on one of our dates, but Pete wasn't having that. But I had a drink with them both several times. Sorry, Dad,' she added.

Bill, who'd looked on the verge of leaping in, bit his tongue and sat back. Mrs Atkinson clearly felt no such inhibitions.

'Drinking! Oh Emily, after everything we've said.'

'Yes, Mum. Sorry,' said Emily, 'but everyone does. Even the nice guys. The ones that aren't criminals,' she added, in an effort to make everything clear.

Her mother took another breath, then thought the better of it and said grimly, 'We'll discuss this at home, dear.'

Jim, trying to get a word in, asked, 'You're sure you recognise this man?'

'Yes,' replied Emily.

'And you met him socially while with the Peter you already identified?'

'Yes.'

'Did you ever see him handle drugs or an unusual quantity of money?'

'Not really. He had wads of cash, but a lot of them did.'

'What made you remember him?' asked Jill quietly. 'What stood out?'

'It was Peter's reaction. He seemed friendly with him, but when he suggested coming on the date with us, Pete was, like, no way. Never. Just keep away, Mack.'

'He called him Mack?'

'Yes. It was his nickname, I think. It was funny,' she added. 'Until then I thought they were mates, but after that Pete seemed scared of him. Didn't want him around.'

20

Into hiding

It was early evening when Ram got the call from the James Paget.

'We've had a problem here,' said the voice identified as Head of Hospital Security. 'This afternoon someone tried to get in to see DI Laurence. Well, at least two someones to be precise.'

'Have you detained them?' interrupted Ram.

'Unfortunately not,' was the reply. 'The first time anything was drawn to my attention was about ten minutes ago. IC1 male, aged around twenty to thirty, wearing dark-blue jacket and trousers, attempted to walk past the nurses' station and into the room occupied by DI Laurence. He got as far as starting to open the door. When challenged he attempted to ignore them and carry on, but one of the nurses got between him and the door and asked him again for his ID. He didn't answer, turned round and started to walk away. At this point one of my guards, alerted by the scuffle, came toward him and also asked him for his ID. The intruder knocked him flat with one punch, then took to his heels. We found a dark-blue jacket on the stairs, so we think he dumped that and then mingled with visitors using the ground-floor corridors. We're checking CCTV footage now, but I don't think we'll find anything. Too many people about.

'It was only after this that one of the nurses remembered another visitor stopping to ask about DI Laurence earlier in the day. That too was an IC1 male, as far as she can remember, rather older than the second. I think that visit was intended to identify the room. The follow-up might have been more sinister.

'In short, I think DI Laurence needs somewhere safer to stay. I checked with the medics. She's okay to be moved.'

'Thank you,' said Ram, when he could get a word in. 'I'll get something sorted. Can I contact you on this number?'

'Yes. I'll wait for your call. In the meantime, I think you need a presence here.'

'I thought we had one,' said Ram. 'I'll get on to that too, never fear.'

His next call was to Chief Inspector Lake.

'I posted a constable at the door,' he said. 'Leave it with me.'

One phone call later, and a much-chastened junior constable was back outside Sarah's room. The coffee for which he had abandoned his post was steaming, forgotten, on the floor beneath his chair. He still had the remains of his embarrassment visible in a red line at the back of his neck, when Ram showed up.

'Any further issues?' asked Ram.

'No, not since...' replied the constable, somewhat at a loss as to how to complete his sentence without embarrassing himself further.

'Okay. Stay there and don't move, not even if the fire alarm goes off,' said Ram. 'A colleague will arrive shortly. Check his warrant card. No one comes in without one.' The staff nurse came over at that point.

'Need any help?' he asked.

'Yes, please. Can we discuss in here?' replied Ram, indicating Sarah's room.

Once inside he sat down on the chair by the window.

'We're moving you to a safe house,' he said to Sarah. 'There's been an attempt by someone to get in here. It could have just been paparazzi, but, in view of the fact they flattened a security guard in the process, I think probably not. In,' – he looked at his watch – 'six minutes there will be a car at the rear entrance, over where stores come in. By then we need you dressed and ready to go. You'll be taken down in the lift on a stretcher.

'I can walk,' objected Sarah.

'I'm sure you can. But you'll be a lot more recognisable vertical and walking than you'll be on a stretcher and blanketed to the eyeballs. The porters are on their way here now, so get a move on. You have help here if you need it.'

Ram returned to the corridor, leaving the nurse to help Sarah. The constable was at his post, and he noted the coffee cup had disappeared. As he went over to him, a trolley approached down the corridor. Ram turned swiftly to the nurses' station.

'Do you recognise the porters coming this way?' he asked the nurse sitting there. She glanced up.

'Yes, it's the usual team,' she confirmed.

'Good. You can go in,' Ram said to the porters, and barely a minute later they reappeared with a blanketed figure on the trolley. Ram turned to the constable. 'You stay on duty here until the end of your shift,' he ordered. 'No one goes in or out, understand?' The constable looked mutinous.

'But she's gone. What's the point of guarding an empty room?'

'So no one realises it's empty,' said Ram with strained patience, and without waiting for intelligence to dawn, he turned to take the stairs two at a time to the ground floor. He noted with relief that crowds of visitors still thronged the space and he lost himself among them before heading for the rear delivery door with reasonable confidence he hadn't been followed.

At the back of the hospital he was met by Jenny, in plain clothes but this time with Turbo at her heels.

'I thought some back-up would be handy,' she said with a grin. 'Plus, I can check out the area round the safe house by looking like a mad dog lady.'

Turbo glanced at Ram, wagged his tail and went back to checking the surroundings industriously. The paw with a bandage and slipper on it didn't seem to slow him up. After a moment he returned to Jenny and sat looking at her.

'No drugs, cash or explosives,' she confirmed as the trolley appeared round the corner. The porters stopped just inside the door and helped Sarah to her feet. A small bag was concealed under the trolley and one of the porters carried it to the waiting car. Turbo checked the bag too, and was similarly satisfied that there was no contraband.

'Get in the back, Sarah,' said Ram, looking round yet again. The only vehicles in sight were a car pulling out of the nurses' car park and an ambulance pulling up to the MRI scanning unit. The rear of the car had darkened windows. Sarah got in, Jenny and Turbo sat down beside her and Ram stepped into the front passenger seat. The constable in the driver's seat glanced over his shoulder and smiled at Sarah, who looked down at the dog, rather than meet his eyes..

'You know Bill Street,' said Jenny to Ram, but Bill had gone back to watching the mirrors.

'Looks okay to me, Boss,' he said. 'Okay to leave?'

'Yes. The sooner the better. Okay in the back there?' he asked.

'Apart from Master Turbo here taking up more than his fair share of seat,' replied Sarah. Ram glanced back and noted that the dog had managed to wiggle round so that Jenny and Sarah were squeezed to the edges, and he had his head resting on Sarah's lap.

The car had reached the end of the hospital drive and had to wait for the lights to change before joining the main road. Ram tapped his fingers on the dashboard as he leaned forward to check the cars to the right.

'Can you see the number plate on the car behind?' he asked Jenny.

She craned her neck and said, 'Part of it. Is there a problem?'

'I'm just playing safe. Ring that one in, and these two on the right. Won't hurt to get them checked. Okay, Bill. Get us home as quick as you can without attracting attention. It would be embarrassing to get pulled over.'

'Where're we going?' asked Sarah.

'A safe house on a Norwich housing estate.'

'Why can't I go home? Surely someone could keep an eye on me there at less expense and inconvenience.'

'It's been decided at a level above me,' replied Ram. 'The view was that you couldn't be kept safe in that small village you call home, certainly not while keeping your neighbours safe as well. The housing estate we're going to is large, anonymous, and the house in question has good security and good sight lines.' As Sarah took another breath, he added, 'And before you complain, you perhaps need to know that the debate was between this or protective custody.' A silence fell. Sarah looked down, fondled Turbo's big ears and sighed. At the steering wheel, Bill was keeping an eye on the traffic around him.

'Car behind has been with us since Gorleston,' he remarked. Ram looked round and picked up his phone.

'Rick,' he said, 'car might be following us. We're just coming up to the usual traffic jams near Tesco. Do you have a car out?'

'Unmarked car waiting for you in the lay-by near the bridge. He'll follow you. Let me know if you think you still have a problem.'

There were a tense few minutes as Bill negotiated the queues by the roundabouts, then took the road that led to the bridge over Breydon Water. There was the sound of a horn as the big BMW in the lay-by pushed into the stream of traffic directly behind them. At the next roundabout Bill took the turning to the Acle straight. The police BMW followed and so did the other car.

'Nothing on the plates,' said Jenny. 'No obvious alarm bells connected with that number. Could be a false plate, of course, but I can't check that for sure. The number belongs to a silver Ford, and while that car is definitely silver, I've no idea what make it is.'

Ram made a swift decision.

'Rick, can your chaps stop the car behind them? Any excuse will do. If they execute a stop just before the Acle roundabout, we can be away down the dual carriageway before they can follow.'

'Agreed,' replied Rick. 'I'll instruct them accordingly.'

A mile or so before the Acle roundabout, the car behind them suddenly produced blue lights and started to slow. To Jenny, watching over her shoulder, it seemed at first as though the silver car started to pull out, then when the blue-lit car swerved to the centre of the road, thought the better of it.

'They've stopped,' said Bill, watching in his rear-view mirror then, as he reached the roundabout, he put his foot down to create some distance between them and any possible pursuit.

21

A new search

Greg and his team were reviewing what they'd learned from Nathan and Emily.

'So, we've got enough to bring Mr Standish senior in for questioning. Jim, can you see to that?' said Greg.

Ned's head appeared round the door. 'I thought you'd like to know this straightaway,' he said before he was fairly in the room.

'You've got the DNA analysis back?' said Greg.

'Yes. And it's what we expected. Samples taken from Mica Gabrys's body match some of the samples taken at Nails Galore.'

'Which?' asked Jim.

'One sample from the neck of an opened bottle of vodka found on the kitchen floor. It'd rolled under a kitchen cupboard, so maybe that explains why it wasn't taken away with them. Two samples from the body of Madame Trieste. There were other results with no matches as yet.'

Greg had been making notes as Ned spoke. 'The samples from Madame Trieste,' he said. 'Where were they taken from?'

'One from under the fingernails of her right hand, suggesting she scratched him in the struggle. The other from her face. That one seemed to be saliva, suggesting he spat on or licked her face.'

There was silence for a while, then Greg said, 'It's helpful, but not enough. It ties him to Nails Galore and Madame Trieste, but the defence could argue he'd visited for other reasons – to use a prostitute, collect money, or deliver drugs. It doesn't definitively tie him to the violence and torture.'

'We've got him on that chap's door camera at the right time,' argued Chris.

'True, but...'

'There's one other thing,' said Ned. 'I was saving the best for last. One other sample was mixed. The technicians thought at first it'd been contaminated, but they persisted. It contained Mica's DNA and Madame's.'

'That's not telling us anything new,' started Greg but Ned interrupted again.

'His sample was from saliva, hers from vitreous humour.'

'Meaning,' said Greg with dawning excitement. The rest of the team looked at each other and Chris punched the air in a silent symbol of triumph.

'Meaning that there's a greater than even chance that he was there when her eyes were removed.'

Greg stood. 'That's enough for me,' he said. 'I'm off to get a search warrant for Horses Mill House. While I'm gone, Jim and Chris, can you organise two teams? One to arrest Standish and search his premises. The second for the Gabryses' place. I want the teams organised, but no destinations given out until we despatch. No leaks. And for the same reason I want both raids to take place simultaneously. Jim, you'll lead on Standish, and I will on Gabrys. In both cases I want all team members in stab vests etc and armed with batons, tasers and CS spray. And in both cases I want armed response on standby just in case.'

'Not necessary for Standish, surely,' objected Jim.

'Maybe not. At least not as regards the man himself. But the people he's been associating with? They're another matter and we're playing safe. Let's aim to go in two hours. Get to it.'

Chris caught up with Greg in the corridor. 'Do you expect any argument from the boss?' she asked.

'Not as regards a warrant. Possibly as regards me leading the raid, but I think I've got the answer there.'

'Which is?'

'There's no one else. Ram is still off dealing with Sarah. Other possibilities are either already involved, like Jim, or excluded from the investigation for reasons of security. So, she doesn't have a lot of choice.'

'Gabrys will scream police harassment,' predicted Chris. 'This, on top of a police officer killing his son...'

'That's one of the reasons I don't think he'll resort to extreme violence. Not on this occasion anyway. It would wreck any future legal action on his part, and destroy his chances of getting out of the mess that his psychopath of a son has landed him in.'

'You don't think that what Mica got up to at Nails Galore and with Madame Trieste was with his father's sanction then?'

'I don't know, but it seems to me unlikely. The violence was too extreme, and too...' Greg paused, at a loss for the right words. 'I mean, there seems to've been too much fun in it for Mica, if you see what I mean. His conversations with

Sarah bear that out. Whereas everything Mr Gabrys senior has touched suggests he's a ruthless, hardnosed business man, not a sadist. When commissioned by him, violence seems to be used as a tool, tempered to the immediate requirement, used with precision. I'm sure he's callous; I just don't see him as insane.'

'So using Mica at Nails Galore was a mistake?'

'Or Mica was never intended to be there, and somehow got in on the act. We may never know for sure. What I do think we have a good chance of finding out now, is precisely how, and how much, our Mr Gabrys is involved in the drug traffic in Norfolk and all its nastier manifestations.'

***

It was already fully dark by the time Greg led his team to Greater Ormesby. They halted their car-and-van convoy in Decoy Rd as agreed. Glued to the radio, Chris awaited the signal from Jim that they too were in place and ready to go, in their case in the affluent suburb of Gorleston where the Standish's had their home.

'What about the team at the Standish offices?' she asked Jim.

'They're ready too,' he replied.

Chris signed off and popped her head out of the car. Greg was in quiet conversation with the driver of the van.

'It's a go,' she said.

'You heard that,' said Greg to the driver, and as the van engine started up he returned to the car and put it in gear. 'Get the helicopter up,' he said to Chris, and led the way to the entrance of Horses Mill House.

At precisely the moment that Greg stood before the security cameras at the main gates of the big house, Jim was knocking on the Standish front door. Behind him stood Jenny and Turbo, returned in the nick of time from Sarah escort duty. Around the back of the house, lurking in the undergrowth of the poorly tended garden, were Steve and Phil, and two of Rick Lake's uniformed officers. As the echoes from Jim's vigorous banging on the door subsided, and neighbours began to respond to his shouts of, 'Police! Open up, Mr Standish!' by sticking their heads out of their own front doors, there was a scuffle in the driveway down the side of the house and the two uniformed constables appeared, separated by a bedraggled figure in a muddy suit.

'Trying to hurdle the back fence, sir,' said one, whom Ram might've recognised from the James Paget. 'Refused to identify himself.' Jim surveyed the sorry figure before him.

'Mr Standish, I presume,' he said. 'I have a warrant to search your property for evidence concerning the concealment, conversion or transfer of the proceeds of crime. A similar warrant is currently being exercised at your offices. Shall we go inside? You look rather cold.'

Round at the front door, the party paused, and everyone looked at Mr Standish.

'Would you like to unlock the door, sir, or would you rather we did?' asked Jim politely, indicating the large red ram held with negligent ease by Steve. Standish felt in his pockets, then with a sulky air, produced a set of keys and unlocked the door.

'Just a moment, sir, if you don't mind,' said Jim, and preceded him into the house. 'Is there anyone else at home?' he asked.

'Not at the moment, as you well know,' grunted the man in the muddy suit. 'My son is presumably with my soon-to-be ex-wife or with social services, depending on how good a tale she's been spinning. Clearly, you've heard his nonsense, or you wouldn't be here.'

'And clearly, you have some reason to fear our presence, or you wouldn't have legged it over the back fence,' replied Jim. 'Just wait here a moment while the team check your house for other occupants, then we'll have a sit down and a little chat.

'You know what you're looking for,' he said to the sergeant in charge.

Once satisfied the house was unoccupied, Jim ushered his reluctant host into the lounge and sat him down, his muddy trousers doing no good at all to the pale cream sofa.

'Just sit here for the moment,' he instructed. 'Once we're done here, you'll be taken to the station for an interview under caution.'

Standish sat, sulky and silent, until a stream of IT equipment, boxes of files and miscellaneous paperwork leaving the house moved him to object.

'You can't do that,' he said. 'That's my business. I can't operate without the tools of my business.'

'I can do it,' said Jim. 'I've got a warrant as I told you. You'll get a receipt for everything.' He gave the nod to Jenny to let Turbo loose, and she nodded back from the doorway and turned away.

'Mr Standish,' said Jim. 'I'm arresting you on suspicion of concealing or transferring criminal property, contrary to Section 327 of the Proceeds of Crime Act. You do not have to say anything. But it may harm your defence if you do not mention when questioned something which you later rely on in court. Anything you do say may be given in evidence.'

22

Horses Mill House

Over at Horses Mill House, Greg was still outside the main gates. The police helicopter was clearly audible overhead, its spotlights visible from time to time through the jagged and mostly leafless branches of the autumn trees. Greg was losing patience and a phone call had been made to the local fire service.

'Please bring Mr Gabrys to the phone or to the gate,' said Greg into the gate's intercom for the third time. 'I repeat, I have a warrant to search these premises and I will execute that warrant this evening, with or without Mr Gabrys's consent. Is that clearly understood?'

The voice on the other end of the intercom was recognisably that of the manservant Greg had met before.

'And I must repeat that Mr Gabrys is busy on the phone to his lawyer and to the Chief Constable. He is not available to come to the gate nor to respond to your demands.' As he spoke, a fire engine and fire service car pulled up in the road alongside.

'Then we're coming in,' said Greg. He turned to Chris. 'Tell the helicopter to keep a sharp eye for any departures via other routes, especially the back gate near the farm road.

'Fred,' he said to the fire chief in charge, 'thank you for such a rapid response. Let's have these gates opened, then you can be on your way.'

It took mere minutes with the hydraulic ram, and one of the gates was off its hinges and flat on the grass verge. Minutes more, the second had been pushed open and the police had free access to the winding drive Greg had driven down only days before.

'Thanks, Fred,' said Greg. 'Brilliant job as ever. I'm sure you'll send in a bill.'

'You owe me a pint too,' replied Fred with a grin. 'In fact, you owe all of us. We're missing the Norwich match! Sure you don't need us any more?'

'I don't think so,' said Greg. 'We should be able to cope at the house. I saw the doors there on my last visit. Bill can sort those if need be. Thanks again.' He waved, and the police car-and-van cavalcade went down the drive, leaving one car behind to secure the gateway.

The helicopter spotlight swept over Greg and Chris as they approached the front door. Gabrys stood on the threshold.

'I have your Chief Constable on the line,' he said, brandishing a phone. 'Anything you'd like to say to him?'

'Not at this moment, sir,' said Greg with a calm that verged on icy. 'If he should wish to contact me, then I've no doubt he will do so through the usual channels. I have a properly executed warrant to search these premises for evidence relating to a murder, an abduction and illegal deprivation of liberty, and the supply and distribution of controlled substances. Would you please stand aside? I would rather we didn't have to damage any more of your property in the pursuance of our duty.'

Gabrys snatched the proffered warrant from Greg's hand, stomped into his hall and off toward the office Greg had noticed during his previous visit. Greg and a uniformed constable followed. Chris paused to direct the remaining team to search the other rooms. Officers and technicians dispersed, and Chris followed on behind Greg.

The house seemed colder than before, the heating off as though the owners had not been in residence long, or were planning to go away. Chris paused and rather than following through to the office, beckoned to a sergeant with the uniformed team.

'Do me a favour would you, and check the drives and garage for cars? I'd like to know which are here, and whether any are prepped for departure.' He nodded his understanding and left through the front door.

At the foot of the stairs, Chris almost walked into Mrs Gabrys, looking if anything frailer and thinner than when they last met, as she lurked in the shadows behind the newel post.

'Mrs Gabrys!' exclaimed Chris, and went to take her by the arm as she looked so shaky, but the older woman shook her head and with face downturned, hurried to join her husband in his office.

Mr Gabrys had read the search warrant, slammed it down on his desk and thrown himself into his chair with such vigour that it almost fell over backward.

'You have no right to make such a search,' he stated with considerable vehemence. 'Even if Mica was guilty of the offences you accuse, which I dispute, he is not here to be arrested. You have no reason to think I or any other of my family were involved.'

'We have Mica's DNA at a crime scene and present on the body of a victim,' said Greg again. 'We have allegations that your accountant has been laundering money generated by the proceeds of sales of controlled substances. Section 8 of the Police and Criminal Evidence Act does indeed give me the right to search these premises.' Chris got the distinct impression that it was not the first repetition, and that Greg's restraint was wearing thin.

There was a crash from the floor above and startled, Mrs Gabrys let out a high-pitched exclamation. Her husband snarled a word neither Greg nor Chris understood and left the room at a near canter. His wife sank into the nearest chair and raised fragile, trembling hands to hide her face.

Chris went to her and asked in as gentle a voice as she felt would be audible above the increasing sounds of disputes from other rooms, 'Is there anyone I can call for you, Mrs Gabrys?'

'No,' she said, rather shakily. 'No.' Chris looked up, but Greg was already leaving the room.

'We need to get a grip on this,' he was muttering.

By the time Chris felt able to leave Mrs Gabrys, Greg had corralled her husband, the manservant they'd met before, and a young woman who was new to her in the sitting room off the hallway. A burly constable with stubble rather than hair was guarding the door, although all involved seemed to have opted to cause trouble by phone rather than in person. At least, all seemed to be spot-welded to their respective gadgets. Chris was tempted to point out they were, in some people's minds, risking brain tumours by so doing, but stopped herself just in time. In the circumstances, that would hardly be tactful, she realised. From her position by the door she could see the procession of boxes, files and IT equipment leaving the building. No smoking guns so far as she could see, and no knives either.

'Wish we'd got Turbo here,' muttered Greg.

'Let's get him over,' suggested Chris. 'He must be finished in Gorleston by now and that's only twenty minutes or so away.' She pulled out her phone and turned away to make the call.

'On his way,' she announced later with a triumphant grin. 'That'll save us some time.'

Most of the obvious possible evidence, mainly paperwork, had been removed to the van by the time Jenny pulled up with Turbo in the back of the car.

'He may not be as fast as usual,' she warned. 'I think he's starting to limp a bit. He's as keen as ever, but I don't want too long a search.'

The excited springer was indeed keen. He stood, his eyes fixed on Jenny and his tail vibrating with barely suppressed enthusiasm. The moment she lifted her hand, he was off. Both the hall and the sitting room got a clean bill of health, and so did the office. The library, however, that called for some energetic quartering of the ground, and Turbo kept returning to the old-style library steps in the corner by the window.

Jenny, puzzled, said 'He's not giving his usual clear signal, but he's interested in something. I wonder if it's too high off the ground for him to check and indicate as normal.'

She pulled protective gloves on and moved the steps some distance from the bookshelves. Sent to review his opinion, Turbo showed some interest in the steps, but the main focus of his attention was now the bookcase. Watching him, Chris was struck by an idea and left the room. Out in the hall, she turned left and left again, then retraced her steps and paced the distances out, counting under her breath. Greg watched her from the library doorway.

'What's your thinking?' he asked.

'That just maybe, Turbo is trying to tell us there's another space between the library and this corridor here.' She tapped on the wall, then tapped again further along.

'Sounds solid to me,' remarked Greg.

'Yes. But the way Turbo is carrying on reminded me of how he showed us the entrance to the crawl space under the barn when we were investigating that explosion at the government laboratory. Remember, where we found the Semtex wrappers? Perhaps this is an original wall, but perhaps the library wall isn't. We should have a look behind the books.'

Back in the library Turbo was still sniffing along the bookcases. Jenny looked up as they entered. 'I was wondering,' she began.

'So were we,' said Chris. The two of them started removing books from shelves where Turbo seemed most interested, and stacking them on the floor. After a brisk few minutes, they stood back and Turbo checked out all the shelves. If anything, his interest had sharpened, but the empty bookcases stared back at them blankly.

'I'm going to trust Turbo,' decided Greg. 'He's always been right before. Jenny, you can stand him down for the moment.

He probably needs a break. Chris, come with me. I'm going to have a chat with the owner.'

'Mr Gabrys,' said Greg, interrupting another diatribe about police corruption and going straight to the point. 'I have good reason to believe there is a hidden cavity or room behind the bookcases in your library. What can you tell me about it?'

'Nothing,' blustered Gabrys. 'You are mad.'

'Look, you have a choice,' replied Greg. 'You can open the concealed entrance to the cavity with minimum damage to your property, or we open it by force. That will be messy. How do you want to play it?'

'You are mad,' repeated Gabrys. 'I will have your career if you do this thing. I will speak to the Chief Constable. To my MP. He is a friend. He will sort you out for me.'

'Fine,' said Greg. 'Chris, get Bill and his tool kit. And have Ned standing by.'

As Greg left the room, Gabrys made to follow but was prevented by the constable guarding the door. 'Sorry, sir,' he said. 'You have to stay here for now.' For just a moment it looked as though Gabrys was going to get physical, but after a pause he sighed and sat down, taking his phone out again.

Back in the library, Turbo and Jenny sat on the sofa side by side, keeping out of the way. Bill had surveyed the shelving with an expert air, first from a distance and then playing his torch over every inch.

'It's well done,' he said, 'but I think there's a crack here. I think we'll try a jemmy, rather than the smasher. Ned, d'you want to take samples first?'

'Yes,' said Ned firmly, and stepped up with swabs and sticky tape. Then he brought up his vacuum cleaner and ran it round the shelving before stepping back. 'All yours,' he said.

Bill tried a chisel first, in the crack he'd identified, then the smaller of his jemmies. Once he'd worked it into the crack, he leaned on it. The wood groaned but held. A bit more wiggling around, then he leaned on it again, harder. With a crack, the panel gave way and Bill only just saved himself from falling over.

Jenny came forward with Turbo now on his lead and held him firmly just behind Ned. Everyone else hovered at Ned's elbows, to the extent he said rather irritably, 'Back off a minute can you, you're all in my light.' He too produced a torch and shone it round the dusty space revealed between the bookcase and the corridor wall. Only three feet or so wide, it ran behind the bookcase for the length of the library, then came to a blank wall. Turning round he looked the other way, and again the narrow space ended with a wall, near the library door.

Pointing the torch upward, he gave a triumphant, 'Aha,' and beckoned to Greg. 'Up there,' he said, indicating with his torch. 'I think we'd better get some photos before we move anything, but I'll be very interested to see what's in those.'

A couple of feet above his head, Greg could now see a long shelf spanning about half the width of the hidden passage and running its entire length. On it were parcels, mainly rectangular in shape and wrapped in brown paper. At the end he could see some other, less regular shapes, some on the shelf, others piled on the floor and also wrapped. On the end of his lead, Turbo was evincing considerable excitement, bouncing on his paws – even the sore one – and emitting little yips. His tail was wagging fit to come off.

'Remind me again what he's trained to detect,' said Greg to Jenny.

'Cash, drugs and explosives,' she replied. 'Mind you, he's pretty hot on Gravy Bones as well!' At the familiar words, Turbo's tail wagged faster.

'I'll be interested to see how many of those we've got here,' said Greg. 'The regular parcels look like cash to me. As for the rest... Come on, Ned, I can hardly wait.'

'All in good time,' said Ned with a grin, backlit by the flashes from the police cameraman. 'Just need to take some preliminary samples, then we can take a look.'

It seemed a long time before the first parcel was handed to Greg and he carefully pulled open the wrapper.

'It's cash,' he said briefly, and held the parcel out for all to see. 'Okay. Two of you,' he pointed at Ned's assistants, 'and Chris, reseal this one. After Ned has fingerprinted everything, count the parcels and organise the transport back to HQ. I don't want any opportunities for anyone to accuse us of mislaying any.

'Ned, let's take a look at the other shapes.'

It was the work of moments to sample the exterior of one and open it. Packages of white powder were exposed. More work for the analysts,' said Greg, then fell silent as he watched Ned open another parcel.

Back in the small sitting room, Greg faced Mr Gabrys.

'Constantin Gabrys,' he said, 'I'm arresting you for concealing criminal property, the possession of controlled substances and aiding and abetting the murder of Madame

Trieste and the abduction of Detective Inspector Sarah Laurence. You do not have to say anything, but it may harm your defence if you do not mention when questioned something which you later rely on in court. Anything you do say may be given in evidence. Handcuff him and take him away.'

Ignoring the explosion of rage-filled Lithuanian he turned to view the whole room. 'Where's the butler chappie?' he asked. They all looked round. He'd gone.

23

One hour earlier

The noise in the elegant sitting room was deafening. Even with the deadening effect of lush carpets, three generously upholstered sofas and double-draped windows, the angry shouts from Mr Gabrys at his mobile phone and the higher-pitched sobs from his wife were peculiarly distracting – like a news commentator with a penetrating voice banging on about the latest exploits of the Kardashians. The man with the black apron over his sober trousers and striped shirt looked at the police officer bent over the weeping wife, and his boss holding his phone slightly away from his ear. He caught his eye for a split second. Mr Gabrys nodded toward the window, then turned toward the door, shouting another sentence at the phone, then demanding of the policeman at the entrance, 'When you let me go, yes?'

Moving nothing except his feet, the man slid back one step, then another, then stepped behind the curtain. He paused for a moment, but hearing nothing, reached behind him and slid the lower sash window upward. Still nothing. He turned to the window, stepped lightly through and onto the terrace, paused again, then stepped quietly over the flags and ran.

The possible next steps flitted through his mind. Main gate? No – guarded. Side gate? But that led on to the same road as the main gate and it was the first place they'd look. On foot through the woods? – too slow and he'd be a dead duck if the helicopter with the infrared camera spotted him. Hot on that thought, he realised the sounds of the helicopter had faded into the distance. Maybe it was running low on fuel. He was halfway to the garage, when he suddenly realised what his boss had been saying as he shouted down his phone. In Lithuanian, and loudly, he'd repeated twice 'Valtis! Valtis!'

Ralph's Lithuanian was rudimentary, but that word 'Boat' had been clear. He had no idea what the rest of the sentence had contained, but it was enough for him to change direction to the boathouse. At the last second, a shape loomed over the edge of the low roof and he realised there was someone standing at the other corner of the shed at the water's edge. He dropped to all fours, paused, then moved silently sideways into the shadow cast by the moonlight. Cursing to himself, he was just about to head back to the garage, with some idea of crashing the roadblock he was sure would be at the main gate, when the shape beyond the shed coughed, spoke into a radio, and headed back to the house.

Ralph paused to collect his breath and his thoughts, then slid through the part-opened door into the boathouse. He dared not put any lights on, and the moonlight through the windows was dim. Ignorant of the remainder of his Lithuanian instructions, or so he now assumed his boss's last comments to have been, he tried to think what was expected of him. Not the electric boat, he hadn't the keys. And not the sail boat, they all knew he was notorious for taking half an hour to sail from one end of the Broad to the other, and half a day to get back! Moreover, the sail would stick out like a spaniel at a cat convention. That left one of the kayaks. Moving cautiously round the edge to avoid falling into the dark water lapping gently near his feet, he hauled the lower of the two kayaks in the rack into the water, and felt along the wall for the paddles in their brackets.

As he recalled, getting in was easy enough, getting in and staying dry was a bit trickier. He did his best to hang on to the decking while sliding into the kayak, but it rolled as he let go of the side and water slopped in. Damn. Now he was sitting in it. Too late to do anything about it, and opting not to bother with the splash apron, he paddled as quietly as he dared to the water entrance of the boathouse and ducked out under the gate.

Once on the Broad, he hugged the margin by the reeds and tried to think where to go next. The decision was simplified by the fact he could only think of one place that was both near a road and easy to beach the kayak – the old staithe.

He paddled on round the edge of the lake, relieved by the continuing absence of the helicopter. The moon cast a clear light over the still water and the reeds loomed black against the sky. He almost missed the staithe, it was so overgrown, but he realised, just in time, why there was a gap in the reeds. He back-paddled a little, then a couple of strokes on the right turned the kayak toward the sloping concrete heavily coated in mud, grasses and sedge. If he'd had some idea of paddling fast enough to beach the kayak on the slope, he was swiftly disabused of the concept. The kayak ran aground the moment the prow left open water, and by the time he'd climbed out he was soaking from the waist down. Luckily, his phone, in a jacket pocket, was still dry. He pulled the kayak to the side in an attempt to conceal it in the reeds, shivering with cold, and reflected that a long walk to the nearest transport had no appeal. He was strongly tempted to ring one of the emergency numbers supplied him by his boss, and took the phone out to do so – hang the risk – when he spotted a vehicle parked by the roadside.

It was a dark van, half hidden by overhanging brambles. He stepped sideways into the edge of the reeds, felt water flow into his already sodden shoes from the squelchy ground beneath and cursed under his breath. If it was the police, he was stuffed. If it wasn't the police, then there was only one organisation it was likely to be. He'd just about decided to risk a move, when the van flashed its headlights. There was just that one brief flash, then the swift fade of the glow, but he hadn't imagined it. He stepped out from his cover, such as it was, and walked toward the van. The passenger door opened and a head stuck out.

As he drew close the man in the balaclava said, 'Ralph? Get in.' Then, as he took in his condition, added, 'In the back,' and gestured toward the rear doors. They, too, opened as Ralph slopped his way toward them, and another balaclava gestured to him to climb in and sit on the floor. His back to the side wall, Ralph sank down and watched as the doors were closed. Then the van drove off.

The man in the van did not seem inclined to be communicative. He sat silent, staring across at Ralph while picking at his teeth with a little fingernail. Dressed entirely in dark clothes, except for a flash of white on his trainers, he looked more like a backstreet drug mule than a commando type, geared for rescue in rough country. Judging by the way the van was swinging round, they were negotiating a series of roundabouts. Ralph guessed they were headed either for Yarmouth or Norwich but had no idea which.

The hatch between the cab and the main van body slid aside and the passenger twisted round in his seat to look in. He seemed inclined to be chattier.

'So, what's happened?' he asked. 'Trouble at the big house?'

'Police,' said Ralph, brevity fuelled by a conviction that surplus words were highly likely to turn septic.

'Taken the boss in, have they?'

'Yes,' replied Ralph.

'He'll be out soon. So, why're we picking you up?'

'Why not?' A silence fell. It seemed his reply was deemed unfriendly. 'I need a safe landline,' said Ralph abruptly. 'And dry clothes.'

'Why?'

'Because that's how the boss wants it. Any more questions?'

The hatch slammed to and Ralph was left in peace until the van pulled up with a jolt on the outskirts of Norwich. He recognised the location and breathed a sigh of relief. The arrangements were holding up. He'd wondered if the organisation might start to fray with its principal out of the way, but it seemed the authority held good. Now all he needed to do was remember the numbers he'd memorised correctly and make three phone calls.

24

Family and friends

When Chris emerged from the house, Greg was on the phone, one finger in his other ear.

'Yes, I understand,' he was saying, 'and I'd love to see you and, yes, spend more time with you, but it's not exactly the best time at present.' He paused to listen some more.

'Problem?' Chris mouthed at him, but he didn't see what she said, so she waited in the drive, flicking through the messages on her phone and trying not to listen.

'Yes, I know that's how it always seems, perhaps that's because it's how this job always is. Bouncing from one crisis to another isn't such a bad description.' There was another pause. 'As I've said, where do I start? One of our valued colleagues was kidnapped and has only just been recovered, alive but hurt. We're also investigating a particularly nasty murder, drug-related activity, money laundering, etc, etc, and Isabelle's ridiculous carryings-on a few months ago didn't help either.

'What d'you mean, how is dear Isabelle?' he exploded. 'Haven't you been listening to a word I've been saying for the last few months? I'm not shouting,' he shouted, then seeing Chris, said, 'Can you wait in the car? I'll be with you in a minute.'

Chris shrugged and went to the car. Sitting scrolling through Twitter in a vain search for light relief, she looked up as Greg threw himself into the driver's seat then sat for a moment, staring through the windscreen, tapping his fingers on the steering wheel.

'Everything okay?' she asked in an ostentatiously neutral tone.

'You judge,' he relied grumpily. 'The parents are coming for a visit.'

'The parents? What? Now? You mean your parents?' she asked, made stupid by surprise.

'Unfortunately, yes. My parents. Whose would you prefer? Don't answer that,' he added. 'At least not until you've met mine. Then I'll accept any judgement you care to make. Whatever it is, it'll probably be fair.' He put the car in gear and they jolted off across the drive.

'I'll be delighted to meet your parents,' she said indignantly. 'I agree, this is not exactly the best time, but I get that there probably isn't a good time and this time...' she paused. 'I'm getting lost with the times,' she said. 'Help me out here.'

'It *is* a bad time. It could hardly be worse but trying to put my mother off when she's in full cry! Well, you've heard of the irresistible force. That's a feeble trickle compared to my mother. On the other hand, I don't want to spend too much time with them because that way lies a row, and at least we have a range of perfect excuses for bunking off. And I'd like you to meet them, definitely. Does that about cover it?'

'I think so. When are they coming and where are they staying?'

'Tomorrow and with me.'

'And what do they know about me?'

'That I think you're wonderful and that you're kind enough to share your life with me.' At last he smiled at her. 'That do?'

'Pretty well. Do they know I share your bed too, or do we have to pretend about that?'

'I think we're a bit old for that sort of pretence,' he replied, turning onto the main road. 'Let's just be normal. There'll be enough odd behaviour from my mother without us making things worse.'

***

Back in the Norwich safe house, the new day saw a steadily recovering Sarah chafing at the bit to go home. The news in a phone call from Chris increased the pressure.

'If you've got Gabrys in custody, then that removes the need for me to be cloistered here. With Mica dead and the big man safely tucked away, where's the risk?'

On the other end of the call, Chris held the phone away from her mouth for a moment, while she considered options.

Making her mind up she replied, 'I sympathise, Sarah, but it's not my call. I'll pass your message on to Greg, but I think he'll need to take it up with Margaret before you get an answer. Please hang on there for the moment. Don't do anything rash!'

Sarah opened her mouth to give the cheeky sergeant a piece of her mind, then swallowed the words. 'Okay,' she conceded reluctantly. 'I'll wait until after lunch at least.'

Chris turned to Greg. 'You heard,' she said. 'We won't be able to keep her there for long.'

'She's overlooking the fact she may be facing charges for the death of Mica,' replied Greg. 'I've got a meeting with Margaret in,' – he looked at his watch – 'in twenty minutes. I'll raise it then.'

'What about Gabrys?'

'He's with his solicitor at present. I'll be interviewing him after I've seen Margaret. Any news about that butler chappie?'

'Nothing yet.'

'Bloody annoying, losing him like that.'

'Any more from your parents?' asked Chris.

'Not yet. But I am certain they'll be on their way.'

By the time Greg joined Margaret in her office, Ram and Jim were already there. The fragrant aroma of coffee was wafting around the room from the large cafetière in the centre of the table. Greg noticed that, judging from the depleted contents, others had already been at it. He hastened to pour himself a cup, not waiting to sit down nor for Margaret's invitation. It had been a long few days.

At the head of the table, Margaret was waiting patiently to begin. 'Let's get started,' she said pointedly, 'now everyone's got coffee.' Then she smiled and the atmosphere lightened perceptibly. 'First, well done, all. I think we've made good progress toward getting a grip on the county lines operation as well as resolving some questions around the murder of Madame Trieste and Sarah's abduction. On the plus side we've identified the murderer beyond reasonable doubt, we've laid hands on large quantities of cash and controlled substances, we have suspects under arrest and most importantly we have

Sarah back, safe if not entirely well.' She held one hand up, as though forming half of the scales of justice. 'On the negative side, our murderer is dead at the hands of a senior police officer, according to the CPS our prime suspect will almost certainly walk when his bail hearing comes up, one of the suspects is away on his toes, we know not where, and I've spent the early hours of this morning trying to scrape an incandescent chief constable off his office ceiling.' Her second hand hit the desk. 'What possessed you to refuse to take his call, Greg?'

Greg took another sip of coffee, refusing to allow himself to be rattled. A hail of raindrops hit the window like bullets as he replied.

'He didn't call me directly, and I'd have been surprised if he had, in the middle of an operation. It was our suspect who offered me a phone, claiming to have the Chief Constable on the other end. I had no way of knowing who was on the call, nor what had been said to them. If it *was* the Chief Constable, then I didn't want to put him in the invidious position of appearing to support a suspect. I knew he could contact me through proper channels if he wanted to. Which was what I told Mr Gabrys.'

'It's what you can tell the Chief Constable shortly,' said Margaret. 'He wants to see you.'

'Not until I've seen Mr Gabrys,' replied Greg. 'The clock's ticking.' It was a statement, not a question. Margaret regarded him with a level gaze for a moment.

'Okay, after you've interviewed Gabrys,' she said. 'Let's park that for the moment.

Ram, how's Sarah?'

'Healthwise, she seems better, and she wants to go home. Now she knows we have Gabrys in custody, she'll be difficult to hold.'

'I've been talking to the IOPC,' said Margaret. 'They're considering charging her with the manslaughter of Mica Gabrys. A lot depends on the conclusion of his inquest.' There was a long silence. 'I don't think that comes as a surprise to you, Ram,' she added at length.

'No, not entirely,' he admitted. 'She makes a good case that she acted to defend fellow officers, but on the other side of that coin is the evidence that she'd seen him fall down after being tasered.'

'She might have believed, in that moment, that her action was necessary,' remarked Greg.

'Yes, and I understand the CPS think a defence along those lines has a reasonable chance of succeeding. And obviously, the coroner will take that into account in considering whether the conclusion is lawful or unlawful killing. Or at least, the jury will.' Margaret looked down at her notes briefly. 'Now, Standish. What've you got out of him, Jim?'

'No comment,' replied Jim. 'I mean, that's all he'll say. An initial look at the material we got from his house and office suggest a pretty naive procedure for money laundering, which fits with what we heard from his son, Nathan. In fact, given the apparent expertise of his alleged boss, Gabrys, it seems strange he'd trust such an incompetent accountant with the cash.'

'On the other hand,' interrupted Greg, 'what we've got lands Standish in bother, but not Gabrys. And so far, correct me if I'm wrong, we haven't got much of the cash except what was found at the House. The stuff Standish squirrelled away through bank transfers does seem to've gone out of reach. So from Gabrys's point of view, employing Standish was not all bad. In fact as a cut-out, he's worked rather well.'

'True,' said Jim. 'It's certainly looking that way.'

'What's the CPS' view?' asked Margaret.

'That we've enough evidence to go without a statement or confession from Standish.'

'Good. At least that shuts off one avenue for laundering money. Be nice if we could recover some more, though. Keep on that. That brings us to Gabrys. So, over to you, Greg.'

Greg stood up and picked up his iPad and phone. 'And I need to be talking to him. Thanks for the coffee, Margaret. I'll report back as soon as I have anything. And he left the room.'

'Don't forget the Chief Constable,' were the words that followed him down the corridor.

25

No comment

An hour and a half of 'No comment' later, and Greg was ready to call it a day. He leaned back in his chair for a moment and exchanged a glance with Chris. Across the chipped and stained table Gabrys and his expensive London solicitor stared at him impassively. Mr Gabrys seemed to have dumped his Norwich legal adviser. The new solicitor from a major London practice had so far said little other than to introduce himself. He had, however, clearly said quite a lot to his client in private and his client had heeded the advice. Gabrys was cool as a cucumber, his well-shaved face belying a short night in the cells. His shirt and suit looked fresh – presumably supplied via the solicitor. His coffee – admittedly pretty disgusting, thought Greg – sat almost untasted before him.

'Interview suspended at,' – he glanced at the clock as he stood to leave the room – 'eleven-forty.'

The solicitor spoke for only the second time. 'If you have no further questions for my client, I assume you will release him?'

'If he'd answered any of my questions,' replied Greg, 'then I might be in a better position to answer yours. However, as he has declined to give any explanation for the materials found hidden in his house, or the activities of his accountant, still less the involvement of his son in a murder case, then I think you might see my problem.'

'You cannot, and indeed have not charged my client with the murder you allege his son committed, therefore why should he answer any such questions?'

'Because he might, as a good citizen, feel inclined to help us with our enquiries. He has, however, been charged with possession of controlled substances and the concealment of the proceeds of crime. I'll be back shortly. Perhaps you might, in the interim, advise your client to consider a more helpful approach.'

Out in the corridor, he turned to Chris. 'Check with Ned to see if he's got anything new. I'm going for my chat with the almighty one.'

The anteroom to the Chief Constable's office was lined with plain chairs – waiting on, for the use of. Greg fidgeted for the ten minutes or so it took the almighty to acknowledge his arrival, then an intercom buzzed on the secretary's desk and, 'He's ready for you now,' said the middle-aged lady occupied with spreadsheets on her desktop.

Greg went in and stood stiffly on the other side the door.

'Take a seat,' grunted the thickset, short-haired individual behind the desk. Greg examined him with some interest, in view of Madame Trieste's accusations about corruption in the Norfolk Police hierarchy and Gabrys's apparent friendship with this man. His face was florid and his nose a little red, possibly indicating a fondness for a tipple, but he met Greg's gaze straight on, and even smiled a little.

'Expecting a bollocking?' he asked.

'Yes, sir,' said Greg.

'If I'd seen you earlier, you'd have got one. But I've had chance to calm down. Plus, Margaret Tayler has spoken up for you. I respect her judgement. But why in God's name did you put me in that situation? Gabrys has the ear of our local MP, who I might remind you is Justice Secretary too.'

Greg was silent for a moment. 'I thought to protect you from embarrassment, sir,' he said at last. 'I had no idea whether Gabrys did indeed have you on the end of the phone, and if he did, I didn't want him overhearing any conversation we might have. I had a properly executed search warrant and as it happens the search did indeed turn up evidence of close links to money laundering and supply of controlled substances. We found drugs, cash, and a gun hidden in Gabrys's home.'

'But do you have any evidence that directly links Constantin Gabrys himself to those materials? Fingerprints? DNA? On any of those goods?'

'Not yet, sir,' Greg admitted. 'But forensic investigations are proceeding.'

'And in the meantime, you're running out of time.' There was a pause. Then the Chief Constable got up from his side of the desk and went over to the window.

'I don't like Mr Gabrys,' he said, staring out into the rain sheeting down over the car park. 'I don't like his attitude, his way of life, or his assumption he can get me to dance to his tune. But given he has the ear of the Justice Secretary, he can cause me and Norfolk Police, a lot of embarrassment if things are not done by the book. We're already in the muck thanks to Detective Inspector Laurence and her killing Gabrys's son.

Whatever the whys and wherefores of that incident, it was a massive cock-up by someone, and DI Laurence is going to have to face an inquest jury.' He turned back to Greg. 'So, no more cock-ups, or I'll nail your balls to the nearest available wall, you see if I don't. Dismiss.'

***

That evening, despite the rush to finish up in the office, Chris presented herself at Greg's, exactly on schedule and unusually monochromatic in dress, albeit the 'chrome' in question was citrus rather than black. But at least the sunshine yellow trousers and top matched in shade and the pink handbag could be lost behind the sofa. That was where Chris secreted it, but Greg was, if anything, disappointed.

'No fuchsia?' he enquired.

'I thought I'd go gently with your mother, at least to start with. How was the almighty?'

'I'll tell you later. And as far as my mother is concerned, I wouldn't bother being gentle,' he said. 'Just be aware that she'll find fault somewhere whatever you or I do, and it's not personal. It's her default setting.'

'And your father?' asked Chris. 'You haven't said much about him.'

'Long since retired from the fray in the interest of a quiet life. Most of his share of any dialogue consists of 'yes dear'. Although he can be interesting about his diplomatic career, if you can get him on his own.'

Chris instantly decided that had to be a main aim. She didn't like bullies, even female ones, and Greg's mother sounded more and more like a bully.

'What're we eating?' she asked. 'Anything I can do?'

'Pork chops, stuffing, well-boiled veg, mashed potatoes and gravy, followed by apple pie and cream.'

'What time are you expecting them?' asked Chris, regarding with a faint horror, the distinctly carbonised pork and the vegetables collapsing into their boiling water. 'Are we having mashed sprouts and carrots as well as mashed potatoes?'

Greg looked harassed. 'I know, awful isn't it? But she'll complain they're not cooked if they're the slightest bit crisp. She doesn't do al dente, or, while we're on the subject of what she doesn't do, garlic, oils, spices, herbs except for mint and parsley and anything else broadly designated "foreign".'

'I see. No wonder you didn't want my help with the cooking. You do realise there's garlic in the stuffing?' she added, picking up the empty packet from the worktop.

'Oh God! Hide that,' exclaimed Greg. 'She'll never know provided she doesn't read the ingredients list. Here they are,' he added as an elderly Volvo pulled up by the, rarely used, front door.

Chris watched with some interest as an older version of Greg, clad in baggy cord trousers and an even baggier tweed jacket emerged from the driving seat and went round to open the passenger door for his wife. The lady who emerged into the last of the watery sunset was both short and slight. Chris's first view was of a slim foot clad in an immaculately polished brown brogue. This was followed by a dark, lovat green tweed skirt, topped by fawn twinset and pearls, grey hair in a chignon and a determinedly bland expression. Picking her way carefully over the muddy grass, Mrs Geldard glanced back in order to give directions about the luggage, then forward to her son by the, now opened, front door.

'Welcome, Mum and Dad,' said Greg.

'Mother,' she replied automatically, 'you know I prefer Mother. Lovely spot darling, but you need a new drive. This must be Christine,' she went on, holding out a gloved hand and blinking slightly at all the yellow. 'How lovely to meet you, my dear.'

'Chris,' said Chris, 'everyone calls me Chris.'

'Do they, Christine?' replied Greg's mother, rather tartly. 'How sad,' she added and sailed into the house. 'Can I have my bag, darling; I need to freshen up before a gin and tonic,' she added over her shoulder.

'Yes, dear,' replied Greg's father.

Greg took the bags from him. 'I'll deal with those, Dad,' he said. 'You go and pour the gins. Chris'll show you where everything is.'

By the time Greg came back downstairs, Chris and his father were getting on like a house on fire. Chris was halfway through a gin and tonic, his father halfway through an anecdote about a ministerial faux pas at a European Council meeting.

'So, he said to me,' he went on, ' "When should I walk out in protest?" And I said to him, "Well, anytime you like, Minister. The tricky bit is working out when to walk back in." ' Greg was heading for the kitchen with a smile and Chris was laughing when his mother appeared in the doorway.

'Not that old story again, darling,' she said. 'I must have heard it a thousand times.'

'Yes, dear,' he said, and falling silent, handed her a generously stiff gin.

Supper went by quite well, considering. Mrs Geldard praised the, rather dry, pork and dissolving vegetables as, 'Very nicely cooked, darling'. But criticised the apple pie (bought from the local bakery) as 'rather heavy'.

'Don't you bake, Christine?' she asked.

'Chris's too busy to bake,' replied Greg, while Chris was still considering her reply. 'She's the best detective sergeant in Norfolk, bar none, and that doesn't leave a lot of time for baking. And while I'm on the subject, you do remember that we're both working tomorrow?'

'I remember,' she said. 'No matter. If you're too busy I'm sure dear Isabelle will have time for us.'

'Isabelle won't welcome a visit,' said Greg. 'She's got a new life now.'

'On the contrary,' said his mother, ostentatiously composed. 'She said she'd be delighted to see us.'

'Well I'm not,' said Greg. 'Not delighted, I mean. Isabelle has a new life and is no longer part of mine. I would be glad if you'd accept her decision and respect her privacy.'

His father muttered, 'Quite right,' then looked slightly terrified of his boldness. 'Told you so, old girl,' he added bravely. 'Time to move on. Absolutely.'

In bed later, curled up together, Chris asked, 'Is she going to call me Christine for ever, do you think?'

'Probably. Sorry. I should've warned you. Abbreviations are another thing she doesn't like.'

'How do you get away with Greg then?'

'I don't. If she's really mad at me she calls me Gregory. The rest of the time she calls me darling. She never uses Greg.'

'Don't waste your time trying to get her to call me Chris,' said Chris with a grin. 'But I think we'll wait a year or two before we tell her it's short for Christabel not Christine.'

'She's done me one favour then,' replied Greg. 'I thought I was going to have to raid the HR files or get you to marry me in order to find out what your name really was.'

A silence greeted him, then a quiet snore. He never did know, then or later, whether Chris was pretending to be asleep or whether she'd heard his last comment.

26

Inquest 1

Two morning's later, Greg waved his parents off with a huge sigh of relief. Much as he loved and admired his father, his mother didn't seem to be getting any easier with age and a couple of days of their company had been enough. Her demand the night before that he sit down and 'enjoy a home-cooked meal' when all he wanted to do was fall into bed, was ill-timed at best and positively mischievous at worst. The menu was so clearly inspired as one-upmanship, with Chris the intended target. His mother had expressed disappointment that 'Christine' hadn't been present to enjoy her homemade steak-and-kidney pie and pineapple upside-down cake.

Greg, well aware of the discarded steak-and-kidney, and pineapple tins, and the empty ready-made pastry packaging in the rubbish bin, was not fooled by his mother's ploy, but dutifully ate what was in front of him and retired to bed feeling like an overstuffed goose intended for the production of foie gras.

Now, despite repeated reminders that he had work commitments, his parents had been late departing, and getting to County Hall in time for the pre-inquest review hearings was going to be tight. With some judicious speeding, he arrived in the Coroner's Court car park with barely minutes to spare and the one remaining parking space verging on the impossible for his fairly large car. Wriggling out of a barely opened driver's door, he sincerely hoped the car would still be undamaged when he returned and ran for the entrance.

While no stranger to coroner's proceedings, it was unusual for him to have two on the go at more or less the same time, and even more unusual that the second concerned the perpetrator in the first.

'Keeping us busy,' was the first comment from the court official in the reception area as she showed him through to Court Number 2. The coroner was taking his place on the bench.

'Sorry I'm late,' Greg whispered to the usher, as he sat at the desk facing the bench.

'You're not, not quite,' replied the sharp-eared man on the bench. 'I don't think we've met. Thank you for coming. I'm Roger Goodwin, the coroner, and this is the court usher, Sally North. Sitting behind you is my officer of the court, Edward Pullen. Attending by live video link we have Maria Laurentiu, sister of the deceased, assisted by an interpreter, Graeme Hardy.

'The first thing I need to do is to set it on the record that although this hearing will be recorded in the court, and recordings can be made available to participants subsequently, it is an offence for anyone else, for example on a video link, to make or distribute a recording. Is that clear?'

There was a mutter from the interpreter, then the dark-haired woman on the video screen shifted in her seat before saying, 'Yes'.

'Thank you,' said the coroner. 'This, as you all know, is the Pre-Inquest Review Hearing, or PIRH, into the death of Adelina Laurentiu, also known as Madame Trieste. The function of a PIRH is to establish what evidence will be heard at the inquest, and by what means. For instance, will it be read into the record from statements already provided, or will witnesses be required to attend.'

The coroner looked up at the video screen. 'But first of all, I want to express my condolences to you, Ms Laurentiu, and the rest of your family, for the loss of your relative in such distressing circumstances.' The dark woman inclined her head and the coroner continued, 'Can I establish how you would like me to refer to the deceased? As Adelina Laurentiu or as Madame Trieste?'

There was a mutter from the video screen and the interpreter spoke up. 'As Adelina, please.'

'Thank you. I also need to explain that the function of an inquest is purely to establish the facts of a death. Specifically, the identity of the person who has died, and when, where and how the death came about. It is not the function of an inquest to attribute blame for a death, even a violent death. That is a matter for other courts. Is that also clear? Good.

'Then the first item on our agenda is to establish the scope of the inquest. Unless I am advised otherwise, I take the scope to be the circumstances that led to Adelina's death on 23rd

October 2019. I shall hear the inquest sitting alone, as there is no suggestion Adelina was in any way in the custody of the state. Any questions?'

Everyone present, actually or virtually, shook their heads.

'Thank you. We have the following witness statements, and I believe you have been provided with translated versions, Ms Laurentiu.

'First, we have the statement submitted by yourself, Ms Laurentiu, concerning your identification of your sister and the circumstances of her work and residency in this country. That will be read into the record. Second comes the statement of DCI Geldard, explaining how, when and where he and Sergeant Mathews came to find the body of Adelina, and the condition of the body when they found it. As this is a statement of fact relating to circumstances after the death had occurred, I propose to read this statement into the record, and you need not attend the hearing in person, DCI Geldard. Does anyone object?' Again silence. 'The next statement is rather different, as it is a statement from DI Laurence, who was present when the death occurred.'

There was an interruption from the video screen and the interpreter said, 'Ms Laurentiu would like the opportunity to ask questions of this witness.' The coroner looked up again.

'Yes indeed,' he said. 'I have already noted the questions she raised by email, and I would be happy to ask them on her behalf or for her to ask them herself. I must, however, urge caution in the framing of the questions, as it is inappropriate for an inquest to conclude by attributing blame to an individual. If Ms Laurentiu was willing to submit her questions via me, that might be best.' Taking silence for consent he continued, ' I think we are agreed that DI Laurence will be required to give evidence, either in person or via a video link. Good.

'The other evidence we will need to hear is the report from the paramedic who attended the scene, finding Adelina to be already dead, and that of the pathologist who conducted the post-mortem and established the cause of death. Her statement lists the causes as: 1a, cardiac arrest; 1b, catastrophic blood loss; 1c, multiple knife wounds, in particular one which punctured the carotid artery. We would normally also have statements from Adelina's GP, but she doesn't seem to have had one.'

There was an interruption from the video screen again and the interpreter said, 'Ms Laurentiu states that her sister was always fit and well and not known to consult doctors.' The coroner inclined his head.

'Thank you, for that clarification,' he said. 'So, I think we have concluded that, with the exception of DI Sarah Laurence, the witnesses need not attend -

The interpreter spoke up again. 'Ms Laurentiu has stated that she might wish to ask questions of the pathologist and requests that they also be available.'

The coroner looked down at his notes, and then up again at the screen. 'I think I need to clarify that in this court we are required only to establish the cause of Adelina's death. I can appreciate, having read the distressing details of the post-mortem myself, that there may be other questions which you and other family members may have for the pathologist, but they may not be appropriate for this court. Having said that, as an interested person, Ms Laurentiu has the right to ask witnesses questions if she wishes. But could you explain to her that if the question is not relevant to the purposes of the inquest, I will be required to disallow it.'

There was more muttering from the video screen, then the interpreter stated, 'She understands but still wants the opportunity to ask questions.'

'Then I will request that the pathologist be present, either in person or virtually. Thank you. Now, it only remains to fix a date for the inquest.'

27

Inquest 2

Looking at his watch, Greg realised he had ten minutes free before the next pre-inquest hearing. One of the volunteers from the Coroners' Court Support Service offered him coffee, but knowing from past, bitter experience that it would be made from granules of cheap instant, he declined politely and went out to the car park to touch base with Chris.

'Not much time to chat,' he said, 'just wanted to keep you abreast. The arrangements for Madame Trieste's inquest are much as we expected. And good luck to the coroner in preventing the family from blaming Mica Gabrys. That's clearly what they have in mind. Next up are the arrangements for Mica's inquest. That's going to be interesting. I just wanted to ask you about tonight. Are you going to be over?'

'Yes,' said Chris when she could get a word in edgeways. 'I'll cook. See you there.'

Back in the reception area, Ram had arrived and the usher was just collecting the folk required for the next PIRH.

'All okay so far?' whispered Ram.

'Yes. Just Sarah and the pathologist to give evidence in person.'

'All rise,' said the usher, and they got to their feet as the assistant coroner came in.

A smart middle-aged woman in a dark suit and white shirt introduced herself as Yvette Granger, and Greg lost focus slightly as she ran over exactly the same introduction as her colleague had an hour before. The only difference was that this time there was no one on the video screen, but a vaguely familiar man in a dark suit was revealed as the legal representative of the Gabrys family.

'Is anyone from the Gabrys family expected to attend?' enquired Ms Granger. The solicitor stood.

'No, ma'am,' he said. 'Not at this hearing, although it is likely they will attend the inquest. I am representing them today.'

'Thank you. Then the first thing I need to make clear is that, as you would expect, I will be sitting with a jury at this inquest, as the death occurred while the deceased was in police custody.

'As regards evidence, I propose to read into the record the evidence relating to the identity of the deceased provided by his father, Mr Constantin Gabrys.' She paused for comments, but there were none.

'The statements provided by the two police constables present when Mica Gabrys met his death will—'

'If it might save time, ma'am, I can inform you that the Gabrys family, through me, will wish to question both those witnesses, the Chief Inspector responsible for planning the raid on the Clean Boats premises, the DI who was allegedly subjected to illegal imprisonment at those premises, the pathologist who carried out the police post-mortem, and the independent pathologist who carried out the second post-mortem. I have a list here,' and he proffered a sheet of paper to the usher.

'Thank you.' Ms Granger took the list from the usher and scrutinised it. 'I think that leaves only the statement provided by Mr Mica Gabrys's GP and the statements provided by the three other persons arrested during the raid as uncontested and therefore suitable for being read into the record.'

'I agree,' said the solicitor.

'One point for clarification,' said the assistant coroner. 'Do the family, as interested persons, wish to question the witnesses themselves, or are you, as their representative, going to do all the questioning?' The solicitor hesitated, and Greg caught Ram's eye.

'I think it entirely possible that the family may wish to ask some additional questions,' he replied.

'They have that right, of course,' she said. 'But I hope that you've made clear to them the very precise scope of an inquest, and the fact that we are not here to attribute blame or criminal liability, and indeed may not express any view that may be so interpreted. Moreover, the jury is also expressly forbidden from expressing any such view or making any comments that may be so interpreted.'

'I have advised my clients accordingly,' said the lawyer, looking harassed.

'Then I suggest you also inform them that I will be obliged to disallow any questions that I judge to be irrelevant to the scope of the inquest.' She stared at the solicitor as he resumed his seat, then went on. 'Thank you. In that case I think we are agreed that the following witnesses will be required to attend the inquest, either in person or virtually, in order to answer questions from interested persons and/or their legal representative,' and she read from the list. 'Finally, we need to set a date for the inquest. The dates I have in mind are the twenty-seventh to the twenty-ninth of November and, in view of what we have just agreed, I think we will need the three full days to complete the inquest. Thank you, all.'

'All rise,' said the usher, and the assistant coroner sailed from the room.

Outside in the car park again, Ram said, 'Not difficult to see where that's going. Clearly the solicitor chappie has little expectation of keeping his clients in order.'

'Certainly looks as though his advice is being ignored,' agreed Greg. 'I think Sarah would be wise to attend via video link. I don't think her and Gabrys in the same space is going to work.'

The car park had begun to empty. Greg made a careful inspection of his car and breathed a sigh of relief. It seemed his neighbours had been careful when they opened their car doors. He waved to Ram as he left, and his phone rang just as he turned into the BP garage opposite County Hall to fill up the car with petrol and himself with a sandwich. To the considerable annoyance of the driver queueing behind him, he paused to take the call before using the pump.

Margaret's voiced assailed him at full volume and he held the phone a little further from his ear.

'Fellowes,' she said without preliminaries. 'We need to sort this. HR are pussyfooting about. See me as soon as you get here.'

'Right,' he said and rang off. 'Okay okay,' he mouthed at the irritable van man behind him and hurried to fill up his car.

28

Consequences

'Take a seat, you're going to need it,' was Margaret's opening remark. 'Fellowes has lodged a counter-complaint against Chris Mathews for bullying and harassment.'

'He what?' Greg sank into a seat, words failing him.

'He complains that she's been on his back since he arrived, shouts at and threatens him, and is biased against him because he's male, thus being in breach of one of his protected characteristics, ie sex. Did Sergeant Mathews indeed call him,' – she consulted her notebook – 'a "plonking, toerag of a dingbat waste of space"?'

'I rather think she did,' admitted Greg. 'And told him he compared poorly to slurry, a view with which I entirely concur.'

Margaret was unable to hide a grin. 'Very eloquent,' she said. 'Sergeant Mathews has, if anything, gone up in my estimation. However, HR insist I have to follow the rules, which means an investigation of both complaints, yours and his, in order to establish what was reasonable, in all the circumstances of the case.'

Greg sighed heavily and crossed his arms. 'Are they serious? Haven't we enough to do?'

'Yes, they are serious and, actually, I think it plays to our advantage, DCI Geldard. You want rid of this Fellowes, don't you? Well now we have the perfect opportunity and excuse to scrutinise everything he's done since he was here, and also look into his record at the Met. I can't believe we won't find a chain of similar behaviour going back years. He's toast, Greg, and if it's at the cost of Chris Mathews having to admit that "dingbat waste of space" was perhaps an injudicious choice of words and that talking quietly might be more effective than shouting, I think that's a small price to pay.'

'You don't have to live with her,' muttered Greg.

'What's that?' asked a tactically deaf Margaret.

'Nothing.'

Breaking the news to Chris from a safe distance on the other side of his desk, Greg was pleasantly surprised by a remarkably low-key response. He was less surprised to discover that she already knew.

'Is there anything that happens in Norfolk Police that you don't know about within minutes?' he asked.

'Well, obviously yes,' replied Chris. 'If I knew everything, I'd have known about those filthy photos sooner. But when it comes to action on the part of HR, and bearing in mind I've worked here for years and know almost everyone, it's hardly surprising that a tomfool complaint from the DWOS comes to my attention pretty promptly.'

'The deewos?' asked Greg, then as light dawned said, 'Oh I see, the Dingbat Waste ... yes, I get it. Perhaps I won't go there, as it seems likely to be termed unparliamentary language.'

'Not by the Chief Super,' pointed out Chris smugly. 'I believe she thought it was eloquent.'

'Now how do you know that? Don't tell me she's one of your informants as well!'

'Not the big boss, no. But one of the secretaries just happened to be passing her door, and it isn't very soundproof.'

Greg decided not to go there either. 'Suffice it to say, thanks to your eloquence, I now have to resource another investigation, this time into one of our own.'

'Not because of me,' argued Chris. 'It was his actions and his damn fool complaint that triggered all this.'

'Yes, well, either way, I'm happy to leave it to Margaret to interview you, but we'll need to put together a summary of his actions that led to the hoo-ha.'

'No problem. I've got it ready. But I also think I should do a bit of digging into his previous background in the Met.'

'Not you, no.' Greg was firm on that. 'Send Bill to me. He can do the digging, then it's clear it's not you pursuing a vendetta, and we avoid an accusation of gender bias as well. Pass the information you've got to HR, then keep out of it.' Chris looked mutinous but agreed.

With Bill given his instructions, Greg was about to head for the canteen when the phone rang.

'You're running out of time,' said the sergeant in charge of the custody suite, 'and I've got Gabrys's London lawyer hopping up and down like a joey with ants up its bum.' Greg checked his watch.

'Damn, you're right,' he said. 'I'll be down in a few minutes, after I've had a word with the CPS.'

***

'Nothing new to report,' he said to Frank Parker of the CPS. 'We've got the evidence from his house and from his accountant, but, yes, it's all circumstantial and, no, I don't have anything that ties him to the death of Madame Trieste or the abduction of Sarah. Both those are down to his son, Mica, so if he claims Mica was acting alone, I don't have anything to prove otherwise.' There was a silence. Clearly there was a lot of thought going on.

'The problem is,' said Frank, 'that while I *do* think we have a reasonable chance of succeeding with the money laundering charges and possession of illegal substances, I'm doubtful we'll be able to keep him off the streets until the trial. His barrister will argue that as well as the evidence being circumstantial, he's a businessman with commitments in the UK and therefore not a flight risk. He also has powerful contacts as you know. So, I'd put his chances of getting bail at better than even. The tactical question for you is, do we charge him now, recognising that he may well be out on bail within days? Or do we hold off on a charge, in the hopes that a little more time will enable you to find the evidence that'll put him away safely?'

It was Greg's turn to think hard. At last, he said, 'I can't prove it yet, but I find it hard to believe that his son would have acted totally on his own initiative. The precise nature of what he did, yes that was probably Mica's twisted preferences at work. But as for the decision to punish Madame Trieste, I'm convinced the guiding mind there was the father's. Moreover, GCHQ tipped us off that action was about to be taken against a "grass". That supports it being a strategic decision of Constantin's rather than a sadistic impulse of Mica's. Sorry, I'm thinking aloud here, but I'm tending to feel that there's still some evidence out there to link Constantin to the murder and, therefore, the abduction, if we can only find it. Perhaps our best bet is to let him go for now and keep a close eye on him. Perhaps with enough rope, he'll hang himself.'

***

Down in the custody suite, the London lawyer bounced to his feet the moment Greg entered the room. 'My client—' he began, but Greg interrupted him.

'Your client may leave now,' he said. 'I'd thank you for your help, Mr Gabrys, but I think we both recognise you haven't given us any. For now, I'm releasing you without charge. I'll probably see you again in the not-too-distant future.'

Gabrys stood, straightening his jacket. 'You will certainly see me when I sue you all for the murder of my son,' he said, waving his arm to encompass the entirety of Norfolk Police.

'That's as may be,' replied Greg. 'As you know, I am not part of the investigation into the death of your son. But I can assure you, Mr Gabrys, that if he were alive to face justice, he would undoubtedly be standing trial for the murder of Madame Trieste and the unlawful imprisonment of DI Laurence.'

There was a moment when Greg thought he was about to be spat at, or otherwise assaulted by the infuriated man opposite. His eyes black with hate, he stared at Greg for a long moment, muttered something in Lithuanian, then turned on his heel and left the room, his solicitor scuttling to keep up.

'Now, I wonder what he said,' murmured Greg as he followed the pair out of the room.

29

At Acle

Looking down at himself in ill-fitting jeans, fleece top and trainers, Ralph was the more convinced that his unscheduled departure from Horses Mill House had been unwise. The message passed on from his boss had reinforced his impression and the behaviour of his new companions had not lessened his concerns. Even allowing for the fact they communicated in a foreign language – foreign to him anyway – grunts seemed to dominate their vocabulary. Their table manners were non-existent – as indeed was a table when he came to think about it – and their manner of drinking recalled the late, great Terry Pratchett's definition of quaffing as being 'like drinking, only you spill more.' This bunch definitely quaffed.

Ralph was not a happy bunny and was rendered less happy by his employer's lack of sympathy. Loyalty had landed Ralph in this predicament, and he feared that loyalty was going to get him into more trouble. At the moment, he assumed the worst he would face was an accusation of being an accessory. There was no doubt that he had known about the stashes of money and drugs. But he'd never been directly involved in anything criminal, but that looked like a line he was about to cross.

Fishing his own clothes out of the tumble drier, he changed hurriedly and went into the living room to wait by the phone as instructed.

It was an hour or two later when the phone rang. Ralph picked it up, not knowing whether to be relieved or disappointed to hear the familiar tones of Constantin Gabrys.

'I have job for you,' he said, without preamble. 'Get one of the men to drive you to Acle. I want you to keep watch and let me know who comes and goes. I'll text you the location. You will watch a property on the other side of the river. You will need wet weather clothes. They will give you.'

'It's not really my sort of job,' began Ralph without much hope he would be listened to. He wasn't.

'You can do. Just do as I say.'

Ralph reflected that, under stress, his boss's language ability seemed to suffer. 'Is Mrs Gabrys okay?' he asked, worried.

'She fine. Nothing to do with you. Just do the job.'

***

By late afternoon, Ralph was sitting in one of the vans, in a side road by the river. Just downstream he could see what appeared to be a sailing club. The muscle who had driven him there had consumed a bag of toffees, put his feet up on the dashboard and appeared to go to sleep. Equipped with a pair of binoculars and an oversized down jacket, Ralph was alternating between watching the river from the rear doors at the back of the van, or wandering up and down the riverbank.

Inspired by the binoculars, he decided he would claim to be a birdwatcher if anyone spoke to him. So far, he'd seen no one, far less spoken to anyone.

As the light faded over the river, he perched on a rotting log and settled down to watch through the evening. By the time half an hour had passed, he was terminally bored. Another thirty minutes and he was cold as well, the damp creeping into his borrowed trainers. He considered ringing the boss and saying there was nothing doing but knew with dull certainty that it would make no difference. He was stuck there until Constantin Gabrys said otherwise.

Around eight o'clock, some lights flickered on the bank opposite, near the dark cottage he could just about see through the trees. Car headlights pulled up to the clump of trees, and, shortly after, lights went on in the cottage. After a moment, a strong flood of yellow light from the conservatory attached to the cottage fell across the opposite bank to the water. A burly man stood in the light, looking at the river. As Ralph watched, a cat climbed up the man to his shoulders. The man turned, paused, and a woman appeared behind him. They both went into a room behind the conservatory. The phone in Ralph's pocket shuddered, and he answered it.

'Anything yet?' asked his boss as he had, several times, during the evening. Ralph reported what he'd seen. 'Good,' said Gabrys. 'You can go home. Be back there five am tomorrow.'

Another miserable night in the Norwich house, and Ralph was back in place on the riverbank. This time, in the pink light of a Norfolk dawn, he could see the cottage had two cars parked beside it. Lights came on around six o'clock, and through his binoculars he could see movement behind the upstairs windows. Vapour rose from what he took to be a heating boiler, and eventually the man and woman came out of the cottage back door. They kissed, then each got into a car and drove away. He didn't see the cat.

He reported to Gabrys again. 'Good,' he said. 'You have done well. Go home. Be ready to go with me this evening.'

'Go where?' asked Ralph, some hope flowering that this uncomfortable part of his life would soon be over.

'To the cottage. Don't be stupid. Tonight, we deal with them.' Ralph gaped at the phone. 'You don't need me for that!' he exclaimed. 'There are others here much better - '

'And I will use them too, where they are needed. But tonight, I need you. Definitely. Be ready and we finish this.'

30

Cat antics

It was dark by the time Chris let herself and her shopping into Greg's house. The outside light had failed to come on as she drove up the drive, so she used her phone as a torch to negotiate the uneven path to the back door. Bobby greeted her as she went in, twining round her ankles and rubbing her head on her leg.

'Mind out,' said Chris, 'you'll have me over.' Then put down her shopping to make a fuss of the cat, currently woogling on the door mat. 'Does that mat feel nice and scratchy?' she asked the cat as she stroked its tummy. 'Come on, Bobby, I'll get you your supper.'

The cat fed, beef mince frying in the pan with onions and garlic, Chris hunted through the cupboard for the tinned tomatoes she was sure she'd seen there. An increasingly frustrated hunt led her to the inescapable conclusion that if there had been a supply of tomatoes in stock, they were there no longer.

'Damn,' she said aloud, surveying the alternatives for her bolognaise sauce. Unfortunately, Greg seemed to be out of tomato purée too, and there were only dregs of ketchup left in the elderly bottle. She could, she supposed, convert her menu from spag bol to cottage pie, but on investigation a lack of potatoes ruled that out. Clearly, she had no option but to nip into town for a tin of tomatoes.

'Back in a minute, Bobby,' she said, and leaving the house lights on for the cat, she returned to her car for the shopping trip. The moon was now out, glowing on the river and silhouetting the bare branches of the willows. This time she didn't need her torch app and used her night vision to make it to the car door.

The other side the river, the two musclemen were now let loose on their own. Having dropped Ralph at a riverside pub, they had, as instructed, returned to their spot near the river bank and dowsed their van lights. For half an hour or so they had followed their orders and kept watch on the cottage opposite. They noted the arrival of a car and lights going on in the house. Time went by, and boredom set in. One started wandering about on the river bank. The other, left to his own devices, started a game on his phone. When the first returned, alerted by the glow of the phone showing through the van windows, he was at first indignant, then philosophical.

'S'pose they're home now,' he observed. 'That's what he wanted to know.' And he too sat down with his phone. He was still scrolling through Facebook when his phone rang.

'Yes, Boss,' he said. 'Yes, Boss. Arrived earlier as we reported. Yes, Boss, both there. No change.' He rang off. 'We're to stay here until the boss says we go,' he said, and went back to Facebook. His partner grunted. He'd not left his game. Neither noticed that there was now no car by the cottage opposite.

The shadows cast by the moon behind the building were impenetrably black, and the next vehicle to bump down the rutted track had no lights on.

At the inn on the riverbank, Ralph sat nursing half a pint of bitter for what he felt was an unrealistically long time. Even the busy bar staff had begun to look at him oddly. When he saw a familiar face come round the door and a hand beckoned, he abandoned his part-drunk half pint and joined his boss in the pub car park.

He was standing by a Range Rover with distinctly muddy number plates. 'Get in,' said Constantin Gabrys. Ralph did as he was told.

'How is Mrs Gabrys?' he asked, as he put his seat belt on. His boss wasn't wearing one, he noticed, and judging from the lack of complaint from the car, the warning sound had been disabled. Gabrys glanced across.

'Fine,' he said. 'Just concentrate on today's job. You know what I want you to do?'

'Keep a look out,' said Ralph, hoping forlornly that that would be the sum total of his tasks.

'Yes. I may need other help,' said Gabrys. 'It depends.' The car turned off the main road and, as it bumped down a rutted track, he turned the car lights off. The moon was bright, lighting the roadway just enough to keep the car on the straight and narrow.

When they pulled up by the cottage, Gabrys looked around, puzzled. 'Can't see a car,' he muttered.

'The lights are on,' pointed out Ralph, and his boss nodded. 'Car must be round the back,' he said. 'Follow!'

They both got out of the car, and Gabrys pulled something from the back. 'Bring,' he ordered Ralph, and handed him a bag that rattled. Looking inside, he saw a hammer and some six-inch nails.

***

Leaving Wymondham at last, Greg was hoping for a swift ride home, when he found himself at the back of a stationary queue of traffic.

'Oh damn,' he muttered, tapping impatient fingers on his steering wheel. After ten minutes of slow crawl, he rang Chris to make his apologies.

'Sorry I can't take your call,' said her answerphone, 'leave a message and I'll get back to you when I've finished saving civilisation as we know it.'

'Stuck on the A11,' said Greg. 'Sorry, Chris. I'll be with you as soon as poss.'

In Acle, Chris had raided the supermarket for tinned tomatoes, ketchup that didn't have a use-by date somewhere in the 1990s, and had then been seduced by the jam doughnuts. As a result, she missed Greg's call.

At the cottage, Gabrys had silently opened the back door using skeleton keys, and gestured to Ralph to stand outside, keeping lookout. Then he went in, producing something from his pocket as he did. Ralph didn't see it clearly, but realised with an icy sensation in his belly that it was a gun. He took a step toward the car, intending to make a run for it, then stopped, finely balanced between horror at what he was getting into, and terror of his boss. As he dithered, something rubbed round his ankles. He only just suppressed a shout, then looking down saw it was a small, tortoiseshell cat. Ralph liked cats.

'Hello, sweetheart,' he said quietly.

Moments later, Gabrys reappeared in the doorway, still brandishing his gun and with an expression of fury on his face.

'Not here,' he snarled. 'They're not here. No one here. Those morons.' He dropped into what Ralph could only conclude was uncomplimentary Lithuanian. 'What've you got there?' Gabrys demanded, seeing the cat. Then he dropped his gun into his pocket. 'Give to me,' he demanded. 'And the tools. If they not here, it have to be the cat.'

Ralph recoiled, the cat still in his arms. Gabrys snatched the cat from him, and all hell broke loose. Bobby, while content to be picked up by almost anyone, was not used to rough treatment and objected violently. Turning apparently within her skin, she raked her claws down Gabrys's face, only just missing his eyes. He dropped her with an oath and as the cat ran back into the cottage, car headlights picked out the scene with brutal clarity.

Ralph dropped the bag he was holding and held his hands over his head. Gabrys, dashing the blood from his face with one hand, reached into his pocket and drawing out the gun, fired it at the lights. One went out with a tinkle of broken glass. Gabrys ran, still firing wildly at the car, which braked so hard it slewed across the drive. The car behind it pulled up in a hurry, narrowly missing a rear-end shunt, and Gabrys fired again.

The car in front was steaming gently from a shattered radiator, one headlight still shining, the other no more than splintered glass. The second car was also stationary, the glass of the windscreen starred from a single bullet hole. In the distance could faintly be heard the sounds of a heavy body crashing through long grass and scrub. Silence fell.

31

Cat-astrophe

Greg was out of his car before the echoes of gunfire had faded. He pointed a finger at the man with his arms in the air.

'You,' he shouted. 'Lie down, hands above your head.' He waited a split second to check the man complied, then turned to Chris's car. He was talking on the phone as he wrenched the driver door open.

'Get roadblocks on the main road to Acle, and at the roundabout,' he was saying. 'The helicopter should spot him with the infrared if he's on foot. Oh God,' he added as he looked at the starred windscreen of Chris's car and the empty driver's seat. The moon shadows obscured his view, then to his immense relief he saw a movement from the footwell and the sound of muffled curses rose from beneath the dashboard.

'You okay?' he asked.

'Apart from the tomato ketchup,' said Chris. Another moment's panic, then he realised the phrase was not a euphemism for blood loss and she really was covered in ketchup.

'How on earth? Those bottles are really strong.'

'Not bulletproof however, and that's where the one through the windscreen ended up. I think bolognaise is off the menu. What's going on?'

Greg reached in to give her a hand out of the car. 'We have someone down here, and another has fled the scene. That was the gunman, I think. Okay, who have we here? You can roll over but keep your hands above your head.'

Revealed in the light from Greg's phone, the man on the ground looked familiar.

'It's the butler,' said Chris. 'I've got handcuffs in my car. Give me a second.'

Moments later, the man was hauled to his feet, handcuffs in place, and hustled into Greg's kitchen.

'You work for Constantin Gabrys, don't you? Name?' asked Greg.

'Yes. Ralph Menton,' replied the man. He seemed badly shaken and unlikely to kick off, but, taking no chances, Greg pulled a kitchen chair into the middle of the hall and sat him down on that.

'Who was the gunman?' he asked.

'That was Constantin Gabrys,' the man replied.

'And where's he gone?'

'I don't know, although I could make some guesses. Look,' he said with a note of desperation, 'this isn't me. I don't do violence or theft for that matter. If you can protect me from Gabrys, I'll help all I can.'

'What was the plan?' asked Chris, standing in the kitchen doorway.

'Don't know for sure, but he was planning some sort of revenge and he came equipped with a hammer and nails. When he found you were out, he said the cat would have to do.'

'Oh God, Bobby,' said Greg.

'Where's the cat? asked Chris.

'The cat's okay. I promise. I like cats. I wouldn't have hurt the cat. But anyway, when Gabrys tried to grab it off me, the cat scratched him, and he let go. Look, there it is,' said Ralph, trying to point with his chin.

Bobby came though the kitchen door, miaowing in indignation and jumped into Greg's arms. 'Hold on to her,' said Chris, and disappeared upstairs.

Greg perched himself on the edge of the hall table, trying simultaneously to calm the angry miaows, keep an eye on his prisoner and decide what to do next.

'I get that he wanted revenge, given the twisted lunatic he is,' he said to the now ex-butler, 'but why here and why now? What did he think he'd achieve?'

'God knows,' said Ralph. 'I think he holds you responsible for what happened to Mica, and the raid on his house was the last straw. If an Englishman's home is his castle, then a Lithuanian's is his fort! You trampled all over him when you took his gate down. He's had someone watching this place for a couple of days.'

'Has he indeed?' said Greg. 'Where from?'

'The other side the river.' Greg went to put the cat down in order to use his phone again, but Chris returned at that moment.

'Hang on a tick, Greg,' she said, and as Greg held the cat she gently pressed on each front paw in turn. As the claws slid from their sheaths, she swabbed beneath them. The swabs went into their cylinders, and she sighed with satisfaction. 'If she scratched Gabrys, we should have his DNA,' she said.

Greg took the cat into the kitchen and closed the door firmly. 'Okay, let's get organised.' He speed-dialled again, then said 'Tell me what's going on.'

'Helicopter's up, roadblocks in place on the A1064, two cars should be with you in a moment or two.' Even as he listened to the phone, Greg heard vehicles approaching down his bumpy drive.

'Any sign of Gabrys yet?'

'Not so far.'

'Seems likely there's another vehicle on the river lane just opposite my place,' he said. How many?' he asked Ralph.

'Two men, as far as I know,' Ralph replied.

'Two,' said Greg into his phone, then rang off. Chris was already on her way out of the door.

'I'll see about transport back to HQ,' she said. 'Neither my car nor yours'll be going anywhere anytime soon.'

In the drive she found Rick Lake contemplating the wreckage of her windscreen and the red smears on the passenger seat. 'In view of this mess, I'm surprised to see you upright,' he remarked. 'Who's the casualty?'

'Mr Heinz,' she replied, and as he still looked puzzled, 'Ketchup. I was cooking bolognaise when all this kicked off. Greg's inside with the one we caught. Gabrys is the one that legged it.'

'No real casualties then?'

'Only the cars. And possibly Mr Gabrys himself, who appears to have been on the receiving end from a very angry cat. We'll find out when we catch up with him.'

Rick's radio crackled and he turned away to respond.

***

High in the ragged, wind-torn sky, police helicopter G-DN5 was circling over Acle Bridge. Blue flashing lights denoted the locations of the roadblocks on the A1064 and another set lit up Greg's yard and drive.

'If he started on foot from there,' – the navigator spoke into his mike and pointed – 'then most likely he'll have headed for the road to Billockby. He'll surely not have headed for the river. And whichever direction he's headed, he's going to have to jump or wade a dyke at the edge of every field. It's not going to be quick.' The pilot nodded and swung the copter over to circle more widely.

'Anything on the infrared?' he asked.

'A few blips. Cattle I think.' He pointed again. 'Take us closer to the junction there, can you?' The pilot brought the helicopter lower, to check out the warm spots.

'Cattle. Definitely cattle,' said the navigator. 'Follow that hedgeline. I think there're some more hot spots along there.'

There were. Two were cattle again, or more precisely, a cow and her newborn calf. The mother looked up and bellowed as they flew overhead. At this lower level the wind was gusting badly, and the helicopter bounced a little in the updraughts from the trees.

'Round again,' said the navigator urgently. 'I think there was something else near the cattle.'

As they turned back, a clear image flowed on his screen. A man, on foot and running toward the road.

'That's him.' Seizing the radio the navigator reported fact and location to control, then switched the floodlights on. The man was seen to stagger in the sudden glare, then he looked round, pointed his arm at the helicopter, and fired. The pilot's reaction was instinctive. Even before the gun was fired, the copter was banking fiercely and turning away. Whatever happened to the bullet, it didn't connect with anything that mattered. The lights remained on, the engine continued running. At the greater, safer height, the pilot breathed again.

'Still got him in sight?' he asked.

'Just found him again,' replied the navigator, refocussing the light.

'Where is he now?'

'Still headed to Billockby. The ground team needs to get hold of him fast. That's a residential area and an armed lunatic on the loose is the last thing we need.'

'Need to turn back soon,' said the pilot to officers on the ground. 'We're running out of fuel. Have you spotted him yet?'

***

Back in his own personal war zone, Greg was startled to realise his hands were shaking. He just managed to complete the handover of Ralph to Rick's team, then went into his conservatory, almost falling onto the sofa. Bobby joined him, and he stroked her for a moment, then pushed his hands under his thighs, trying to still the tremors. The image of the starred windscreen of Chris's car, and the apparently empty front seats kept recurring in his mind's eye. Across the river he could see flashes of torches on the bank opposite, and realised some colleagues were probably looking for the two spotters. Moonlight flooding the garden still offered the brightest light, together with the reflections of the blue flashes from the police cars.

'I wish to God they'd turn those damn lights off,' he said aloud.

Behind him, Bill coughed and said, 'I'll deal with it. Ned's here now, and he'd like a chat.'

'Send him in here would you, Bill, thanks,' said Greg, not moving, in case the shaking hands became visible.

'Will do. I'll bring you a coffee too.'

Chris appeared before the coffee, closely followed by Ned. 'Do you two need a paramedic?' he asked. 'You look terrible.'

'Well thanks a lot,' said Chris.

Just as Greg said, 'No thanks. At least not for me. A coffee will do.' He looked at Chris and added, 'You don't look too great.'

'Nor do you,' she replied. 'Being shot at does that. I've just thrown up. How's the shock taking you?' He grinned, struck again by her practical good sense.

'Shaking hands,' he said. As he held one up, Bill stuck a hot mug into it.

'That'll help,' he said, and Greg detected the comforting aroma of whisky rising in the steam.

'What actually happened here?' Ned asked.

'In summary,' said Greg, sipping the coffee and whisky, 'as I turned into the drive off the main road, Chris followed. Been shopping I gather. We drove in convoy down to the house and just as I arrived, my headlight was shot out. A second or two after, what I think was the second shot hit Chris's windscreen, and then the shooter took off across the fields. The second man was standing, apparently frozen, in front of the back door. I told him to lie down while I went to check on Chris, who I found covered in ketchup, then we handcuffed him, went looking for Bobby, and rang for assistance. Not sure in what order.'

'We found a bag of nails and a hammer by the door,' remarked Ned, as neutrally as he was capable.

'Yes. I gather they were meant for me, then when he found I wasn't here, for Bobby. But Bobby got her retaliation in first.'

'And I swabbed her claws,' said Chris. 'That Ralph chappie says she scratched Gabrys's face, so there should be DNA in the samples.'

'Assuming we catch him soon, the scratches should be pretty evident anyway,' replied Ned. 'Not sure the DNA will add much. But well done for thinking of it,' he added in a hurry, as a distinctly mulish expression was crossing Chris's face. 'I don't think there's much else I need to do here, so I'll be off.'

Bill was on his radio again. 'They've spotted what they think is Gabrys from the helicopter and they're closing in on him in Billockby,' he said. 'Chief Inspector Lake's on the scene and says to get something to eat while you've got the chance. What's for supper?' he added hopefully.

'I can tell you what's not,' said Chris. 'Spaghetti bolognaise.'

32

Cornered

The last moments of flying time were passing swiftly, when, 'Got him, there!' said the navigator, pointing. 'He's in the field by the junction with the B1152,' he said into the mike. 'I had him in the spotlight for a moment, then he dived into the hedgerow, and I lost him.'

'We have to go now,' interrupted the pilot. 'Absolutely right now,' and the helicopter dipped as it turned away.

On the ground, Rick Lake shouted into his radio, 'Go! Go!' and six men, all he could round up in a hurry, poured out of the blue-lit cars and ran toward the junction from all three directions. Moments later they met in a confused huddle.

'Nothing?' asked Rick.

'Nothing.'

'Then spread out down the hedgerows and take another look.'

As they scoured the tangled undergrowth with their powerful torches, the man panting in the ditch held his breath and readied his gun. In the mist eddying around the willows, the torches wavered, then passed over him. Two constables moved on up the side road and the man scrambled out of the dank, nettle-strewn dyke to run across the road with a curious, scuttling gait, rather like a large crab. The sound of his footsteps was drowned in the noise of the departing helicopter, but he was very lucky to make it over the road and the boundary before any of the searchers turned round. He lay by the fence he'd just hurdled, getting his breath back, then looked round. He was in a small garden, not very tidy, but not completely neglected. The lawn needed a mow, and the flower borders were overgrown, but there was evidence of some activity in the spade stuck in some recently turned earth. The smell of the disturbed soil reached his nostrils as he picked up the spade.

First, dry clothes; second, a vehicle, he thought. Although he could hear voices in other gardens nearby, coming from folk who had been distracted from their TVs by the helicopter circling low over their roofs, the nearest residents seemed undisturbed. Flickers of light in one window suggested a television screen in active use. He prised open the back door using the spade, then just in case they'd heard anything, he moved swiftly through the kitchen to the sitting room. He burst in, throwing the door open in approved commando fashion, and waved his gun at the couple sitting on matching armchairs by the fireplace.

'Be quiet and stay still. No harm if you stay quiet and still.'

The two looked at him with mouths identically agape, then the woman screamed. Gabrys stepped forward and put his gun to the man's head.

'Any more noise and I shoot,' he said. The man went so pale Gabrys thought for a moment he might faint, and the woman sat with her mouth open but now, thankfully, silent. 'Turn the TV off,' he ordered. The man reached out a shaking hand holding a remote control, and the TV also fell silent.

'You! Don't move,' Gabrys said to the man. 'You,' he gestured to the woman, with the gun. 'Fetch me dry clothes, trousers and jumper. Something warm. And your car keys.' The woman started to speak, but he barked over her, 'Silent. Do as you're told, otherwise I shoot him.'

After a few moments, which Gabrys filled by peering round the curtain at the road outside, she returned with a dark tracksuit and a jumper.

'These belong to my son,' she said. 'I thought they might fit better.' She gestured toward the short, slight man sitting greyly motionless in his chair. Gabrys held up the trousers. Not his normal choice, but warm, dry and dark. They would do.

'Over there,' he gestured with his gun. 'Sit on his knee and put your hands on your head. And in case you have any ideas, a bullet from this gun would go through you and into him behind. No trouble.'

They did as he instructed them, the woman visibly shaking. Gabrys looked at them for a moment, decided that rebellion was unlikely, and put the gun down on the small table at his right hand.

'I can pick up in seconds. Don't forget,' he said, then he swiftly stripped off his wet things and pulled the dry clothes on.

Dressed again, and gun in hand again, he said, 'Right! Car keys, then we go.'

The woman looked round at the face of the man behind her and swallowed nervously.

'That's what I tried to say,' she said. 'We haven't got a car.'

***

Out in the road, Rick Lake was on his radio again, then turned to the two new arrivals. Jim and Greg both looked at him.

'We heard you've lost him,' said Greg in a flat tone. Rick raised an eyebrow at Jim, who just shrugged slightly. He'd thought Greg coming onto the scene was a poor idea, but hearing the updates over the radio, Greg had been determined.

'We don't know that yet,' replied Rick. 'I've roadblocks on all three approach roads to this junction. Nothing's got past them, so unless he's taken to the fields again, he's somewhere inside this circle.' He pointed to the map spread on the bonnet of his car. 'There're a few outbuildings here and here, a sizeable livestock farm here,' – he pointed again – 'but I don't think he'll have got that far, unless he's an Olympic-standard cross-country runner. Most likely he's gone to earth in one of these properties close to the junction.'

'Armed response?' asked Greg.

'On their way from Norwich. Should be with us in,' – he checked his watch again – 'around fifteen minutes. So, I think we start a house-to-house, cautiously. Anything that arouses suspicion, we back off until armed response gets here.'

'Your chaps know not to take any risks?' asked Jim.

'They know.' Rick's voice was grim. 'I'm aware some of them haven't exactly covered themselves with glory recently, but they've been briefed very thoroughly for this exercise, and they know they'll have me to answer to, if they so much as breathe in the wrong direction.

'Okay. We'll start at the Fleggburgh end of the village, working our way towards Acle and then up the road to Clippesby. A second team will take the back road and meet us at the end of the line. Hopefully, by then we'll have him or at least know where he is.'

Greg and Jim waited by Jim's car near the roadblock. 'Chris okay?' asked Jim, keeping his voice low. 'I didn't get chance to ask on the way here; the radio was never silent for long enough.'

'She seems fine,' replied Greg. 'Better than me, to be honest. The moment I looked at the bullet hole in her windscreen and couldn't see her... Just thinking about that gave me the shakes. She seems mostly upset about the ketchup all over her front seats. With luck, she's gone to bed with Bobby.' He looked up at the thin line of light forming in the east of the big Norfolk sky. 'Not much of the night left now,' he added.

'Much damage to your car?' asked Jim.

'No idea. I know he shot a headlight out and the radiator's not looking good, but whether it did much other damage, I've not had time to check.'

'And there's no doubt it was Gabrys?'

'None. Even if the glimpse I got wasn't enough for the court, we have the evidence of his man, Ralph. He's definitely had enough. I think the criminal activities normally went on out of his sight, and he was able to pretend it was nothing to do with him, or even that it wasn't happening. Tonight brought him face to face with the real thing, and he didn't like it.'

'Brave man, to give evidence against Gabrys, after what happened to Madame Trieste.'

'I've had to promise him protection. He wouldn't say a word without that. I just hope the CPS are willing to play ball. Hang on, I think something's happening.'

The two men raised their pace in order to join Rick three houses down the road. The moon was still high, notwithstanding the encroaching dawn, but the fronts of the houses were in shadow. One had a light on, but the hefty bang on the door by the senior constable in the team had produced no immediate response. A voice spoke up from the back door of the adjacent bungalow.

'They're an elderly couple,' said a middle-aged man in pyjamas and dressing gown. 'They may not've heard you, or they might be too nervous to answer. Would you like me to come round and give them a shout? They might find a familiar voice reassuring.' He made to step over the low fence between the two properties.

'No, stay where you are,' said Rick sharply. The man paused, one leg over the fence, the other still in his garden. 'Don't move,' said Rick, and the man twitched uncomfortably.

'Back up to me,' said Rick to his two men. 'I don't like the look of this.'

The two constables at the door looked over their shoulders at Rick, then turned to move back down the short garden path to the gate on to the road. As they did, there was the flat crack of a gunshot, accompanied by the crash of breaking window glass. The man straddling the fence fell into his flower bed and emerged on his hands and knees. The two policemen by the door ducked involuntarily, then accelerated along the path and through the gate as though engineered by Ferrari. They joined Greg, Jim and Rick behind the hedge.

'Let's get behind the car,' said Greg, viewing the straggly hedge and its lack of bullet-stopping ability with a marked lack of enthusiasm. They crouched in the lee of the vehicle, its cover barely sufficient for five, Rick already issuing orders over the radio.

'Well, that's one thing,' he said. 'At least there's no doubt where he is. Anybody done the hostage negotiation course recently?'

33

Siege

'You haven't!' Words failed Gabrys and turning away from the couple he slammed the gun down on a small occasional table, causing irreparable damage to a cluster of china dogs. The woman yelped and Gabrys turned back in a rage, face purple, eyes popping. He shouted a flood of Lithuanian and shook the gun at them again. The two cowered into the chair and Gabrys took a deep breath. He had to get control of himself. All was not yet lost. Perhaps he could get out the back and escape through the gardens. There must be cars somewhere along this road.

He waved the gun at them again. 'You stay. Don't move,' he snarled. And with one eye on his prisoners, he glanced quickly through the door to the kitchen behind. All looked dark in the tatty garden, and he took another breath as he moved toward the back door. Then the air whistled out of him, and he stepped back into the sitting room, leaving the door ajar. He'd seen stealthy movement in the moonlit garden, under the shadows of the tall hedge. There was no way out by that route. Keeping an eye on his prisoners he went to the front window and peered cautiously round the curtain, then reversed quickly. A couple of policemen were approaching the door. As he watched, another man, a neighbour by the look of his pyjamas and dressing gown, appeared at the fence and appeared to speak to the police. Strain as he might, Gabrys couldn't make out what was said.

At that moment, a small sound alerted him to movement in the room behind him, and turning he saw the man reaching for a telephone on the table nearby. He snarled a 'No!' at the man, took the safety catch off his gun and out of the corner of his eye saw through the window what he thought was an attempt to force the door. Without clear volition, the gun in his hand went off and a bullet shattered the glass in front of him. As the echoes faded, the policemen disappeared, and the woman screamed again.

Silence fell over the room, except for the whimpering behind him.

'Shut up,' he commanded, took another look out of the window then turned back into the room. It seemed unlikely they'd rush him just yet. He had two hostages. They'd want to negotiate. He looked round and pulled the other armchair until he could see the door, the window and his two hostages without turning his head.

'May as well get comfortable,' he said. 'We're going to be here a while. You,' he pointed the gun at the woman. 'Your name?'

'Mary,' she said, and closed her mouth tight.

'If you're sick, Mary,' he said, 'you'll clear it up.' She shook her head and he turned his attention to her husband still squashed under her not inconsiderable weight.

'Your name?' he asked.

'Clive,' he replied.

'Okay, Mary, you go make me coffee. Bring me something to eat. And remember, if you make a sound or leave the house, I shoot your husband in the knee. Very painful and he never walk again. Don't forget. Go.'

***

Rick signed off his radio and looked at Greg.

'You heard all that?' he said. 'Margaret wants you to keep out of the way. No offence, but she thinks you'll antagonise him still further and we need a more neutral negotiator. She has someone in mind. In the meantime, I'm still in overall control. Any thoughts?'

'On a practical point, I assume you'll be evacuating immediate neighbours,' said Greg. 'You'll need somewhere to send them. There's a community hall in the next village, Fleggburgh, and a school, but I think you might be best to contact the village pub – The Kings Arms. The chef-owner lives on the premises. I'm sure he'll be glad to help. I have his number. Hopefully this'll be over quick enough you won't need an ops room as well, but, if you do, that still leaves the village hall.

'Incidentally, I'm not surprised by Margaret's decision. I'd already concluded that if he's mad enough to come after me for revenge, I'm not exactly a good choice to talk him out of the mess he's in. Do we know how many hostages he's got?'

'Seems likely it's two. Their neighbour says it's an elderly couple – Mary and Clive Westerby. He also says they don't have a car, so he's going nowhere anytime soon.'

'Then that's obviously going to be his main demand,' said Jim. He was interrupted by the arrival of a black BMW X5 at the roadblock, followed closely by another car. 'I thought the road was blocked back at the turning to Stokesby,' he added.

'It's okay. That's one of ours,' replied Rick. 'It's the armed-response team.' He pulled out the radio again. 'Approach with caution,' he instructed. 'He's already fired into the road once.'

From their vantage point behind the car, Greg and Jim saw four figures deploy from the BMW and move silently behind the houses. Two more from the other car, heavy with body armour and helmets, came down the road, pausing just out of line of sight of the target bungalow. The radio crackled again.

'I need you out of there,' said the firearms team commander. 'Wait on my command.' There was a silence, then he shouted, 'Okay, I have men covering. To me, fast as you like. Go.'

Led by the two constables, the five left the car's cover and ran down the road. There was no response from the dark bungalow behind the shabby fence.

'Are the neighbours clear?' asked the man in body armour bearing 'Inspector' insignia.

'Yes,' replied Rick. 'My lads have cleared the two houses to either side of the target property and are checking the remaining houses down the road, working away from the incident.'

'What's he armed with?'

'We don't know for sure,' said Rick.

'I saw a handgun, but we don't know what else he's got,' Greg added.

'Negotiator on the way?'

'Yes. What specialists do you have with you?' asked Rick.

'Two rifle officers and two specialist firearms officers besides me. Okay, my perimeter should be in place now. The light's improving all the time, so we can pick the best spot for the sniper team soonest. Then we wait for the negotiator.'

'On that, I've got a suggestion,' said Greg. 'Gabrys's home isn't far from here and I'd expect his wife to be there. I think we should go and have a word with her. She might be able to help talk him out.'

Rick thought for a moment. 'Worth a try,' he said. 'You and Jim okay to go and have a chat with her? I'll mention it to the negotiator when he gets here.'

Jim nodded. 'No problem.'

In his car, Jim turned the heating up full as they headed for Greater Ormesby and Horses Mill House. 'Do you think she'll be any help?' he asked.

'Not sure, but worth a try. I think she might be willing, but she may not be very effective. I don't get the impression Gabrys listens to her very much. And he wasn't exactly comforting when they were told about their son's death. But if we don't ask, we won't find out.'

Jim slowed at the turning to the house in case the drive was blocked, but the entrance gates were still lying on the grass verge where the police had left them. As they negotiated the broad sweep of the drive and parked by the main entrance they were surprised to see lights on in ground-floor rooms.

'What time is it now?' asked Greg, and looking at his watch was surprised to see it was already six-thirty. 'They're up early,' he commented as they got out of the car. The early morning air was still and there was an elusive scent of something sweet from the garden as they approached the front door. Jim had his hand raised to knock, when the door swung open. A young woman he didn't recognise was standing in the doorway, a mug of something steaming in one hand.

'Yes?' she asked. Jim and Greg both held out their warrant cards.

'We're police officers,' said Greg. 'DCI Geldard and DI Henning. We'd like to see Mrs Gabrys.'

'She's not up yet,' said the girl. 'Can you come back later?'

'I'm afraid not,' said Greg. 'I'm sorry to disturb her so early, but it's important. May we come in?'

The girl stood back from the door and gestured them toward the sitting room they remembered from their last visit. 'You can wait in there,' she said. 'I'll see if she's awake.'

'And you are?' asked Greg as she turned to leave the room.

'Her daughter,' she replied.

Greg and Jim looked at each other as they sat down in a couple of upright chairs.

'Interesting,' remarked Jim, but didn't have time to say more before the girl returned. They scrutinised her with renewed interest. Her long, light brown hair was pinned up carelessly on the back of her head. Her eyes were light too and appeared to be assessing them with calm intelligence.

She hesitated by the door, then said, 'She'll be a while getting dressed. Would you like a coffee while you wait?'

'Yes, please,' said Greg. 'One black, one white, please.'

She came back after a few moments with three mugs and a plate of biscuits on a tray, putting it down on a table near the two officers.

'Help yourselves. Oh, sorry I forgot the sugar.'

She turned to go again, but Greg said, 'It's okay, neither of us take sugar,' and she sat down in the corner of a large sofa with her mug in her hand. They watched her silently for a moment, taking in the slim figure casually dressed in jeans and sweater with slippers on her feet.

'What do you want with my mother?' she asked, just as Greg began his question. 'Are you living here, Miss Gabrys?'

'Helen,' she said. 'Call me Helen. It's not what I was christened, but it's the English version and what I go by. No, I don't live here any more. I'm at uni in York, but I came back when I heard about my brother.' She sipped her coffee again. 'You haven't answered my question,' she observed.

'First, can I give you our condolences on the death of your brother,' said Greg.

She interrupted. 'You can skip that bit. I don't imagine you're at all sorry about the death of that mad bastard, and nor am I. I think the only person who is, is probably my mother. Which is why I'm worried about her.' Greg looked into the clear pale eyes and decided to come to the point.

'Your father is currently holed up with two hostages in a cottage not far from here,' he said bluntly. 'He's armed and dangerous. We want to ask your mother if she could come with us and help persuade him to come out peacefully.'

There was a long pause. Helen put her coffee mug down on the tray and picked up a biscuit. Greg noticed that she wasn't quite as calm as she was pretending. The fingers holding the biscuit had white knuckles.

'Won't work,' she said, and took a bite of chocolate Hobnob. She chewed and swallowed, then went on. 'My father stopped listening to my mother at least twenty years ago, if he ever did. And she'll have hysterics at the thought. It'd better be me.' Greg was startled.

'You're offering to help, Ms Gabrys ... I mean, Helen?' he asked.

'I'm offering. I don't know how effective I'll be either, but I'm your best bet. Where is he?'

'Billockby,' replied Greg.

'Then I'll just tell my mother where I'm going and grab a coat, and I'll be with you. You can tell me what's been happening on the way.'

The sound of loud voices and weeping from the floor above fulfilled Helen's assessment of her mother's likely reaction. After a short delay, there was a clatter of footsteps on the stairs and Helen reappeared, pulling on a long, padded coat.

'I've left her with the maid,' she said. 'Okay. I'm all yours.'

Greg opened a rear door, then got in beside her for the short drive to Billockby. Jim glanced round to check seat belts were on before he drove off.

'What are you reading at York?' asked Greg. She glanced up, a cheeky smile overlaying her general air of worry.

'Law', she replied. Greg smiled back.

'You're very different from your brother,' he observed, and the smile vanished.

'Yes. He was definitely a one-off,' she said. 'Okay, what's happening now?'

Greg decided to be blunt. 'Your father raided my home, fired off some shots then ran for it. He's currently holed up in Billockby with two elderly hostages. We need to talk him out with no one else getting hurt. How much influence do you have?'

She shifted in her seat then admitted, 'Not much, as a daughter that is. He never had as much time for me as he did for the son and heir. Even though said heir was mad as a box of frogs. But as lawyer, there I might be able to help. He can be persuaded by logic, provided he's not in a rage. Why did he raid your home?'

'Revenge?' said Greg. 'Don't know for sure, but I think he blames Norfolk Police generally for the death of your brother, and as the person who raided his house and knocked his gates off, I guess I make a good scapegoat.'

'Revenge,' said Helen thoughtfully. 'Never a good idea.'

By the time they pulled up again at the roadblock, a familiar figure was getting out of a battered four-by-four.

'Neil,' said Greg in recognition. 'It's Neil Simpson.'

'Neil?' asked Jim.

'The psychologist I saw after the bombings at the Science Park. He talks a lot of sense. He must be the negotiator. Let's introduce Helen, then I'll get out of the way as Margaret wanted.'

Neil was being brought up to date by Rick as they joined the group. 'We have the landline number from their neighbour,' he was saying, 'so when you're ready we can give them a ring and find out what he wants.'

'This is his daughter, Helen,' introduced Greg. 'She's very kindly volunteered her help.' Neil made a swift assessment, just as Helen did of him. Both seemed to like what they saw and smiles blossomed both on Helen's thin face and behind Neil's bushy beard.

'Okay,' said Neil. 'Let's take time for a quick chat. I'll outline my approach and you can tell me what you think might work. Then we'll take it from there.'

Greg waved a goodbye and got back into Jim's car. 'Are you okay to run me to Wymondham, or should I ask Rick for a driver?' he asked. 'I need to catch up with the boss and pick up a pool car while mine's *hors de combat*.'

'No problem,' said Jim, and got behind the wheel again. 'I've stuff I need to do in the office.'

34

Negotiations

Margaret took one look at Greg and leaned out of her office door. 'Coffee,' she ordered, and her PA leaped to her feet and seized a large cafetière. 'You look terrible,' she said, turning to Greg. 'When did you last sleep?' Greg sat down and had to think about it.

'Not sure,' he mumbled. 'Night before last?'

'Then as soon as we've finished this conversation, you're going home,' she said. 'In fact, I'm not sure we should even have this conversation until you've had some sleep.'

'I'm here now,' said Greg, nodding his thanks as the PA returned, placing a full cafetière and a mug in front of him. 'What's come up?' Margaret sat down.

'Another Fellowes-related problem,' she said, and hesitated. Greg poured the coffee and sipped.

'Another?' he asked.

'Look, I think this is best left until tomorrow,' said Margaret. 'You've had a sleepless night, been shot at, had your home invaded, chased a homicidal maniac across the marshes and—'

'And now I'm worrying about Fellowes again, so better deal with it, then I can go home in peace. Because I think you're right, I'm not in a good state to face a whole new day. Some sleep and I'll be right as rain.'

'Okay. He's made another complaint. Specifically, he alleges that you and Sergeant Mathews are in an inappropriate relationship, in that not only are you cohabiting but that she is your junior officer and is receiving unfair benefits, career-wise, from the relationship. He also manages a sideswipe about you being a married man, which is plainly out of date, so we can ignore that. But I'm sorry to say you *will* have to answer to the other two elements of his case.' Greg sighed and drank the rest of his coffee.

'You know I transferred the line-management relationship to Jim Henning specifically to avoid an accusation of this kind. You also know that any favourable treatment of Chris is earned by her sheer unadulterated competence, as compared with Fellowes's general lack of any sense, intelligence or integrity. You've commended her yourself, ma'am.'

'I know, I know,' said Margaret, holding up her hands. 'Unfortunately, the accusation, once made, has to be answered.'

'Then, as you said in the first place, I'll answer it tomorrow, when I've had some sleep.'

'One other thing,' said Margaret. 'The date for the two inquests has been brought forward. It's next week.'

***

At Billockby, in the bright sunshine of the new day, the rifle team had selected their lookout. The front bedroom of the house opposite was far enough back from the road to afford a clear line of sight over the perimeter hedge. They were now well placed to keep watch on both the front door and living room windows opposite.

In the road, rendered even more rotund by body armour than nature had provided, Neil made his first call. The phone rang unanswered for some minutes then reverted to answerphone. Neil rang off, then rang again. He repeated the process some four or five times, until eventually it was answered by a person.

'Who are you?' growled the voice.

'My name's Neil,' said Neil. 'I'm here to talk.'

'I don't need to talk,' replied Gabrys. 'I have two hostages. Get me a car, or I shoot one.'

'Would you like some hot food?' asked Neil. 'I gather Mr and Mrs Westerby were expecting a food delivery today, and clearly that's not going to happen. I could get you some pizza. Or fish and chips?'

'So you can dope it?' sneered Gabrys. 'I'm not a fool. Get me a car or I shoot the woman. She tells me she can't drive, so she's just a waste of space. She won't be missed.'

'I'll order some pizza anyway,' replied Neil. 'It's your choice whether you eat it. It won't be drugged. Oh, and I have someone who wants to talk to you.' He held the phone out to Helen, but Gabrys had rung off. Helen looked at him, dismayed.

'He's gone,' she said.

'Don't worry. These are just the opening manoeuvres,' said Neil with more confidence than he felt. 'Do you think he's capable of what he threatens?'

'Yes.' Helen had no doubts. 'Don't push him too far.'

Reporting back to Rick, the latter was in no doubt. 'He doesn't get a car,' he said, 'and we can't risk him killing hostages. If we think he's a serious risk, then the sniper team take him down. Or we go in with stun grenades. Or both. Make his daughter understand that he has no option other than to come out. But don't spell out the details, obviously.'

'Got it,' said Neil. 'But don't rush things. We have some time yet.'

During the next phone call that changed. 'You are wasting time. You have one hour,' Gabrys said as Neil handed over the phone to Helen.

'Father,' she said, 'it's me. Helen.' There followed a torrent of what sounded like angry Lithuanian, and Helen replied, 'I have to stay in English or they won't let me talk to you. You have to come out, Father. You won't get away. Come out in peace and we can get the lawyers to free you. There will be a legal solution. But if you shoot someone, there's no going back. No way out.' She listened to some more Lithuanian then replied, 'I'm not a traitor. I'm looking out for you. There is a legal way, believe me. I can think of at least three ways, but only if you don't hurt anyone. If you fire, I can't help. Believe me.' More Lithuanian, then she said, 'Of course I can't explain with everyone listening, but if I can think of three ways, your expensive barrister can probably think of more. Trust the law. It's the best way out believe me.

'He's rung off,' she said to Neil. 'But I'm fairly sure he's thinking about it.'

Ten minutes later, and this time Gabrys rang them. 'Less than half an hour now,' he said, and rang off.

Rick looked at Neil. 'Can we afford to wait?' he asked. 'What's your professional judgement?' Neil looked through the car window at Helen pacing up and down outside, the wind blowing strands of her hair across her face.

'It's all going too fast. He's piling on the pressure, and she thinks he's capable of carrying out his threats. So, no, I don't think we can afford to wait,' he said slowly. 'I think he's very unstable.'

'Can you get him over to the window?'

'Doubt it, he's not stupid.'

'Okay, can you get the hostages over to the window, or at least at the front of the house?'

'I'll see what I can do. The pizzas should be here any minute.'

'Okay. In that case, do your best to separate Gabrys and the hostages, at least by a few feet. Leave the rest to us. I'm off to have a word with the firearms team.'

As the pizza delivery van drew up by the roadblock, Helen turned round. 'Let me help deliver them,' she said. 'Let me get nearer and see what a direct appeal will do.'

'I can't let you do that,' said Neil, uncomfortably. 'I'm under orders. And you have no body armour. Sorry, Helen.' He picked up the phone.

'I'm going to leave the pizza delivery on the doorstep,' he said. There was some muttering on the line, and he suggested, 'Get Mrs Westerby to pick them up. She'll still be under your eye won't she?'

The house was still when he approached the front door. No one visible, not even as shadows behind the broken glass of the front window. He placed the boxes on the doorstep in a single pile and took a step back.

'Get back here,' said Rick's voice in his earpiece and he started back down the drive. The sound of the front door opening made him turn his head, and he saw Mrs Westerby emerge onto the step and pick up the boxes.

'No clear shot,' said the sniper, lowering his rifle as he saw Gabrys pushing Mr Westerby in front of him while he watched the pick-up from the window.

'Go! Go!' was the next thing Neil heard, and as he ran for the cars the almighty bang of a stun grenade threw the elderly couple and their captor backward. The Westerbys landed on the floor, Gabrys on the armchair he had so carefully placed near the window. The sniper raised his rifle again and a bright dot appeared on Gabrys's head.

'Am I cleared?' asked the sniper. Then there was another bang and Neil was pushing Helen into the back seat of the nearest car.

'What happened?' she almost screamed.

'I don't know,' he said, suddenly breathless. 'We'll have to wait for Rick Lake.'

35

Survivors

Only the exercise of extreme self-control kept Neil in the car. And only his iron grip on her arm kept Helen with him. It seemed a very long time, but was only a matter of minutes, before they saw more activity by the Westerbys' bungalow and then the emergence of two frail figures wrapped in blankets. They were ushered into the property opposite, and all fell quiet for a moment.

'So they survived,' said Helen at last. 'Does that mean my father didn't?' Neil was unable to answer her, so kept quiet. More time passed, and eventually two more figures emerged from the bungalow.

'That's Rick and the firearms team leader,' said Neil. 'We should have some answers soon.' He tightened the grip on her arm as she showed signs of opening the car door. Just as the two men reached the vehicle, an ambulance on blue lights appeared from the Fleggburgh direction and was allowed past the roadblock. Rick leaned an arm on the car roof, while the other man spoke into his radio, just out of earshot.

'Your father's alive, Miss Gabrys,' he said, and Helen heaved a huge sigh of relief. 'He's been arrested and is being taken to the James Paget Hospital under guard.'

'In the ambulance?' asked Helen. 'Can I go with him?'

'No, the ambulance is for his hostages. The gentleman may be suffering a heart attack and they both need a check-up. A squad car will take your father to the James Paget. He's unharmed except for his hearing. The stun grenade went off close to him, and the intensity of the bang has deafened him, hopefully temporarily.'

'Shouldn't he go in an ambulance?' asked Helen, and Rick raised an eyebrow.

'Hardly appropriate that he share an ambulance with his victims,' he remarked. 'Frankly, he's a very lucky man. He nearly got a bullet through the head!'

'What's he been arrested for?' asked Helen, shifting her ground. 'What exactly is the charge?'

'Breaking and entering, false imprisonment and attempted murder,' replied Rick. 'That's just for the moment. There may be other charges.'

***

Arriving home in a police pool car, barely able to see straight, Greg did, nonetheless, notice that both his and Chris's cars were missing. Clearly someone had been busy. Fumbling in his pocket for his keys, and then with the key in the keyhole, he eventually managed to get the door open. The whole experience reminded him of getting home drunk as a teenager, only without the heady euphoria and the damage to a hedge where he had fallen into it. There was a note on the kitchen table.

Car with BMW Norwich. Got them to tow it away. They say should be fixed within a couple of days, assuming the new radiator and headlight arrive from Germany on time. Mine was just the windscreen and got that fixed here by the call-out crew. Popped into the office. May see you there, otherwise back here this evening. Love C

He said hello to Bobby, twining round his ankles, and stumbled off to bed. He was returned to sudden consciousness by a car door slamming and leaned over to look at the time. 17:30. Okay. Probably time he got up anyway, or he wouldn't sleep this evening and he needed to be fresh tomorrow to prepare for the inquests. And to catch up with what had been happening in Billockby. The car door sounds were replaced by footsteps and then a ring on the doorbell. Feeling distinctly drowsy from his daytime sleep, Greg went over to the window and peered out. The top of the head looked familiar. Opening the window, Greg stuck his head out and hollered, 'Ram! Hi. Give me a moment and I'll be down.'

Ram spent the time admiring the view of the river. At this point on its journey to the sea at Great Yarmouth, it was wide and deceptively slow moving. Lazy eddies showed where underwater obstructions interrupted its smooth glide to salt waters. A quiet plop from the brambled bank opposite marked the descent of an otter into the waters, but city-bred Ram was too slow to see it.

Greg came up behind him. 'Coffee?' he asked. 'Or something stronger? Beer?'

'Coffee, please,' replied Ram. 'I've just come from another chat with Sarah.'

'How's she getting on?'

'Well, I think. She'd like to come back to work. I told her that was a matter for you and Margaret, but that I thought it unlikely until the inquest on Mica Gabrys was over. The main thing is, she's sticking to her line that she acted to defend colleagues from attack. And personally, I think she'll get away with it, on the grounds that her belief Mica was an immediate threat to life was reasonable at the time.'

'Get away with?' queried Greg. 'You mean you don't believe her?'

'I mean I don't know, but the more I talk to her, the more I think there was a strong element of revenge.'

'What do the IOPC think? Which way are they going to come down?'

'I'm pretty certain they're anticipating a conclusion of lawful killing at the inquest, in which case she'll be in the clear and able to return to work. Although whether she should, here in Norfolk? Well as I said at the start, that'll be up to you and Margaret. Now they've brought the inquest date forward. I thought you should know.'

'Yes, thanks.' Greg stirred his coffee thoughtfully. 'Have you heard what happened at Billockby? I was about to ring Rick Lake.'

'Gabrys arrested and shipped off to the James Paget under guard.'

'Shot?' asked Greg almost hopefully.

'Stunned and deafened,' replied Ram.

***

In Wymondham, Chris had just heard about the latest from her bête noir, the DWOS. Her cry of *'What!'* had echoed down the corridors all the way to Margaret's office. The door slam that marked her exit had similarly shaken the Chief Constable's office door until it rattled, then everyone had relaxed.

36

None so deaf

At the James Paget Hospital, Rick Lake and Jim Henning stared at the audiologist with identical expressions of irritation.

'Is he deaf, or isn't he?' asked Rick, speaking for both of them. The audiologist, a young man with a brown beard and floppy hair who, in Jim's estimation, wouldn't have looked out of place in the cast of *Pirates of the Caribbean*, sighed heavily.

'I wish I could give you a definitive answer,' he said. 'Proximity to an exploding stun grenade is well known to cause temporary blindness, temporary deafness and balance disorders. Permanent deafness is also recorded in the literature, but it's much rarer. I've examined Mr Gabrys and I can find no damage, for example to the eardrum, and his responses to some of the testing are equivocal. My guess is that he's fabricating deafness in order to avoid answering your questions. There are some more tests I can run that would help clarify matters.'

'Such as?' asked Jim. 'I mean, are they incontestable?'

'Nothing's that, at least not in a court I believe. But taken together they do give a clear result. Some depend on the capacity of an undamaged ear to generate sound. Others catch the malingerer out by comparing the responses of people who are genuinely profoundly deaf to those of people who are just pretending. It's surprisingly hard to keep up a pretence consistently or convincingly, mainly because most hearing people don't know enough about deafness. I don't have the time, or indeed the equipment here, to carry out the more objective test. But there is one thing I could do.'

'Then what are we waiting for? Let's go for it.'

'Okay,' said the audiologist, rising from his chair. 'Provided Mr Gabrys is willing to cooperate obviously. To be clear, any further, more complex tests would need to await another day, but I can run a Lombard test now.' He went back across the waiting room to where Gabrys, handcuffed to an alert constable, was sitting in the consulting room. After some discussion, the constable unlocked the handcuffs and left the room. As the door closed behind him, Jim saw Gabrys being fitted with headphones and handed a card. Less than fifteen minutes later, the audiologist returned.

'He's faking it,' he said. 'I'm sure of it. I handed him a card with printed instructions and fitted him with headphones. He had to read out the words on the card, and I played some sounds through the headphones. When the sounds got louder, he raised his voice. It's a natural response, but it doesn't happen if the subject is deaf. A profoundly deaf person can't hear the sounds in the headphones.'

'Thank you,' said Rick. 'Jim, we'll take him back to the station and interview him there. If he persists in this nonsense we can commission more tests, but with this information it's worth having another go. Thank you, Doctor.'

Gabrys was sullen and silent when he was taken to the squad car, and remained so all the way back to Great Yarmouth. When he realised he was being taken to an interview room he stopped dead in the doorway and in a harsh, loud voice demanded his solicitor.

'He's on his way,' replied Jim. The demand was repeated, as though he hadn't heard the response, but Jim ignored it and left him with another constable on guard.

Joining Rick, he found him in consultation with said solicitor and Helen Gabrys. 'I've just explained to Ms Gabrys that she can't be present when we interview her father, but that obviously his legal representative can. I've also explained that we have medical evidence that the deafness of which he complains is not real. That he's malingering.'

'You can't know that for sure,' the solicitor blustered.

'We can,' replied Rick. 'We're very sure. Google a "Lombard test" if you doubt me. The best advice you can give your client is that he drops this pretence and cooperates with our investigation. Otherwise, the inferences that will be drawn will do him no favours. I'll leave you to discuss matters with Ms Gabrys and then your client.'

It was almost an hour later when Rick and Jim sat down opposite Constantin Gabrys and his London solicitor. Tape on and running, the police officers having identified themselves and the solicitor likewise, they waited for Gabrys to comply. He sat staring at the table top and refused to engage.

'Mr Gabrys,' said Rick again, 'the charges facing you are serious and this masquerade of deafness has gone far enough. You failed the Lombard test and we have testimony from the specialist concerned that you have not suffered permanent hearing loss from the events of last night.

'You were arrested in the home of Mr and Mrs Westerby, in possession of a handgun, and according to them had threatened to kill or injure them both. What do you have to say about that?'

Silence.

'Prior to that, you called at the home of DCI Geldard, attempted to slaughter his cat, fired a bullet at his car, a second one at the car of a work colleague, then left on foot. Where did you obtain the gun and ammunition from? How do you explain your presence at this place?'

The silence continued until interrupted by the solicitor. 'My client is now profoundly deaf, thanks to the actions of the police,' he said. 'This questioning is pointless.'

'Possibly, but not for the reason you put forward,' said Rick, keeping a sharp eye on Gabrys. 'Let's cut to the chase, shall we? We found large quantities of cash, some cocaine and heroin concealed behind the bookcases of Mr Gabrys's Ormesby home. We found his DNA on the packages of cash and under the claws of DCI Geldard's cat. We have three witnesses who place him at the home of DCI Geldard the night before last, and multiple witnesses to his taking Mr and Mrs Westerby hostage at their home in Billockby that same night. The plain fact is, we don't need a confession or a statement from your client. We've enough evidence to land him in prison for the rest of his natural life, and that's before we start on his involvement with Clean Boats Inc, the illegal imprisonment of DI Laurence, the death and torture of Madame Trieste and the trafficking of immigrants to work as slaves in his cannabis grow-houses, nail bars and so on.'

'The drugs belonged to his son, for personal use only,' started the solicitor, but was interrupted by a low growl from his client.

'You have nothing. You *will* have nothing. Nothing, do you hear me?' The voice was rising from a growl to a roar. 'No one will give evidence. What do you have? I go to talk with the man who defends my son's murderer. The man who plots against me. His cat attacks me, I flee, and you accuse me? You have nothing. You are nothing. You will never hold me.'

Rick waited calmly for the tirade to end. When Gabrys eventually paused, his chest heaving, spittle on the table in front of him, only then did Rick respond.

'Constantin Gabrys, I'm arresting you for the crimes of the possession and concealment of the proceeds of crime, possession of controlled substances, breaking and entering, the attempted murder of DCI Geldard, the false imprisonment of and assault on Mr and Mrs Westerby, occasioning grievous bodily harm. You do not have to say anything, but it may harm your defence if you do not mention when questioned something which you later rely on in court. Anything you do say may be given in evidence.

'Oh, and I may yet add other charges to the list. Take him to the custody sergeant for processing,' he said to the constable in the corner, and left the room.

Jim caught up with him back in his office. 'We need to do something about witnesses,' he said. 'That was a straightforward threat to witnesses. If we don't protect witnesses from intimidation, if they change their evidence or refuse to testify, it weakens our case. And from past experience with this chap, once one falls over, they all do.'

'Point taken,' said Rick. 'Make a list. Prioritise who needs protection and how we give it. I'll talk to Margaret and the CPS.'

37

Inquests part 2

Greg's arrival at the Norwich Coroner's Court was almost identical to his last visit, save that the pool car was a lot easier to fit into the one remaining space. He was even greeted by the same Court Service volunteer.

'They're running a bit late on the preceding inquest,' she informed him. 'Coffee?'

'No thanks,' he said hastily, just like last time and for the same reason. 'Do you know how far they've got?'

'Closing stages I think,' she said. 'All the witness evidence that was going to be read into the record has been. When I was last in the courtroom, they were about to hear from DI Laurence.'

'I'll sit in then,' said Greg, and picking up his notes he crept into the public seating, bowing to the bench as normal. On this occasion there was a reporter at the media desk, and at least another taking notes from the public gallery. Greg sat down and looked up at the TV screen on the wall.

The screen was divided into four, with another small image at bottom left, showing the coroner on the bench.

Greg recognised the pathologist Dr Paisley at top left, Sarah Laurence top right, two faces at bottom left whom he recognised from the pre-inquest hearing to be Madame Trieste's sister Maria and her interpreter, while the final quarter screen was occupied by Helen Gabrys and what he assumed to be a Gabrys family solicitor. It seemed Sarah had given her evidence and was now responding to questions.

As I stated at the start,' said the coroner, Roger Goodwin. 'Maria Laurentiu, sister of the deceased, has submitted some questions, which I will be asking on her behalf.

'DI Laurence, you have stated that when you arrived at the property, Adelina Laurentiu, or Madame Trieste as you knew her, was already dead. You need not rehearse the precise circumstances in which you found her,' he added hastily. 'That evidence has already been read into the record.'

'That is correct,' replied Sarah.

'I am directed to ask whether anyone else was present at the property.'

'Yes,' said Sarah. 'A young man subsequently identified as Mica Gabrys, and an older man.'

'What happened when you arrived?'

'The younger man struck me on the head with a blunt instrument and while I was dazed, the older man seized me by the upper arms and pushed my head down on the kitchen table.'

'Could you see Adelina Laurentiu from your position on the kitchen table?'

'I could.'

'Are you confident she was dead at this point?'

'I believe so. She made no movement nor sound and although severely wounded, her wounds were not bleeding actively. I therefore concluded that she was already dead.'

There was a sound from the TV screen, and the interpreter said, 'May Maria ask further questions?' The coroner looked up at the camera focussed on him.

'Provided she bears in mind what I have already explained about the purposes of an inquest, she may put further questions,' he said.

There was some muttering on-screen, and the interpreter said, 'She wishes to know what happened next.'

The coroner intervened. 'That is not a question material to this inquest, as Adelina Laurentiu was already dead,' he said, 'although I appreciate it may be relevant to further legal proceedings in other courts.'

'Then one other question,' said the interpreter. 'Did Mica Gabrys kill her sister?'

There was a lot of scribbling from the reporters present and the coroner was quick to intervene again.

'That is also not an appropriate question for this inquest, as we do not and are explicitly forbidden from apportioning blame. If there are no further questions, we will move on. Thank you for your evidence, DI Laurence.'

'The final witness to be heard is the pathologist, Dr Paisley, who has also submitted a statement, in which she lists the causes of Adelina Laurentiu's death as: 1a, cardiac arrest; 1b, catastrophic blood loss; 1c, multiple knife wounds, in particular one which punctured the carotid artery.

'Dr Paisley, for the clear understanding of everyone not medically qualified, am I correct in interpreting this as meaning that the ultimate cause of death was cardiac arrest, which was caused by catastrophic blood loss, which itself was caused by multiple stab wounds?'

'That is correct,' said Dr Paisley.

'Thank you. I believe the family may have further questions. Ms Laurentiu, the same restrictions apply as I explained earlier.' The interpreter spoke up again.

'Were Adelina's eyes removed before or after she died?' Dr Paisley opened her mouth, then thought the better of it and waited for the coroner.

'You have, I believe, seen a copy of the post-mortem report,' he said gently. 'That will answer your question. But the question itself is not material to this inquest, as it does not pertain to the cause of death. Dr Paisley, you need not answer that question at this time.'

There was a pause as the interpreter struggled to translate 'pertain to the cause of death'. Ms Laurentiu looked mutinous but remained silent.

'If there are no more questions, I will adjourn for thirty minutes to consider my conclusion.'

'All rise,' said the usher, and the coroner left the room.

The TV screens froze then went blank and Greg left the courtroom for the reception area. As he helped himself to a bottle of water from the fridge, there was a rattle from the automatic door as Ram came in from the car park.

'You haven't missed much,' said Greg. 'The coroner's just considering his conclusion. They're running a bit late.'

'So I gathered. Are the jury here for the next inquest?'

'No idea. I imagine so, as it was due to start an hour or so ago. Who's attending from the family, do you know?'

'The sister, Helen Gabrys and their lawyer are attending in person and Constantin Gabrys on a live link from Norwich prison.'

'Helen's attending in person? She was on a link just now.'

'Yes, I believe the link was from a solicitor's office in the city, so they're only a few minutes away. I expect she'll arrive any minute.'

'Not the mother?'

'No. I don't think any of the witnesses are attending in person either. It was agreed that Mica's GP's evidence would be read into the record, and same for most of the police evidence, especially as the body-worn-camera footage has been made available.'

'Yes, I saw it. It doesn't help much either way, does it?'

They were interrupted by the door swinging open again to admit Helen Gabrys and the lawyer. She came over to shake hands with Greg.

'This is Mr Johnson, our solicitor,' she said.

Greg introduced Ram and added, 'I saw you on-screen just now.'

'Yes. I thought we should at least keep an eye on proceedings.' She turned to help herself to a cup of tea, just as the usher returned.

'We'll be reconvening shortly,' she said, and they all returned to Courtroom 2. Helen and Mr Browne took seats in front of the coroner's desk. This time the only faces on the TV screen were those of Maria Laurentiu and her interpreter.

'All rise,' said the usher, and they stood as the coroner returned to his seat behind the glass screen. He coughed and looked round the room.

'As I said at the start of this inquest, we are here for a very specific purpose and to answer four specific questions as set out in the Act. Our purpose is to identify the medical cause of death, and the four questions set by law are: who died, where, when, and how did they come by their death. I may not express opinions on other matters and nothing I say may imply criminal liability. And I must make a determination or conclusion.

'On the balance of probability and in the light of the evidence heard over the last two and a half days, I find that Adelina Laurentiu, also known as Madame Trieste, a Romanian citizen, resident at the time in Norwich, on 23rd October 2019 died at the nail and beauty salon Nails Galore. The causes of death were: 1a, cardiac arrest; 1b, catastrophic blood loss; 1c, multiple knife wounds, in particular one which punctured the carotid artery.

'My conclusion is that this was an unlawful killing.'

There was a long pause. No one commented.

'I would like to repeat my condolences to the family and friends of Adelina Laurentiu for their sad loss in these tragic and traumatic circumstances.'

Another pause, and then, 'All rise,' said the usher again, as the coroner left the room.

Back in the reception area the different groups, by common consent, divided themselves among the separate circles of chairs.

'Are we going to have to wait long for the next round?' wondered Greg aloud.

'Not long,' replied an usher passing behind him. 'As the next is being heard by the assistant coroner, it'll start in Court 1 in twenty minutes.'

38

Witness protection

Back in Wymondham, Jim had got his head together with Chris over the issue of witnesses.

'With you in a moment,' she'd shouted, and dashed off. Now she was back.

'Close the door, Chris,' he said as she came in encumbered by a teetering pile of laptop, charger cable, files, coffee and some paper bags that looked encouragingly greasy, and added, 'You didn't!' as she placed the pile on the spare desk and the paper bags slid off. He reached out hurriedly to rescue them from hitting the floor.

'I did,' she replied as the alluring aroma of bacon rose from the bags. 'I didn't think you'd have eaten, and we can't keep running on empty.' Jim was already tearing a bag open.

'Egg as well,' he said, ecstatic. 'Messy but delicious.' Chris was temporarily unable to respond, her mouth being occupied by a huge bite of bacon and egg butty. The following few moments were bereft of conversation, albeit not exactly silent.

'That was marvellous,' said Jim at last, screwing up the eggy paper and tossing it, inaccurately, at the bin. 'Okay. To work. What've we got?'

'A long list,' said Chris. 'I think we can eliminate some, but let's start wide and go narrow.'

'My thoughts precisely,' replied Jim. 'You start.'

'Okay. Well I've got on my list, roughly in date order, the Methodist minister and his wife who got involved with Dragan Bakalov in the aftermath of the modern slavery case; Cara, the girl who was at Clean Boats with Sarah; Nathan Standish and his father – mainly his father; Emily Atkinson, the other of the two teenagers who gave us evidence at the school; Peter or Patrick Ashfield/Shinfield/Ashton, whatever he's calling himself, the chap who groomed Emily and didn't have much time for Mica; Ralph Menton, Gabrys's butler chappie; and the Westerbys.

'Yes, all worth considering,' said Jim, looking at his notes. 'The only ones you've missed, by my reckoning, are Sarah, Greg and yourself.'

'Well, you can scratch us two off for a start.' Chris's response was predictably robust. 'Goes with the territory, doesn't it? And we can look out for each other.'

'So long as you *do* both take precautions. In fact, I'm going to put you top of my "take precautions" list,' said Jim. 'Looking at the others, I think we can just keep a watching brief as far as the Thetford minister is concerned. But if we have a "keep an eye on" list, Nathan and Emily and their families are top of that. I'll come back to Standish senior. Likewise, the Westerbys.'

'In the case of the latter, there's not a lot they can add that police witnesses can't,' agreed Chris. 'Wouldn't have thought he'd waste a lot of effort on them.'

'Which leaves us with the top priorities being Mr Standish senior, Peter/Patrick and Ralph Menton. And they're all in custody.'

'I think there's more evidence to be got from the last two,' said Chris. 'In fact, I'm sure of it. But we won't get it unless they feel safe, now and in the future.'

'I agree. They're the three top priorities for witness protection. I'll talk to Margaret.'

'And in the meantime, I'll have a word with uniform about keeping an eye on the others?'

'Yes, Chris, do that. Thanks.'

A quick skip through the corridors, and Jim was lucky to catch Margaret just before she left for a meeting. She heard him through in silence as she pulled her jacket on.

'You really think there's potential in those two, Patrick Ashton and Ralph Menton? Yes, Sally, what is it?' she asked as her PA burst in through the door.

'Message from the Chief Constable's office to say he's in a hurry and can you get there asap.'

'Tell them I'm on my way,' replied Margaret, snatching up her bag. 'Jim, you have my authority to contact witness protection for those two. It doesn't sound as though Standish has much he can add to the evidence collected from his office, so no point extending it to him, although we'll need to be careful which prison he ends up in. Get on, Sally,' she added. 'Or we'll have him charging down the corridor like a mad rhino.'

The PA shot back to her desk and picked up her phone as Margaret left at a trot. Jim returned to his office to look up the contact details for the witness protection team. This was a new one for him.

When Chris came back into his office, he was on the phone. 'I'm speaking to the Protected Persons Service. They've agreed that, from the descriptions I've given, our two chaps are probably eligible,' he said quickly to Chris. 'Okay, got it,' he said into the phone, and rang off. 'It's down to us now. We need to talk to those two and spell out the implications. If we think either or both might want to take up the offer, I get back to Protected Persons.'

'Ralph's still here, awaiting transfer,' said Chris. 'Let's talk to him first then whip over to the prison to talk to Peter.'

'Okay. But I think we'll avoid using names from here on. Just in case. We'll refer to them as, oh I don't know, Mutt and Jeff? Have you spoken to Greg?'

'I texted him at the Coroner's Court. He agrees.'

'Let's go see Mutt.'

***

Hustled into the interview room by a constable Chris didn't recognise, the ex-butler looked shrunken and nervous. He was already developing the prison pallor of someone deprived of fresh air, or he was just plain terrified.

'That'll be all, thanks,' Chris said to the constable, 'we can take it from here. Sit,' she said to Ralph, and pulled out a chair from the table. He sat and fiddled with his sweatshirt cuffs while Jim shuffled his paperwork, largely for effect. Chris sat down next to Jim and glanced at the recording equipment to make sure it was off.

'I'm going to be blunt,' said Jim. 'While you may not initially have been directly involved in Constantin Gabrys's criminal activities, it's very hard to believe you didn't know what was going on. And that all changed this week. At the very least you can be charged with aiding and abetting and, as I'm sure your defence solicitor has pointed out, if convicted the sentence is the same as for the principal offender.'

'Why isn't my solicitor here now?' muttered Ralph.

'Because I want to make you an offer, and the fewer people know about it, the better.' The pale man opposite stopped picking at his clothes and looked up. 'Have you heard of witness protection?' asked Jim.

'Yes,' said Ralph, an expression of hope crossing his face.

'That's what's on the table,' said Jim. 'If you stand up in court and bear witness against Constantin Gabrys, we can arrange for you to disappear. You'll get a new identity and a new location: a new start, free of associations with organised crime.'

'But there's something you need to understand,' added Chris. 'This is not an easy option. You must move away from everything and everyone you know. You can't share your new identity or location with anyone, not by phone, email and especially not on social media. If close family go with you, then the same applies to them. It's not easy. And it's not a free pass to a life of luxury. If you live in a council flat now, then that's what you get in your new life. And if you work in a call centre now, the same applies. The offer is like for like, not a life of luxury at government expense.' There was a pause.

'Do you want to think about it?' asked Jim.

'How would it work for me?' asked Ralph. 'Butler jobs are few and the world is small.'

'True, that's a complication,' admitted Jim. 'I imagine the team would look for something comparable in the service sector.'

Ralph tapped his fingers on the desk, whistling under his breath. 'I have no close family,' he said. 'No wife, no children. I haven't seen my sister in a while. That wouldn't be a problem.' Jim and Chris looked at each other.

'So, you're interested?' she asked.

'I'm interested, but how sure are you, you can protect me? Gabrys has a long reach and his revenge would be terrible.' If possible, he turned even more ashen at the thought.

'The system is well-practised and efficient,' promised Jim. 'It's run by a specialist team independent of us. The next step, after we've taken a new statement, would be to refer you to the team. They'd take you to a safe place rather than you going into custody, and after the trial you'd be given your new identity, new job and new home.'

There was more tapping and whistling. 'And you don't charge me with any of the offences you've been hanging over me? I go free? I don't have to go to prison?'

'That's the offer,' said Jim, 'provided, of course, that you stick to your side of the bargain, undertake to keep clear of crime and provide us with evidence. And while you're thinking about that, you might like to bear in mind that the better the evidence against him, the longer he'll be sent down for.' Ralph seemed to make his mind up.

'When do you want to take my new statement?' he asked.

'Now,' said Chris, turning the recorder on.

'The first thing I want to say,' said Ralph, barely giving them chance to complete the official warning and note who was present, 'is that I heard Mr Gabrys ring his son and tell him to go to Nails Galore and make an example of Madame Trieste.'

There was a pregnant silence. Then Chris asked, 'In English? I'm surprised the conversation wasn't in Lithuanian.'

'It was in Lithuanian. But then he got on the phone again, and this time he spoke in English. He said, "the bitch is sorted. It won't happen again".'

'When was this?'

'The morning she died.'

'Did Gabrys know you'd overheard?'

'I don't know. He came out of his study and saw me in the hall. He asked me if I didn't have something to do, and I said yes, I had just cleared out the wood burning stove. I had a bucket of ashes in my hand. He just grunted and I carried on with my day.'

'Exactly where were you when you heard this conversation?'

'On my knees by the log burner. The door to the study was open the whole time.'

Jim checked back in his notes. 'And what about the drugs?' he asked.

'I know very little about anything outside Horses Mill House. I knew there was something dodgy in the hidden space by the library, but I took care not to know too much. I'm guilty of turning a blind eye, yes,' he said. 'But not much more.'

Half an hour later, statement signed and 'Mutt' safely back in a cell awaiting collection by the Protected Persons Service, Jim and Chris were on their way to Bure prison to see 'Jeff'.

'Remind me, why Bure instead of Norwich?' said Chris.

'Because Gabrys's long-term enforcer, Dragan Bakalov, is in Norwich. And as someone accused of a sexual offence, Bure prison seemed a good alternative.'

Navigating the narrow country lanes near Coltishall took concentration and a satnav. Even then, the first attempt landed them in the light industrial units that had been set up in the old RAF base.

'Fencing seems a bit inadequate,' remarked Chris, just as Jim cursed the satnav, and returned to the main road.

On the second attempt they succeeded in negotiating some rather more stringent security to enter HMP Bure, home to most of the convicted male sex offenders of East Anglia.

'I'd have thought you'd been here before,' remarked Chris. 'In a professional capacity, obviously.'

'I have, but the road closures confused me,' said Jim, choosing to ignore the implied aspersions cast on his morality. 'Anyway, we're here now. Let's see what Jeff has to tell us.'

It took some negotiating to achieve a suitably confidential space for the interview. Once that was done, Jeff was brought in and he sat down rather sulkily.

'Why am I here?' he asked. 'Where's my brief? I'm not saying anything without him present.'

'We have an offer to make,' said Jim as he had to Mutt. 'Hear me out, then decide how you want to proceed. You know perfectly well that with Emily's evidence you are going to be convicted of grooming, as well as possession and supply of Class A drugs. No, hear me out,' he said, holding up a hand to ward off the immediate reaction from the young man opposite. 'The question is, do you want to go to prison for years, then come out and continue the life you've been leading, or do you want a fresh start? You're an intelligent man, more intelligent than some of these lowlifes you've been consorting with. You're a good-looking lad too and, perhaps more importantly, I think you still have a vestige of a conscience. At least, protecting Emily from Mica suggests that to me.

'So, my offer is, you give us the evidence that will put Constantin Gabrys away, and undertake to turn over a new slate. In return, we'll provide you with a fresh start – new name, new cover story, new location, new home, new job.'

There was a silence. 'I do that, and I'm not safe in here,' said Jeff.

'The fresh start starts from here,' replied Jim. 'The Protected Persons Service collects you from here and takes you to a safe house. Your new life starts after you've given evidence at the Gabrys trial.'

'And the charges are dropped? They just go away?'

'Provided you keep clean from here on. It's a new life,' said Chris. 'Think about it.'

'I don't need to. I'm in. What do you need to know?'

39

Inquests part 3

Two days later, Greg was back in the Coroner's Court for the final day of the inquest into the death of Mica Gabrys. Ram had sat through the whole preceding two and a half days, and according to him, the image of Constantin Gabrys on the TV screen had become stonier and stonier as evidence of the events at the Clean Boats premises had been presented, questioned and challenged.

'How did it go, after I gave my evidence and left?' asked Greg.

'We spent hours crawling over the planning of the raid, and the justification for it. The argument seemed to be that if the unjustified and badly planned raid hadn't gone ahead, Mica would be alive today,' said Ram.

'I suppose if the raid hadn't gone ahead, he might well be,' said Greg. 'But the fact he died doesn't necessarily mean it was badly planned and certainly not that it was unjustified. We did find Sarah there after all. And she had been kept prisoner.'

'We're about to hear from Sarah now,' said Ram.

As they filed into the public seats, Greg checked the TV screens. Sarah, top right, was virtually cheek by jowl with Gabrys, top left. The jury, five women and four men of mixed ages ranging, Greg estimated, from around to thirty to seventy, were in their places opposite the door. Helen Gabrys and the solicitor had returned to sit in court in person. She nodded at Greg, then turned her attention to the assistant coroner, just taking her place behind the glass screen.

They all sat down, and Yvette Granger ran through the preliminaries, then went on.

'Before our adjournment, we heard the detailed statement from DI Laurence. That raised some questions, and I requested the footage from a body-worn camera that had been mentioned in earlier evidence. It has been provided. I have reviewed it and we are now going to see that footage in court. As it was taken by a camera worn by one of the officers who sought to restrain Mica Gabrys, I must warn you both that it is at times blurred and that it shows some distressing scenes. If you're ready,' she said to the court usher, who stood and fiddled for a moment with controls on the screen.

The image flickered, then showed a scruffy corridor. The wearer obviously turned because the picture swung dizzyingly and focussed on a door. A loud bang and a lot of shouting, and the door swung open. A short, slight young man was revealed, half turned from the camera. He spun round, a knife blade flashed, then there was the snap of a taser, and the man fell twitching to the ground and out of range of the camera lens. When his body next came into focus the handle of a carving fork was standing out of his chest and another officer was beginning CPR. In the background could be seen a woman wearing a brightly coloured, shiny wrap.

'Thank you,' said Yvette Granger. 'DI Laurence, is that you in the background of that picture?'

'Yes,' said Sarah.

'Could you describe, please, what we have seen in the video from your perspective.'

'You saw the door open and Mica Gabrys standing just inside it. Immediately prior to that moment, he had been threatening me with the knife in his hand. When the first officer came through the door, he stabbed him with that same knife. Immediately after that I pulled the carving fork from under the mattress on the bed and went to defend my colleagues. He turned again as I did so and the fork went into his chest.'

'This was the fork that, as you described in your statement, you found in the kitchen and hid in the room where you were being kept.'

'That's right.'

'Was Mica tasered before or after you stabbed him?'

'I don't know. It all happened very quickly.'

'Was he on the ground when you stabbed him?'

'I don't know. I don't think so, but he may have been on the point of falling. It's all a bit of a blur.'

'Did you keep hold of the fork after you stabbed Mica with it.'

'I don't think so.'

'One of your colleagues, PC Smith, said in his evidence that he tasered Mica before you stabbed him.'

'He may have, I don't know. As I said, it all happened very quickly. I was threatened with a knife, then I saw an officer stabbed with the same knife and I reacted.'

There was an interruption from the TV screen and Constantin Gabrys shouted, 'Ask the bitch why she stabbed an unconscious boy!'

The assistant coroner intervened immediately. 'That is an inappropriate question asked in an inappropriate manner,' she said. 'I make allowance for your grief and distress, Mr Gabrys, but if you can't treat this court with respect, I will be obliged to restrict your access.

'Are there any other questions for DI Laurence?' As silence ensued, she moved on. 'Then we will now hear the evidence of the pathologists who, separately, carried out post-mortems on the deceased. All interested parties have copies of Dr Paisley's statement, which we will now have read into the record.'

With a few stumbles over medical terminology, the usher read the statement into the record, slowing over the final conclusions. 'So, I conclude that the death of Mica Gabrys was caused: 1a, by cardiac arrest; 1b, catastrophic blood loss, which was itself; 1c, caused by a penetrating wound to the dorsal aorta. Dr Paisley, the police pathologist, and Professor Bailey have kindly now joined us by virtual link. A second post-mortem was carried out by Professor Bailey from University College London, at the request of Mr Gabrys.

'Professor Bailey, I believe you concurred with the conclusions reached by Dr Paisley as to the cause of Mica's death.'

'Correct,' said the lean, dark man now visible on-screen.

'Bearing in mind the objectives and constraints of an inquest, does anyone wish to ask any questions?'

Gabrys senior waved his hand and spoke up. 'Is it true that my son had a brain tumour, and that this would have affected how he behaved on that night? That, in short, the police not only killed a man who was already restrained, but one who was sick as well, and not responsible for his actions!'

'Professor Bailey, would you care to respond?' asked Ms Granger.

'It is correct that Mica Gabrys had a small frontal-lobe tumour, and that some authorities suggest such a tumour can affect behaviour. I cannot state with any certainty that his behaviour on that night was affected by the tumour.'

'Did the tumour contribute to his death, directly or indirectly?' demanded Gabrys.

'It is all a matter of timing,' replied the professor. 'It did not contribute to his death directly, although it may well have proved terminal at a much later date. It is unlikely it indirectly contributed to his death that night.'

'Dr Paisley, do you wish to add anything?'

'No, thank you, ma'am.'

'But not impossible that it contributed to his death,' shouted Gabrys from the TV screen.

'Not impossible, no,' said the professor.

There was a pause while Yvette Granger looked through her notes, then she looked at the jury.

'Members of the jury, I must remind you that an inquest has a very specific duty and very specific limitations. You are required to reach a conclusion on the medical cause of death of the deceased and to answer four questions: who died, where, when and how?

'In dealing with the requirement to decide how Mica Gabrys came by his death you might like to consider the following questions:

'What was the ultimate cause of his death as determined by the pathologists?

'What was the chain of events that led to this death?

'Were there any other contributory factors?

'There may be other questions which you consider important, and I am not telling you what to say. What you find and how you express it is entirely a matter for you. I am merely helping you with the sort of words you might use if you so choose.

'In answering the question of how Mica Gabrys came by his death you must make findings of fact. The law says that you must not make recommendations or express opinions. And your findings of fact must, of course, not only be brief, neutral and clear but they must also be based upon the evidence which you have seen and heard in court, from witnesses and in documents and from the CCTV evidence.

'Once you have agreed the facts, then and only then should you move on to consider your conclusion. Let me now direct you about the possible conclusions.

'As I explained at the start of this inquest, we are encouraged to use, wherever appropriate, short-form conclusions and I am required to direct you as to the conclusions appropriate for your consideration. In the light of the evidence we have heard, the possible conclusions open to you are two:

'Lawful killing, or

'Unlawful killing.

'To assist you in making your choice between these alternatives, you need to be aware of the distinction the law draws between a lawful and an unlawful killing.

'A killing may be regarded as lawful if a person fears for their own safety or that of others. In such circumstances, it will be considered lawful to use reasonable force against the threatened danger. It is not required that the assessment of danger was correct. It does not matter whether a mistaken appraisal of immediate danger is foolish or in any way unreasonable – all that matters is whether the mistake was honestly made.

'The question you must answer is, therefore, in the light of the evidence you have heard, was the level of force used against Mica Gabrys reasonable in all the circumstances of the case?'

A middle-aged lady juror on the back row stood up. 'Can we add comments or recommendations to our conclusion?' she asked.

'If you choose to do so,' replied Ms Granger, 'then you should be mindful that a narrative conclusion, as this is known, should be a brief, neutral, factual statement; it should not express any judgment or opinion. It should not attribute blame or liability either directly or indirectly. And it is not necessary to use a narrative conclusion where it does not add anything to a short conclusion.

'I will note, for the record, that Mr Constantin Gabrys, as an interested person, requested that I exclude lawful killing from the options available to you, because he does not believe such a conclusion to be correct. I have declined to do so, because it is for you to reach a conclusion based on the evidence you have heard, not any other person no matter how involved.' Ms Granger stood and

'All rise,' said the usher.

Out in the waiting area, Ram and Greg looked at each other. 'I'm going to stay,' said Ram. 'What about you?'

'I'd better get back. I have someone I want to interview. Let me know what happens will you, Ram?'

'Of course.'

40

Safe house

Greg looked at his watch as he hurried from the Coroner's Court, then reached for his phone.

'Chris, where're we meeting?' he asked. 'I was assuming it was at HMP Bure, then remembered you'd got the Protected Persons lot involved. Have they moved Jeff yet?'

'They have now,' she said. 'Had a quick chat following our conversation with him, satisfied themselves he was serious, then took him home to pack a case and moved him to a safe house.'

'Just one case?'

'That's right. And he hasn't been able to tell anyone where he's gone. I imagine his neighbours assume he's back in the prison. He said no one was visiting, so it may be a while before anyone outside realises he's not in the prison system.'

'He's happy with that?'

'I think he's happy to get away, to get a fresh start. But I think he's still terrified of the Gabrys network. Wouldn't you be?'

'So, where're we headed?' asked Greg as he joined the main road past County Hall.

'Bacton. It's an old holiday property not far from the beach. In fact, not a million miles from where our serial killer took his last victim. I've texted you the postcode. I'll meet you there.'

When Greg pulled off the not-very-main road in Bacton, he had to acknowledge that it was a perfect site for a safe house. The cottage lurked at the end of a long drive closed by six-feet gates. On one side were more holiday properties and on the other, open fields. Once he ID'd himself to a man in jeans and fleece with 'Potters Property Services' written across the back, the gates were opened, and he parked next to Chris's car. Another chap in logoed clothing opened the door and showed him into the living room.

Chris was sitting in an armchair by the unlit electric fire, a young man with neat black beard and matching cropped hair in the chair opposite. He got to his feet as Greg came in, started to hold his hand out, hesitated – not sure what to do – then held it out again.

Greg shook it, saying 'Take a seat. How are you getting on here, Peter?'

'It's okay.' He shrugged as he looked round the room. 'The wi-fi's a bit slow, but there's TV and radio, etc. I can see me getting a bit bored if I'm here for long, but it's no worse than HMP Bure. In fact, it's a lot better than getting boiling sugar water thrown in my face, so I suppose I can take a bit of boredom.'

As he spoke, Chris had been setting up the recording equipment. 'We're good to go,' she said.

'Okay,' said Greg. 'Now, I'll just remind you you're still under caution, Peter. As you know, we're looking for evidence that clearly ties Constantin Gabrys to the drug manufacturing and distribution businesses in and around Great Yarmouth. But I stress evidence, not fantasy. Don't succumb to the temptation to embroider. We know a lot already and if you start to make things up, well,' he shrugged, 'we'll know, and we won't trust you again.' There was a silence while Greg let that sink in. 'As I said, we already have some documentary and forensic evidence, but first-hand experience of how he works and what he's been involved in will be invaluable. That's why the protection officers were willing to help. But you need to be clear, this isn't a get-out-of-jail-free card. There are two conditions. First, that you testify, and second, that you undertake never to get back into crime.'

'Yes, they explained all that,' said Peter.

'First then, how much direct contact did you have with Constantin Gabrys?'

'Very little,' admitted Peter. 'In the normal way of things, none at all. I only saw him when things were going wrong.'

'Was he involved in recruiting you?'

'Not as far as I know. If he was, it was behind the scenes.'

'Who did you normally deal with?'

'No idea. My instructions came by text message. I've given you the number, but I'm sure it was a burner phone. My pay arrived along with the drug packages, always cash.'

'Who set the system up? You surely didn't get involved purely on the back of text messages?'

'No, of course not. In the beginning it was a man at a gig that approached me. I was dealing,' admitted Peter. 'In a small way, that is. Just to friends. But the chap supplying me passed me on to a bloke named Dragan, and he said he had a better job for me, one more suited to my talents. I wasn't sure what he meant at the time. Then it was explained to me they wanted me to line up young girls to do the transporting because you lot were too thick to spot them. Sorry,' he said, 'but that was what they said.'

'When you spoke to us before, you told us about your contacts with Emily. Was she the first girl you groomed?'

'No.'

'How many others?'

'Four I think, no five. Emily was the sixth.'

'And what happened with the others?'

'The first blew me off. She wasn't very impressed by my technique. The others, they all carried drugs as instructed.'

'We'll need names.'

'I've already given them to her,' he said, nodding at Chris, who held up a crumpled piece of paper with a short list of names.

'Okay, thank you. Who told you who to target?'

'I said, I got my orders by mobile. Usually text message. Mostly they just said what they wanted, you know, what area they were looking at, where they wanted the drugs taken. All the normal messages came by text.'

'What wasn't normal?' asked Greg.

'Occasionally there'd be a rush on, or once, they needed someone to make a meet in town at short notice because one of the couriers had got ill. Then I got a phone call.'

'From whom?'

'Once it was Mica. Once, one of the big ex-wrestler types who ran the grow-houses. Once it was Gabrys himself.'

'How did you know?'

'Because that time it was a rush job. I'd had to call at the grow-house myself to pick up the package that needed passing on. There'd been some trouble with the workers, and Gabrys senior had called round to sort it out. He was coming down the stairs when I got there. I'd just picked the package up and he gave me a funny look, as though I shouldn't be there. The grow-house manager said something like, "This is Patrick, he recruits and organises the delivery teams".'

'What did Gabrys say?'

'He said, "Ah, Patrick. Yes. Patrick. I'm told good things about you. Good with the girls?" I said something like, "Yes, I think so," and he said, "Hurry up with that package. I've got another that needs to go to Norwich when you've despatched that one".'

There was a pause, then Greg said, 'You're quite sure about that? You have first-hand evidence that Constantin Gabrys was involved in the business of growing and distributing the drugs in Great Yarmouth and to Norwich?'

'Yes.'

'And you're willing to give evidence saying that?'

'Yes.'

'Let's take a break,' said Greg. 'I'll get you a coffee or whatever, then we'll carry on. Okay?'

He and Chris retired to the kitchen. 'Okay if we make a brew?' he asked the logoed sweatshirt.

'Fine,' he replied, putting his mobile away in his pocket. 'I guess you'd like a bit of peace. I'll be in the garden if you need me.'

Greg put the kettle on while Chris scouted in the fridge for milk. 'They're a depressingly healthy lot, this bunch,' she grumbled, pulling out a bottle of skimmed milk. 'No biscuits either. They'd better have some sugar. What else do we want?'

Correctly interpreting the question to relate to the investigation rather than the comestibles, Greg replied, 'Ideally I'd like to know what happened to send Mica to Nails Galore. It bothers me no one has faced justice for what happened to Madame Trieste. If we can tie Constantin to the decision to send Mica, then, who knows?'

'Ralph Menton said he overheard a phone call,' said Chris.

'Yes, I read what he said. But he made a lot of assumptions about what was meant. I don't think it stacks up as evidence,' replied Greg.

Clutching two steaming mugs in one hand, Greg pushed open the door to the living room. Peter hadn't moved. He was still in the armchair by the fire, staring into space, his eyes blank. He shivered as he took the mug from Greg with thanks, and Chris leaned over to the fire before switching the recorder on. The flickering mock flames added a little warmth even before the radiant element kicked in.

'It's just starting to sink in,' Peter said.

'What's that?' asked Chris.

'That I'm not going back. Ever. That I won't be popping down the Horse and Groom for a pizza and a pint. That I won't have the where-am-I-going-for-Christmas argument with my mother. That the holiday I booked in Spain won't happen. I won't see any of the gang at Carrow Road to watch Norwich lose again.'

'Not all bad then!' said Chris.

'That's right,' Greg replied. 'On the other hand, you won't have to seduce children to carry drugs, you won't have to deal with the likes of Gabrys, senior or junior. You have a unique chance to start again. A new job, a new home, new friends. maybe someday a new family.'

There was a long silence while all three sipped hot drinks. Eventually Peter looked up.

'I've made a lot of mistakes,' he said. 'Some of them weren't my fault, but a lot were. If I really can go back and start again, well I'm young enough to do that.'

'Tell me about Mica,' said Greg. Peter shuddered, and it wasn't just the slight chill in the air.

'He was a nutter,' he said. 'There was something twisted up here.' He screwed a finger into his forehead. 'The crowd around me could be pretty rough and ready but Mica was something else. He really enjoyed inflicting pain, and he liked to do it up close and personal. There were others in that crowd who'd shoot someone if they were told to do it. Or maybe even if they got in a temper. At least, that was the rumour and I saw some with guns from time to time. But Mica didn't wait for orders and he preferred a knife. There was one girl...' he stopped and took another drink from his mug.

'The girl,' prompted Chris, as he seemed to have ground to a halt.

'This was a girl Mica picked up at a rave. I was there because I was keeping a check on one of my lot. He was with this one girl all evening, dancing, drinking, chatting. I went round the back to...' he hesitated.

'You were dealing?' asked Greg.

'Yes. At least, I was passing a parcel on. I'd arranged to meet one of my girls round the back. She was a bit wobbly, so it took longer than I intended. In the end she teetered off on her high heels, gave me a little wave as she got to the corner, and walked straight into Mica and his girl. I saw Mica pull a knife. She kicked her heels off and ran. Mica was left standing, with the girl he'd been chatting up all night and a knife in his hand. I stayed in the shadows,' he admitted. 'I didn't like the look of it.

'I saw Mica push his girl against the wall. He seemed to be giggling. She was trying to get away, I could hear her talking but her eyes never moved from the blade. He was waving it in front of her face, then he moved closer. If it wasn't for the knife I'd have thought he was going to, you know, but she stayed pressed against the wall as though she was trying to melt into it, and then she fell silent. I saw Mica push the knife under her eye and I didn't know what to do. I thought he was going to cut her up right in front of me, but I'll be honest, I was scared to death of what he'd do to me. Or what his father would do. The only thing I could think of was to make a noise. There was a bin near where I was standing. I pushed it over and got back into the shadows. It made quite a clatter and when Mica turned round, the girl took her chance and ran for it.

'Then I ran too, only the other way, back right round the building and in through the entrance. I couldn't see the girl, but there was a lot of excited chatter and a whole bunch of young girls by the ladies, so I assumed she was in there with her mates. Mica had gone.'

'Was that why you kept him away from Emily?' asked Chris.

'That's why I kept him away from any girl I could. He scared the living daylights out of me. And I don't think I was the only one. Even the musclemen were wary of Mica. That's how I knew it was going to end badly when he was told to go to Nails Galore.'

'How did you know that?' asked Greg.

'I was there, standing next to him when he got the call from his father.'

'Did you hear what was said?'

'I heard his voice, his father's voice I mean, but he was speaking in Lithuanian. It was Mica who said, "I've got a job to do at Nails Galore. An enforcement job for my father. See you later." Then he got in his car and drove off.'

Outside on the drive, Chris said, 'It's the link we were looking for. The direct link from Constantin Gabrys to the murder of Madame Trieste and it's the second time we've heard the same story.'

'And it's hearsay,' said Greg, smacking his hand on the roof of his car in frustration. 'Dammit it's hearsay. You know the CPS won't like that and defence will wipe the floor with us.'

A few miles down the road, Greg had an idea and reached for his hands-free button just as his phone rang. It was Chris.

'I've had an idea,' she said.

'So have I,' he said. 'Let's see if it's the same one. You go first.'

'The funny buggers were recording Gabrys's phone calls,' said Chris's voice.

'What if they recorded that one?' finished Greg. 'Snap! Let's find out.'

A few miles further, and Greg's phone rang again. 'Another idea?' he asked, without looking at the caller ID.

'Not exactly,' said Ram's voice. 'But we do have a conclusion from the inquest.'

'Ah, that, yes,' said Greg. 'Sorry, Ram. I thought you were someone else. What's the jury said?'

'Lawful killing.'

'Did I hear that right? There was no 'un' in that sentence?'

'That's right. Lawful killing. I gather the delay was while they argued about whether to add a narrative to their conclusion, but in the end they decided to stick with the short form. And you didn't hear that from me.'

'Okay. That's Sarah off the hook then.'

'As far as the inquest is concerned yes, although Constantin Gabrys was ranting about miscarriage of justice and a private prosecution when the coroner cut him off.'

'We might have something else to keep him busy. I'll brief you when I see you.'

41

January 2020

It was one of those Norfolk big-sky days; a day when there seems to be more blue dappled with white above, than there is ground beneath. Greg paused outside Norwich Crown Court to enjoy the fresh air, before disappearing into the maw that was British justice, chewing through the evidence exceeding slow. At his elbow, Chris was fussing with her coat zip which, in the rush to leave that morning, had become entangled with the fringe of her scarlet scarf.

'He'll tell you to lose the scarf anyway,' remarked Greg, apropos the well-known views of Frank Parker, the senior CPS prosecutor, with regard to colourful clothing.

'I know,' she said, tugging fruitlessly at the scarf, 'which will be difficult if I can't get it out of this damn zip.'

Greg looked at her affectionately out of the corner of his eye and remembered a certain recent conversation with his boss, Margaret, a sudden lump in his throat. He was going to miss moments like these.

'Got it,' said Chris, having recourse to her teeth, and looked up with triumph in her expression and red wool in her incisors.

'Just need to get it off my choppers now. How do you think it's going? How was yesterday?'

'Yesterday was the Standish evidence, father and son, but mostly endless poring over incredibly boring accounts and balance sheets. Boring to me anyway, and I think the jury were losing the will to live.'

'But did they bring it home to Gabrys? Are we going to get him on the money laundering charge?'

'I think so. I didn't stay until the end of the session. Once I was sure they wouldn't need me, Frank let me go. He seemed happy.'

'So, they've heard about the drugs and cash we found at his house and they know about his attempt on us. They've heard about the activities of his accountant; they know what we found at Clean Boats Inc. and they've heard from his own butler. How did Ralph stand up to cross-examination?'

'I wasn't there for that bit, but as I said, Frank seems happy they'll convict on money laundering. The involvement in the supply of drugs is perhaps a bit shakier, even with Ralph's testimony about what was hidden in the house. Apparently, defence were suggesting it was nothing to do with the father, it was all down to the son apparently.'

'Who is conveniently dead.'

'As you say. But today we hear from Peter Ashfield.'

'I see he's got the screens round the witness stand,' remarked Chris.

'Yes. Ralph Menton didn't have them, but Peter made his case and they were granted.'

In the courtroom they took their seats at the back and noted the arrival of Helen Gabrys in the public gallery, escorted by her solicitor and a Witness Service volunteer.

'No Mrs Gabrys again,' whispered Chris, as they rose for the arrival of Her Honour Judge Helena Westlake, QC. She took her seat on the bench, exchanged a quick word with the usher and then looked across the court at prosecution counsel.

'Please call your next witness, Sir Frederick,' she said.

In the glass-walled dock, Gabrys leaped to his feet, his shouting obscuring Sir Frederick's words. 'Let the coward face me,' he said. 'Let him face me.'

'Sir Bernard,' said Her Honour to defence counsel, 'please advise your client that he is doing his case no good at all by this behaviour, and that I will have him removed if he cannot restrain himself. We had enough of this behaviour yesterday.' Sir Bernard turned his leonine head, but his intervention was not necessary. Gabrys had resumed his seat, with some muttering. Sir Frederick coughed and began again, addressing himself to the figure behind the screen.

Greg was distracted for the next few minutes by a note passed him from Chris. 'Saw Margaret yesterday. Think we need a chat.' He turned to Chris, she was smiling but not wholly convincingly and there was a tiny wisp of red wool still in her teeth. He nodded, and turned his attention back to the court, but his mind was spinning.

'In your statement, Mr Ashfield, you explained that you were recruited to Mr Gabrys's organisation in order to groom young girls and persuade them to carry drugs for you. How did you know this organisation was connected to the defendant?'

'I met him at one of the grow-houses in Great Yarmouth.'

'How did you know it was Mr Gabrys?'

'He was pointed out to me, and he's sitting there in the dock,' said Peter.

'To pre-empt my expert colleague here,' said Sir Frederick indicating Sir Bernard, 'he could have just been passing.'

'No, he was definitely involved,' said Peter. 'He spoke to me.'

'What did he say?'

'He said "Hurry up with that package. I've got another that needs to go to Norwich when you've despatched that one".'

'And this package was?'

'Drugs. Weed and ketamine to be exact.'

There was more noise from the dock, but, on this occasion, it was more of a rumble than a yell and Her Honour decided to overlook it. Sir Bernard bent a severe look on his client, knowing all the while that it would have little effect.

'Let us then turn to the matter of conspiracy to commit murder,' said Sir Frederick, flicking through the bundle of papers on his desk, more for effect than need. 'You have stated that you overheard a telephone conversation between the defendant and his son, but that you couldn't understand the detail because it was in Lithuanian.'

'That's right,' said Peter behind the screen.

'And that the defendant's son, Mica Gabrys, told you, and I quote, "I've got a job to do at Nails Galore. An enforcement job for my father. See you later".'

'That's right.'

Sir Bernard rose to his weary feet. 'The witness can have no personal knowledge of what was said in the conversation, as he has admitted he speaks no Lithuanian.'

'If Your Honour and my learned colleague will bear with me for a moment, I will explain that I am not relying on the witness for the content of the conversation, rather that the conversation took place.'

'You may proceed,' said Judge Westlake, 'but don't waste the court's time, Sir Frederick.'

'Thank you, Your Honour. Mr Ashfield, when did this conversation take place?'

'It was the day the lorry was found in Essex with lots of dead refugees inside it. It sticks in my mind because Mica leaned over and read the headlines over my shoulder. He said it wasn't one of theirs. That's why I remember,' he repeated.

'That date, Your Honour, was 23rd October 2019. I am now going to introduce into evidence the transcript of a mobile phone conversation of 23rd October 2019, obtained from GCHQ, together with a translation into English. I can provide the recording if wished, and also an expert witness happy to testify that the voices on the recording are those of the defendant Constantin Gabrys and of his son.' Sir Frederick flapped some photocopied papers and the usher hurried to take copies to the judge, to the jury and to Sir Bernard. 'I apologise for the late arrival of this evidence, Your Honour, but I only received it last night. You will note that the translation bears out the essence of the conversation as offered by my witness, ie "Get yourself to Nails Galore, Mica, and sort out the Trieste bitch once and for all. I don't want to hear anything from her again".'

***

Outside in the fresh air again, court in recess, Greg looked at Chris leaning on the bonnet of her car. 'I thought all hell was going to break loose,' he said. 'Sir Bernard wasn't a happy bunny was he?'

'Nor was Gabrys. I thought he was going to have a coronary then and there. He was puce! I wonder what he was shouting at Peter Ashfield.'

'Threats I would think. We can find out from the court transcript later. He's certainly a man who likes his revenge, judging from what happened at Nails Galore and his attempt on us.'

'Didn't get him very far in the long run, did it?' said Chris. 'In fact, if he'd managed to resist the temptation to take revenge, he might still be in business, and we might still be struggling to put him away.' Pursuing that train of thought, she added 'Sarah's revenge on Mica hasn't worked out well either.' There was a pointed silence. 'Don't worry, I won't say that to anyone else,' she assured him. 'In the legal sense, the inquest conclusion was perfectly sound. But whatever she believed at the time, she certainly got her revenge, and it's trashed her career.'

Greg raised an eyebrow, but decided a change of subject would be timely. 'Chris, what're you doing tonight?'

'Nothing special. I'm going back to the office now, then home.'

'Can I pick you up from home and take you out for dinner? As you said, we need a chat and I'd rather not do it at the office.'

'Did Margaret give you the same ultimatum?'

'You mean, about us not working together. Yes. But let's not talk about it here. Let's talk tonight.'

'Okay. But, Greg, if one of us has to fall on their sword...'

'Tonight,' he interrupted. 'We'll talk then.'

***

Sir Frederick returned to the conspiracy charge toward the end of his closing speech.

'My learned friend has already tried to cast doubt on the evidence of the crucial telephone conversation. He has, at one and the same time, sought to suggest that the speaker was *not* Constantin Gabrys, or that it *was* Mr Gabrys but the translation was faulty, or that the translation was accurate but that the interpretation put on the words was wrong. You have heard from expert witnesses both on the identity of the speakers and on the translation. You will make your own minds up as to whether, in all the circumstances of this case, there can be any reasonable doubt that when Constantin Gabrys instructed his son, his unstable and violence-loving son, to "get yourself to Nails Galore, Mica, and sort out the Trieste bitch once and for all. I don't want to hear anything from her again" he was ordering her death.'

***

'Guilty on all counts,' reported a triumphant Greg to Margaret Tayler. 'We've got him at last. I don't know who's happiest. Frank Parker, Sir Frederick or me!'

He listened in silence for a moment, then said, 'I'll let you know tomorrow. I'm on my way to collect Chris now.'

Chris was ready and waiting when he pulled up outside her tiny cottage and tooted his horn. She came hurrying out and leaped into the car in a flurry of pale pink jeans and fluffy angora top, with a tasteful counterpoint of bright orange tote. He pulled his sunglasses down from the sun visor and donned them.

'Oh, ha bloody ha,' said Chris equably. 'But take them off to drive, do, or we'll be hitting something.'

Greg drove back onto the Billockby road and turned toward Acle. 'Where are we eating?' asked Chris.

'It's a surprise,' he said. As they approached the bridge over the Bure, Chris was certainly surprised when he turned off the road and went down the track to the riverbank.

'I hope we're not eating here,' she said. 'January is a bit nippy for an alfresco dinner on the riverbank. According to the papers there's enough flu about already, without us going out of our way to catch it.'

'I just thought I'd like to have this conversation here by the river.' Leaving his phone in the car to ensure no interruptions, he led her down the bank to the water's edge, then turned and looked at her. Apart from the intermittent glow of cars passing on the road above, there was little light but the moonlight reflecting on the river and shining in her hair. 'Here, where you saved my life. Chris, I've loved working with you. You make every day a joy and you bring so much skill and knowledge to every investigation. But as you know—'

'Look,' she interrupted, 'if you're trying to tell me gently that after the complaint from the DWOS, Margaret's put her foot down and we can't go on as we have any more, then—'

'I'm trying to ask you to marry me, woman!' shouted Greg, exasperated. 'I had a whole romantic speech rehearsed and now it's gone straight out of my head.'

'Say that again,' said Chris.

'I said,' said Greg taking her by the elbows and turning her toward him, 'that I can't imagine any greater joy than working with you, other than being married to you.'

'Was that the romantic speech?' she said critically, 'because if so, it wasn't bad, but it could do with a bit of work.'

'For God's sake, will you marry me?' demanded Greg. 'Yes, or no?'

Chris opened her mouth, but her phone rang. 'Leave it,' said Greg as she glanced at the screen, but she held up her hand.

'Sorry,' she mouthed, listened, then put it on speaker phone.

'I've been trying to get hold of Greg, but he's not answering,' said Margaret's voice, sounding very strained. 'I assume he's somewhere near you. Can you tell him, there's been a leak somewhere. The Protection Service got Peter Ashfield away from the so-called safe house, but it was a close thing and they've taken casualties. They've had to change their plans for him. And we need a good hard look at how this supposedly confidential information got out. Tell Greg I need him here soonest.'

Chris closed her phone and looked at Greg. 'You heard,' she said.

'I heard, but I haven't heard an answer yet.' He pulled her close. 'Will you, Chris?'

'Of course I will, you silly sod. Now get us over to Wymondham. It might be our last case together.'

THE END – FOR NOW

Printed in Dunstable, United Kingdom

68885831R00180